ARKIE'S PILGRIMAGE to the NEXT BIG THING

LISA WALKER

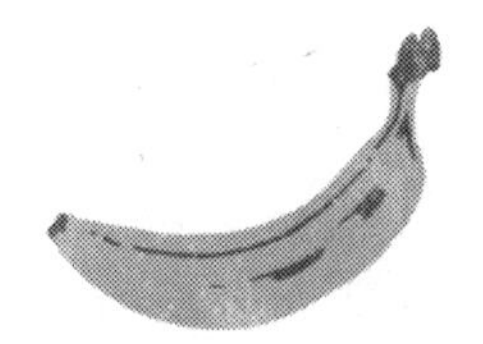

BANTAM
SYDNEY AUCKLAND TORONTO NEW YORK LONDON

A Bantam book
Published by Random House Australia Pty Ltd
Level 3, 100 Pacific Highway, North Sydney NSW 2060
www.randomhouse.com.au

First published by Bantam in 2015

Addresses for companies within the Random House Group can be found at www.randomhouse.com.au/offices

National Library of Australia
Cataloguing-in-Publication entry

Walker, Lisa, author.
Arkie's Pilgrimage to the Next Big Thing/Lisa Walker.

ISBN 978 0 85798 440 1 (paperback)

A823.4

Cover illustrations and chapter heading illustrations by Chris Nixon Illustrations
Cover design by Christabella Designs
Internal design by Midland Typesetters, Australia
Typeset in 12/17.5 pt Fairfield Lt Std by Midland Typesetters, Australia
Printed in Australia by Griffin Press, an accredited ISO AS/NZS 14001:2004 Environmental Management System printer

Random House Australia uses papers that are natural, renewable and recyclable products and made from wood grown in sustainable forests. The logging and manufacturing processes are expected to conform to the environmental regulations of the country of origin.

For Simon, in his twenty-first year

Part One

'If only you knew it, you are in luck not to have a heart.'
The Wonderful Wizard of Oz, ***L. Frank Baum***

One

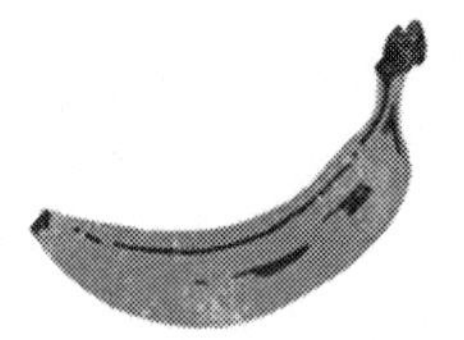

It has been precisely a year since Adam left me.

On the streets, New Year's Eve partying is in full swing, but here on the station, all is quiet. Byron Bay has turned out to be not at all what I needed. Despite determined efforts to be cheerful, to smile at strangers, to exercise and swim, even to have a reiki treatment, I have slid further and further over the line.

My feet are placed squarely on the white mark beyond which you may not pass. Two steps and I will be over the edge.

Why a train? Why not pills, drowning or a blade? Perhaps I was thinking of Anna Karenina – the snow, the rushing wheels, the final jump. I always have been fond of trains.

How did I come to this point? Perhaps it is as simple as a loss of pleasure. That's how it seems. The world feels tuned to black and white. This black and white world has been mine for a year now. It no longer seems likely that it will change.

A Dali print used to hang in the bathroom that Adam and I shared. Every morning and evening, the drooping clocks mesmerised me as I brushed my teeth. They hung off tree branches and walls like melting cheese on a hot summer day. If time was really as soft as a camembert cheese, would I bend it back and do things differently now?

A raindrop lands heavily on my head and a clay-like smell drifts towards my nostrils. I check the battered timetable I have plucked from the drawer in my motel room. The train from Sydney arrives at twenty-one twenty. I do the figures again. Fifteen more minutes to wait. I tap my feet on the concrete, watch spots of rain decorate the rails, try to focus my mind, so I will be ready.

'Excuse me.'

The voice is an unwelcome distraction. I thought I was alone.

'Would you like play bingo?'

I turn.

The girl is a strange figure in this setting – neatly cut hair, glasses, a short-sleeved collared shirt tucked into too-high jeans. A briefcase hangs from one hand. Most of the Japanese I've seen in Byron are hip. They have jagged-cut bleached hair and low-slung shorts. This girl shares one thing with them – a surfboard in a silver cover is slung over her shoulder.

She doesn't look like a surfer.

Bingo. I could almost laugh. Do I want to spend the last moments of my life playing bingo? With a girl who has no dress sense? Let me just think about that. *Hmm, no.* I picture the irony. *Did you hear? She was playing bingo. Before she jumped. Sad. She used to really be someone.*

'No, thank you.'

The girl bows. 'Sorry.' She turns to go.

I feel bad. She seems lonely. She wants to play bingo. I don't want to leave this life feeling selfish. Pretentious and delusional maybe, but not selfish.

'Wait.'

She swivels back, her eyes apologetic behind her glasses.

'How do you play bingo with two people?'

She smiles. 'I show you.' She beckons with her hand towards the rear of the platform.

I'll be back, I tell the white line. *Don't go anywhere.*

We sit down on the bench, one at each end so there is room between us. Pulling a small box out of her briefcase she gives me a card with numbers marked on it.

'We must be quick,' she says.

'Because the train is coming?'

She shakes her head, her silky hair swinging against her face. 'Bingo starts at twenty-one fourteen.' The girl inspects her watch, then hands me a pencil. 'Thirty second. Then we start.' She pulls out some cards and places them on the bench between us. 'We take turns to turn over.' Her eyes follow the hand of her watch. 'Now.' Her tone implies great urgency.

I want to ask her why the rush, but there doesn't seem to be enough time.

'Twenty-one.' She giggles, crossing the number off her card.

I flip up the next one. 'Two.' One for me.

'Sixteen.'

'Thirty-six.'

The pile of cards diminishes between us.

'Nine,' says the girl.

'Bingo.' I wave my card with mock excitement. Thank Christ that's over. Now I can get back to it. I start to rise.

'You win.' The girl opens her briefcase and hands me a parcel. 'Your prize.'

It is a facecloth, sealed in plastic and decorated with pink flowers.

'Sakura.' The girl points. 'Cherry blossoms.'

'Did you bring this with you from Japan?'

She nods.

'Just for bingo?'

'Yes.' She taps her briefcase. 'I am ready.'

'Thank you.' I turn it in my hands. Wonder what they'll make of it. After.

She smiles. 'You are welcome. I am Iida. Miss Iida.'

'I'm Arkie. Ms Arkie.' I exhale, lower myself to the seat again, stick out my hand. Going through the motions. A good hostess.

Miss Iida looks at my hand, then puts hers out and clasps it briefly. 'Misaki? This is Japanese name.'

I don't bother to correct her. *Misaki.* I quite like it. I glance at my watch.

'Train almost here,' says Miss Iida.

I nod. I am resigned to being stuck with her now. I hope she's not squeamish. I edge to the furthest point of the bench in preparation, measure the distance with my eyes. *Five steps.*

'Beautiful blossom,' says Miss Iida.

'Pardon?'

'Your name – it mean beautiful blossom.'

'Oh.' That almost makes me smile. *Misaki. Beautiful blossom.*

'On the train, we will have soba noodles,' says Miss Iida. 'At twenty-two fourteen.'

I can't let this pass. 'Why the timing? Why soba noodles?'

'Fourteen minutes past the hour, because we are going to 2014. It is . . .' She pauses.

'Lucky?'

'Yes, lucky. And we have soba noodles, because it is traditional.' She gives a quick bow. 'And they are delicious. It is optional, of course. You don't need to have, if you don't want.'

I glance at her slim briefcase. 'You have them in there?'

She nods.

'What else have you got?'

'A prayer. That is for twenty-three fourteen. And a present. For twenty-four fourteen. I think we are in Brisbane then.'

I'll never get to see them. I brush the thought away. It will take more than a prayer and a present to deflect me. I think of telling her that the train only goes to Murwillumbah, but it seems too hard.

Miss Iida inspects her watch again. 'Train is late.'

'Not really.' It is only nine twenty-five. 'In Japan they run on time, right?'

Miss Iida nods. 'Five twenty-two train comes at five twenty-two. Not five twenty-one or five twenty-three.' There is something hesitant about the way she says this.

'That's good, isn't it?'

She nods in an indeterminate way. 'Sometimes I wish . . .'

I wait.

'Sometimes I wish it is less perfect.'

My eyes meet hers for a moment. She has nice eyes, dark brown behind her glasses. 'Sometimes I wish it was more perfect here.'

She smiles. 'We like to organise. In Japan.'

She is distracting me. I drum my fingers on the bench, tap my feet, tense my muscles so I will be ready. I twist my hair back from my face and secure it with a clasp. I need to be able to see what I'm doing. *Five steps, then a jump.*

Adam used to say that my hair was the colour of autumn. Now it is like autumn leaves chewed by caterpillars. *Autumn leaves with flecks of snow.* Stress has not only ruined my hair, it has made me lose weight. Once, I would have killed for the hips I've got, but now I miss my curves.

On the positive side, my clothes sit better on my body. Tonight I am wearing my cloudy night outfit – floaty black with flashes of silver. *Stars glimpsed through curtains.* Such things will be noted – by those who care. I am no longer one of them.

'In Japan, sometimes train is late.' Miss Iida gazes out at the platform. 'When it hit people.'

I catch my breath, stare at her face, but there is nothing to see. I cough. 'Does that happen much?'

'Yes.' Her gaze doesn't shift from the rails.

I am expecting her to say more, but she doesn't. 'So, what happens after the prayer and the present?' I hadn't even known I was going to speak.

She turns to me. 'After present, is bedtime.'

I like the precision, the direction given. Outside the train station drunken revellers crowd the street. 'We don't do it like that here. We drink. We kiss at midnight. Everything else is . . .'

Miss Iida waits politely.

Everything else is so bloody complex, so fraught with possibilities that will never be fulfilled. 'Negotiable.' I look down the tracks. Where is that train?

'On New Year's Eve we make fresh start. Leave old troubles behind.'

Ha. It is a nice idea, but it never works. We are silent for a while. 'You're surfing?' I nod at the surfboard, now under her knees. Will I still be making small talk as I jump?

'I have been surfing. For one week. Now I go home.'

'One week? You came all the way from Japan for one week?'

She nods. 'I have one week holiday only.'

'Only one week a year?'

'Yes. And I am finding surfing so enjoyable. I am exciting every day. I surf from nine until five. No stopping for lunch.'

'Nine until five? No stopping?'

'Sometimes I have cup of coffee only. Then I am surfing again. It is too much pleasure.' Her eyes light up with excitement. 'When I am in water, I am happy.'

'So you work fifty-one weeks a year?'

'Yes. That is why I am surfing all day. Not stopping for lunch.'

'How do you stand it? Fifty-one weeks a year . . . Only one week to live.' The irony of this question strikes me as I ask it. Here I am, all the time in the world, not the faintest idea how to enjoy it.

'It is what I must do. That is my life.' She sounds not exactly serene, but fatalistic.

'But how? How do you accept that?' I lean forward, the words falling from my mouth in a rush. 'How do you learn to stop wanting?'

'I enjoy simple pleasures – food, company. Like you and me, here. It is pleasure talking to you, Misaki.' She gives a shy smile.

Pleasure. 'It is a pleasure talking to you too, Miss Iida.' This is almost true. She is undemanding company. My eyes dart to the platform edge. *Five steps.* I tune back in to find

Miss Iida talking about pencils. It seems that she works in a pencil factory.

'. . . Japanese pencils are best in the world,' she says, not boastfully, but as if it is an undisputed fact.

I have never contemplated a pencil before. Never imagined a competition, real or imagined, where pencils might play a part. 'What makes them the best?'

'They are smooth writing, very sharp. They are pleasure to look at. Pleasure to hold.'

I like the idea of taking pleasure from something so simple. From a pencil. It seems a particularly Japanese thing to do. I almost make a note, then remember that such things no longer concern me.

We both check our watches.

'Train is very late now, I think?' says Miss Iida. 'Almost time for soba noodles.'

She is right. I pull out my timetable, read it again.

She does the same. Her timetable is like mine, crumpled and faded.

It is only then, as I double-check the timing, that I notice the fine print down the bottom. *Train service discontinues May 2004*. I read it twice, disbelieving, then hold it out to her. A silent howl wells up – *can I do nothing right?* Why did they leave a ten-year-old train timetable in my motel room? Only a woman with a tenuous grip on reality would wait for a train on a disused railway station. *And a Japanese tourist.* I look at my companion. Aren't the Japanese supposed to be well organised?

Miss Iida laughs uproariously.

I am a little taken aback. I thought Japanese girls only giggled, not guffawed.

'No train?' She glances at the timetable in her hand. 'I take from backpackers. I didn't know was so old.'

I shake my head, crumple the timetable in my hand. What now?

'I will catch bus to Brisbane tomorrow, I think.' She giggles. 'I came down on bus, but I thought something different to go back. What about you, Misaki? Are you in hurry?'

I glance at the edge of the platform. 'I don't know. I thought I was. Now . . .' Now I am not sure. I breathe deeply and a faint scent of flowers enters my nostrils.

'You can catch bus too. On New Year's Day we do something lucky. Something with friend. Then we have good year.'

Miss Iida pours noodles out of a thermos into two plastic bowls, also decorated with cherry blossoms. 'Noodles mean long life,' she says.

We eat soba noodles, sitting on the platform. I slip them into my mouth with my chopsticks. They are salty and chewy. 'Here's to long life.' *Or not, as the case may be.*

'Soon we will say a prayer. For peace and happiness.' Her glasses sparkle in the station's lights.

'Here's to peace and happiness.' The ghost of a weight slips off me.

'No train.' Miss Iida giggles. 'But I met you, Misaki.'

'And I met you.' I find I am smiling.

Two

Bangs, crackles and loud cheers from the street signal the stroke of midnight. I try not to think of the last time I heard fireworks but each bang is like a blow to the heart.

Miss Iida leans over to her briefcase and extracts a small red drawstring pouch. She checks her watch, then places the pouch in her lap.

This must be my present. I eye it surreptitiously. It looks like a bag of marbles. Perhaps we will play marbles next.

At fourteen minutes past twelve precisely, Miss Iida holds the pouch out to me in cupped hands and bows. 'Happy New Year.'

The silk pouch rattles as I take it. I bow back. 'You shouldn't have.' Pulling open the cord at the mouth, I tip a jumble of colourful wooden objects into my palm.

'Lucky Gods,' says Miss Iida.

The main fireworks are over but firecrackers pop in the streets around the station as I arrange the gods carefully on the bench between us. One, two, three, four, five, six, *seven* . . .

Good things come in sevens. The seven wonders of the world, the seven dwarfs, the seven colours of the rainbow, the seven stages of man, the dance of the seven veils . . .

Seven is strangely significant in all religions. The world was created in seven days, the biblical Egyptians had seven years of plenty followed by seven years of famine. There are seven worlds in each of the Hindu universes, seven chakras in the body, seven doors to the Islamic hell –

'You like them?' says Miss Iida.

My eyes focus and I nod, gazing at the figurines. My Seven Lucky Gods look a little like the seven dwarfs. They are all plump and smiling. Each one is about the size of a thimble and dressed in brightly coloured robes.

'Shinto Gods bring good fortune,' says Miss Iida. 'Especially seven together.'

I think it will take more than that but as I pick them up and place them on my lap the firecrackers stop at last, so who knows? Their gaudy colours blaze against the dark material of my dress. Like lorikeets at dusk.

Miss Iida puts out her finger and touches one of the gods. 'Hotei, the laughing Buddha.'

Hotei is the fattest of the gods and the one with the widest smile. His round stomach is bare.

Miss Iida places her finger on Hotei's belly and looks into my eyes. 'You must rub for good luck.' She yawns. 'After present is bedtime.'

'You go right ahead.'

She lies down, places her head on her briefcase and falls instantly asleep.

I toy with the idea of sneaking away but I can't find it in me to leave her alone on a station at midnight. I suppose that catching a bus to Brisbane is as good a plan as any. I have no reason to be back in Sydney. No reason to be in Byron Bay. There will be plenty of trains in Brisbane. I can jump under one any time I want.

I contemplate my Lucky Gods as Miss Iida sleeps. Good things might come in sevens, but bad things come in sevens too – the seven deadly sins, the seven gates to the underworld, my seventh lover . . . Is that just a coincidence? I don't think so. A shiver travels down my spine and I reach for Hotei. It's about time some good luck came my way.

The air is humid and the scent of flowers strong as I rub Hotei's belly. A flicker of optimism warms me. I am forty-one years old but perhaps it is possible . . . Can my life begin again?

The streets are quiet in the pre-dawn light as we walk out of the station and across to the bus stop some hours later. I haven't slept at all but I don't feel tired. Since I hadn't expected to see this morning at all, just being here feels like a bonus. My Lucky Gods are in my hand, the string of the pouch around my wrist. I can feel them through the silk – one, two, three, four, five, six, seven.

Miss Iida inspects the timetable in the corner of the bus shelter. 'Bus come at six am.'

We sit down.

'Maybe?' she adds.

The night revellers are sleeping it off on the beach or in their beds, or those more sturdy may have climbed to the lighthouse for the sunrise. All is quiet. All is possible. We could be in an alternative universe where the bus will never come.

'Maybe,' I agree.

But, at precisely six am, we see headlights. A bus rounds the corner and we climb on. We are the only passengers. Our driver nods. We purchase tickets in complete silence – it seems to be called for. I take a seat next to a window and despite the many seating options Miss Iida perches beside me. We rumble through the town and out onto the almost empty highway like passengers on a ghost ship. We are quiet – as if to speak would break a spell, turn our carriage into dust. Or a pumpkin.

As the bus sways around a corner Miss Iida leans closer and speaks in a whisper. 'On New Year's Day Lucky Gods travel together on treasure ship, visiting houses.' Her breath tickles my ear. 'Before go to bed, you put picture of Lucky Gods under pillow. If you dream about good luck, then you will have lucky year.'

I nod, rolling my Lucky Gods between my fingers like rosary beads.

'Don't tell anyone your dream, or it won't come true.' Her voice is an urgent murmur. 'If you have bad dream you make picture float away on river or sea to stop bad luck.'

'Thank you. I'll do that,' I whisper back. I have no intention of doing any such thing. I have no intentions at all. I feel as if I am barely here.

We relapse into silence. As I sit beside Miss Iida on the bus I don't feel anything unusual. No tingle, no presentiment. I see a round-faced, pale-skinned girl in a button-up shirt. I don't notice how special she is. I don't see that her nerdiness is just a disguise. I am too wrapped up in myself to realise what I have found.

Later, I shudder when I think how easily I could have let her get away.

We are almost in Brisbane when her eyes alight on my handbag and she breaks the silence. 'Vintage?'

It might be only one word but it catches my attention. Her voice seems different, less diffident – a combination of soft and hard, quiet but determined. Yes, there was a lot going on in that word. And was that a hint of an American accent? I hadn't noticed it before.

I look at her again. The morning sun streams in through the window now, casting a glow around her. And at once I see what I'd missed before. What I would have seen straight away if I had been myself.

On her dazzlingly white sneakers, she has drawn some feet. They are lifelike – it is as if her shoes are transparent. Her too-high jeans stop short above her ankles, exposing red socks. I was wrong to think she had no dress sense. I get it now. She has something going on – something subtle and clever.

I nod, suddenly wide awake, as if set free from an enchantment. 'You like vintage?'

She shrugs. 'Yes, you know – the connection with past, simplicity, grandmother thing. It is still good. But . . .' Her English suddenly seems much more fluent.

A twinge of excitement stirs me. I swallow, lean towards her. 'But what?'

'It is . . .' She waggles her head with a slight grimace.

I know what she means. It is on its way out. 'What do you think is next?' I say this casually but it takes an effort.

Miss Iida looks out the window, gesturing at a girl on the street with her chin. She is wearing blue, a floating dress. 'I see that a lot. In Japan more.'

'What does it make you think of?'

She is quiet for a moment and I want to reach out and shake her, but then she speaks. 'Flow.'

'Flow?' I can't pretend disinterest anymore.

'Ocean, river, word, poetry, music. Anything that flow. Shade of blue, long hair, fountain, chiffon skirt . . . ' Miss Iida gazes into the distance with a far-off look that I recognise. She is channelling. 'River journey, surfing, poetry on T-shirts . . .'

I can hardly breathe for excitement. I look at her and I see myself.

At the age of twenty I would collect fragments like a bower-bird, building them into a fabulous prophecy with a barely discernible effort. My reputation rests on being the first person to predict that mobile phones would become more ubiquitous than Filofaxes. I also foresaw that grey would be the new black post-9/11, that juice bars would be the new hamburger joints and that animal prints would move out of the jungle and into the shopping mall. Call it mysticism, call it sensitivity to the universal consciousness, or call it luck. I call it my mojo. Out of my subconscious came pure gold.

For more than twenty years I forecast trends as easily as breathing. It was an animal intuition, not a science. I walked the streets and a collective intelligence soaked into me. I would stride into a meeting, pronounce *magenta is the new blue*, and everyone would take notes as if the oracle had just spoken.

Last year, my mojo evaporated like fairy dust. From this first misfortune flowed many others. Or did the misfortune flow the other way?

I had never met anyone else who could do what I did, though not for want of looking. Plenty of bright young trainees came my way, but none could take the leap from pupil to master. They were all good with spread-sheets, with figures, with sales. But what none of them understood is that trend-spotting is more like magic than logic.

'What is your first name, Miss Iida?' I say.

She smiles, exposing the gap between her teeth. 'Haruko.'

'Do you really have to go straight out to the airport, Haruko?' I say as the bus pulls into the middle of Brisbane. 'Why don't I buy you a cup of coffee first?'

Haruko glances at her watch. 'Okay.'

I smile with relief. I'm not sure what I would have done if she'd said no, but I suspect it would have been demeaning.

When we get off the bus, Elizabeth Street is like a vision of purgatory. Washed-out bodies flop in cafes and slump on benches. It is New Year's Day after all. Those who haven't stayed up all night pondering suicide have obviously been partying hard.

Haruko and I sit down in a cafe and I put my Lucky Gods on the laminex table. They have been in my hand since Byron Bay. The background noise fades. Our surroundings are irrelevant. We are like two actors spot-lit on stage.

We lock eyes across the table and I feel it then. There is something between us. Something I haven't felt before with anyone else. Not sex. I know what that feels like.

I'm sure Haruko feels it too, but she turns away. She isn't going to let herself fall in deep with a woman who was contemplating suicide only hours before. I am certain, now, that she knew.

Of course she knew.

I come out with it as soon as the coffee is on the table – a job offer. I can't hold on to my excitement any longer. I am expecting her to jump at it. *A life raft. A soft landing. An escape.* There will be no commute to Tokyo and it won't be fifty-one weeks a year. Brisbane isn't far from the surf. She seems to like Australia. And – the major selling point – I will pass on my hard-won knowledge of how this trend-spotting game works. Many would cut off their right hand for that offer. Although there is no way she could know that.

'No, thank you, Misaki.' She drains her coffee. 'I must go back to Japan.'

I breathe deeply; I must try not to seem desperate. 'Just stay one more day. Change your flight. Think about it. I'll pay your expenses.' I have no money, but I'll find some. I can't let her go.

She gazes into my eyes with a look that is way too knowing for her years. It seems to come very naturally to her, that look. I can see her thinking, *what does Misaki want from me?* Maybe she has learnt that you don't get anything for nothing. There is always a catch. *Always.*

As Haruko shakes her head again her phone rings once. A text. She glances at it. Her eyes linger for a moment longer than is necessary, then she looks up. 'Okay,' she says. 'I will stay one night.' Without another word, she makes a call and changes her flight to the next day. As soon as this is done, she stands up. 'I am going to Lone Pine. I have always wanted to hug koala.' Her English is almost perfect now, with just a hint of an American accent. She pulls out a business card and places it on the table. 'My phone number.' She bows.

I know I should reciprocate, but I don't have a card. Such things have been left behind. I have nothing except my vintage handbag and the clothes I am wearing. I hadn't expected to need luggage where I was going. 'I'll call you.'

Haruko bows again, smiles, and is gone.

On the second of January I meet her again. Same humdrum cafe. I hardly recognise her. She has transformed overnight from nerd to punk.

She smiles as she sees me take in her look and touches her zippered black jacket. 'Doom and disaster with distressed fabric.' She is speaking in code. Fashion code. Trend code.

Two can play at that game. 'Black is not a colour, it is an answer,' I reply.

Something passes across her face then – recognition. I think that is when she makes up her mind.

She sits down and again it happens. The air around us goes still. The eye of the storm. A solar eclipse. The curtain rises. I feel something in my brain. *A tickle. A tease.* I offer her the job again. I have checked the visa situation and she is allowed to stay for a year.

This time she barely hesitates before she says yes.

I had never been in any doubt that she would. The night before I had followed her instructions and drawn a picture of the Lucky Gods. I placed it under the pillow in my cheap inner-city hotel room and when I dreamt, I dreamt about Haruko.

Three

'Pilgrimages are so hot right now. I think they are the next Big Thing.'

This is the kind of thing Haruko always says. And always with the conviction of youth. With Haruko's help I am back in the trend-spotting game, albeit in a more low-key way than before.

For one week now she has been channelling for me. We could build a small clientele among furniture designers and clothing retailers – it would be easy money – but I am looking for the Big One, the one that will put me back on the map. Trend-spotting is a fast-paced field. Standing still is going backwards. The only way I want to re-enter is with a bang.

I know it is only a matter of time until we find the Big One. Haruko is the real deal. I can hardly believe my luck.

Now, I tap my pencil on the desk. 'Why pilgrimages?'

Haruko picks up a blue marker, scrawls four words on the small white board I have set up near the table. *Transition. Penance. Sacred. Journey.* 'Very now,' she says. 'Particularly walking pilgrimages.'

I nod. 'You got some stats?' I know she will. Haruko flies by the seat of her pants, but she also prepares.

We are in the lounge room of my Spring Hill flat, which I am renting by the week. Soon, I am sure, we will be able to set up an office, but for now we have a white board and a table. I had to call in some favours to get this far.

It is not just inertia that has kept me in Brisbane, although that is partly true. Heading back to Sydney would have been too much, too soon. Too many memories, too many expectations. In Brisbane, no-one knows me. I don't have as far to fall.

Haruko pulls her phone towards her and slides her black-framed glasses down from the top of her head. Today she wears a ruby-red faux-flapper dress and shiny gold sneakers, which she has left next to the door. I have told her that it is okay to wear shoes inside, but she never seems to remember. Her fingernails are parrot green. Looking at Haruko makes me feel that Christmas is just around the corner even though it's still January.

'Camino pilgrimage in Spain, now over 200,000 pilgrims each year, compared to six hundred in 1985. Shikoku pilgrimage in Japan, five years ago 50,000, now 150,000 pilgrims every year.' Haruko looks up.

I like the sound of it. *Shikoku pilgrimage.* The words spread ripples in my mind. I gaze out the window. A heat haze rises off the footpath of my steep, narrow street. 'That's it?'

'There are lot of other pilgrimages, but . . .'

'You haven't got the figures.'

She nods. 'Still, you have to admit, Misaki . . .'

The name Misaki has stuck. I am fond of it. I wonder now if Haruko ever really thought it was my name or if she was just playing. Haruko has layer upon layer. I'm not sure if I will ever know her.

I steeple my fingers together. The ripples from the pebble are spreading. *Shikoku.* I feel something. It is not the tingle I get when my mojo is working, but it is an echo of it. 'Tell me about the Shikoku pilgrimage.'

'Shikoku pilgrimage is best in Japan, I think. You walk 1200 kilometres, to eighty-eight temples.' Haruko leans back and puts her bare feet up on the table. Her toenails are parrot green too. She sees me looking at her feet and blushes, pulling them down. 'Sorry, Misaki. I have very bad manners. Everyone tells me.'

'No, no. Please. Put your feet up.' I wave my hand.

But Haruko shakes her head as she pulls the tab off a can of her favourite drink – Fanta. In her hands, even Fanta takes on the aura of cool. Haruko could make joining the Girl Guides seem hip if she wanted to. 'I have done, myself. One week, only. Eleven temples, not eighty-eight.'

'So, why would someone undertake a pilgrimage?'

Haruko's eyes meet mine. Her lips are now faintly stained with orange. I can feel our brains aligning as they always do when we talk trends. It is like I can channel through her. I have the experience, I know what questions to ask, but she is my connection to the ether. Together, we are almost as good as I used to be. One day the pupil will overtake the teacher and she won't need me anymore. I don't like to think about that.

'Traditionally, religion,' Haruko says. 'You are cleaned of your sins.'

Cleansed. Forgiven. Redeemed. The idea is like a clear and glassy pond. I have much to be forgiven for. 'Right. You'll spend less time in purgatory.'

'Purgatory?' says Haruko.

'It's a Catholic thing. You have to wait in a place that is neither heaven nor hell. Were you brought up religious?' Instinctively, I touch my Lucky Gods. They are set up on the table and my finger runs along them, stroking their heads like charms. I keep them with me at all times. While they haven't brought me too much luck yet, who's to say what might have happened without them? A run-down one-bedroom flat is better than no flat at all. And Haruko did stay – at least for now.

Haruko gazes at me over the top of her glasses. Her hair bobs around her face. 'Japanese pray to Shinto Gods for success at school and work. Buddhism is for funerals. We do both. You?'

'No. I made my parents send me to Sunday School for a while, because all my friends were going. It was more about boys than bibles though, so I don't know much about purgatory. What can you find out?'

Haruko types the word into her phone and scans it for a moment before looking up. 'You must balance out your sin before you enter heaven. If you are little bit bad, you spend time in purgatory being cleaned up ready for entry to pearly gates.'

'So purgatory is betwixt and between, you are neither in nor out.'

'It is state of transition,' says Haruko.

'And a pilgrimage gives you a *go direct to pearly gates* pass. Yeah, I can see why you'd do that. What about the Japanese though? It must be different for them. Do you have pearly gates?'

'For most Japanese, pilgrimage is about reward in this life, not next. Like praying to Shinto Gods. We ask for practical help.'

'So, you get lucky now, instead of later. Works for me. But pilgrimages aren't just about religion, are they? Not these days. They're about transforming yourself.'

'Yes. You come back changed,' says Haruko.

'You come back healed.'

'Maybe you meet hot pilgrim, find love.' Haruko's tongue flicks out over her orange lips.

'Maybe.' And I think perhaps we will talk about love but then Haruko slurps loudly on her soft drink and the moment is gone. 'You leave one world and enter another,' I say.

'Everyone want that.'

'Just look at Harry Potter.' I love it when ideas fly between us like this.

Haruko smiles. She is feeling it too. 'You pass through gateway from one world to next,' she says.

I gaze out the window at my suburban street. *Transition* . . . Could pilgrimage be the trend that puts us on the map? *Transformation.* It has the ring of authenticity. I can feel it. If my mojo had been working, I wouldn't have needed to wait for Haruko to tell me that pilgrimages were so hot right now. I would have known it myself.

'You're right, Haruko. This is very now.'

'How can we use it?' she asks.

This is my department and the only reason Haruko needs me. She is my link to the zeitgeist. I am the goblin who spins her gift into gold.

That night, I take Haruko out to dinner. We walk down the hill from Spring Hill, past the Tibetan flags on falling-down terraces. Homeless men gather on the street corner in the fading light for coffee and sandwiches. They will spend the night on park benches, but they still call out a cheerful hello as we go by.

I am on a mission to discover more, to understand this mystifying girl I've found. We have been practically joined at the hip for one week, but yet I still know so little. She comes across as cool, in control, but I can sense sometimes it takes an effort. Haruko is like surrealist art – she can be interpreted in many ways. Or not at all.

We eat Italian and share a bottle of cheap wine. As we finish our tiramisu, I ask her about her job. 'Are you missing it?' I find it hard to conceive. A pencil factory! A girl with her talents could do anything.

Haruko giggles, putting her hand up to her mouth. 'I am very naughty. I have never worked in pencil factory,' she says. 'That was just a story, for Miss Iida. It fitted her. I was playing. Sorry, Misaki.'

As she says this, it makes perfect sense. Of course she never worked in a pencil factory. Why would a girl like Haruko do that?

'So, what do you do back home? Are you a student?' I don't even know how old she is. She looks about eighteen, but she acts older.

Haruko drains her wine glass. 'I go with men for money.' She says this with no more emotion than if she'd said she worked in a cafe.

I try to hide my surprise, my shock, but probably don't succeed. I wonder if this is just another story and if there are others to come. But I sense at least an element of truth in it.

Haruko waves her hand breezily. 'All girls do it. Even school girls. I am almost too old now.'

'How old are you, Haruko?'

'Twenty.'

Twenty. I nod. Somehow I knew she would be twenty.

'Men like girls in school uniform very much,' says Haruko. 'I still fit mine. That is how I buy ticket to

Australia.' She stands up. 'I go to bed now, I think? See you tomorrow.' She bows and heads for the door.

I watch her as she walks past the window – a ruby-red dress on a grey street. It must be windy out there; her hair blows across her face. She walks quickly and soon she is gone. I touch my chest, soothing a sudden ache. I feel no closer to understanding her, but at least I know how old she is. Although, perhaps, I already knew.

After I pay the bill I walk, aimlessly, and find myself in the Queen Street Mall. I pass an all-night Internet cafe and a door advertising showgirls. Up a side street a sex shop displays items that baffle me. I stop and study them, their purpose slowly becoming clear. Do people really do that? I suppose they must.

A group of Goth kids is slumped in a doorway of a closed department store. They are young, no more than early teens. I wonder if their parents know where they are. Maybe they don't care. Their eyes slide over me as I pass. In their world I don't register.

Eventually, I find myself at the river. I lean on the railing of the bridge and gaze down at the muddy waters. *I work in a pencil factory. I go with men for money.* Adversity affects people differently – some go soft, some go hard. I haven't known Haruko long but I think her life has given her a shell that's difficult to prise open. *Closed windows keep the rain out.*

I am the opposite. Survival has made me soft. I lost my shell along with my marriage. Now the world just flows on in. I don't know how I dare to let it, but I do.

Four

I touch the Lucky Gods with my finger, one by one, as I do every morning now. Outside it is already thirty degrees and it isn't even ten o'clock. Inside, a sluggish fan shifts the air around. I suppose it is better than nothing.

On the other side of my lounge room, Haruko is working up a pilgrimage concept plan. I could do it in half the time, but she needs the experience. If I were a little more ruthless I would bring Haruko in only for ideas. I would keep to myself the nuts and bolts of turning dreams into dollars. Ideas are one thing – getting people to pay for them is quite another. I did a marketing degree solely to learn how to make money out of this gift of mine. I could easily ensure that Haruko continues to need me as much as I need her. A year ago I might have done that. But then, a year ago I was a sinner.

I pause when I get to my favourite – Benzaiten, the only goddess in this group. Benzaiten wears pink. Her black hair is piled up on top of her head in a bun and a gold heart adorns her chest. She is the goddess of music, fine arts, beauty, eloquence and literature. In fact, Benzaiten is the goddess of all that flows. And more than anything, I want what she offers. I want that flow of ideas, of connectedness, to return. I want my self back.

Benzaiten's virtue is amiability, a most female virtue, and one that I seem to have misplaced along with my husband and my mojo. I don't like myself as much as I used to. These days I am brittle, impatient, quick to find fault. Except with Haruko.

I watch her typing, thinking, typing. She is lost to this world, her face wrapped in contentment. I see her and I see myself. I see the way I used to be.

I touch Benzaiten's head in the hope that some of her good nature will flow on to me.

'Benzaiten is very brave.' Haruko is looking up from her work. 'When she met a dragon that was eating children, she married it and used her good influence to subdue it. They had fourteen sons and one daughter.'

Amiability, fertility and wifely competence. Yes, Benzaiten has everything that I do not.

'Benzaiten's shrines are near water,' says Haruko. 'Sometimes she has eight arms, in order to protect against disaster.'

'That's a good feature.' I consider my Seven Lucky Gods and wonder in what way their luck will manifest itself. I hope it happens soon.

I have always been suggestible, superstitious even, one of those people who sees links, connections, meaning in things that are meaningless to others. For a while this was my strength, before it came to be my weakness. Over the time that I have had my Lucky Gods I have pondered their meaning, because I know they have one.

Although not the trend-spotter I used to be, I still find myself analysing portents and symbols for hidden significance. The world seems deeply mysterious to me in a way that it isn't to others. A crow outside my window, a dog following me home, a dream of a shipwreck, any of these things can set my mind off on a tangent of cause, effect and meaning from which it may take some time to return.

I understand totally how people can come to believe they are Jesus or, worse, the other guy. I understand, but I don't go there. I stay on the right side of sanity. Mainly.

I watch Haruko typing and I can't help thinking that there is a reason she is here with me – a reason beyond the obvious. I remember the text message she got in the cafe on New Year's Day. Was that the moment she decided to stay? I hope she isn't disappointed with the way things are turning out.

My eyes roam around my dingy lounge room – the leatherette sofa, the two innocuous and almost featureless landscape prints . . . Why can't people be a bit more daring with their art? It's not like it costs any more to be adventurous.

When Adam and I moved into our first house together we crammed it with cheap surrealist prints. Dali brushed up against Tanguy, Miro came face to face with Magritte. It's a wonder that our Blossom Road terrace didn't explode with the energy, angst and creative audacity crowded inside it. There is nothing restful about surrealism.

Surrealism, in a way, is what brought Adam and me together. He had an exhibition at the university where I was a student; he was studying art there as it turned out. Adam has always painted in the surrealist style. I admired his work, he admired me, I admired him back, and so it went . . .

I have always loved the surrealists, always felt that I was on their wavelength. Trend forecasting is a lot like surrealist art – you tap into the subconscious, you mix and match, you try unusual combinations until you find one that sings. If I was an artist, I would be a surrealist.

I stand up and take down the brown-hued landscapes. It is an improvement I think, but still . . . My eyes scan the room. This is such a far cry from my Sydney trend-spotting business. Haruko could do better.

I am grateful to her for so much, but I'm not sure if she's grateful to me. I suspect she will leave me as soon as she figures out how to do this trend-spotting thing on her own.

Thinking about Haruko leaving makes me nervous. Without her I'll be back where I was – back on that station in Byron Bay. I chew my hair as I always do when

I'm anxious. I'd have thought I'd get over this by the time I turned forty. All this chewing isn't doing my hair much good. I should get it cut, but I am resisting the commandment that women of a certain age should bob their hair.

Before lunch Haruko gives me her pilgrimage concept outline. It is the first she has done all by herself. She places it on my desk like a child with a school project. She wants my approval. I can hardly bear to look at it. I can tell at a glance it is as good as anything I have ever done.

'I'll read it after lunch,' I say. 'I'm a bit tied up right now.'

Haruko returns to her desk – the kitchen table. Her shoulders slump a little in her red jacket. Today she's dressed like Minnie Mouse. Teased-up pigtails poke out from the sides of her head and the jacket is teamed with a short blue skirt. False eyelashes brush her eyebrows. I have never seen Haruko wear the same look twice. She is a genius of metamorphosis.

When she goes to the toilet I flick through her proposal. I was wrong. It is better than anything I've ever done. She doesn't need me anymore.

I look down at my desk – at the envelope I have been trying to ignore all day. What I am actually tied up with has nothing to do with trend-spotting. What occupies me is a package that came by Registered Post this morning. This innocent padded post bag holds a ticking bomb. It contains a letter from my husband's lawyer requesting a divorce.

How I carelessly lost my husband, the short version:
Mea culpa. I strayed. I fell in love, or something like it, with another man.

We bonked enthusiastically for months. His wife found out. When the music stopped with only two chairs left, he and his wife were sitting in them. My husband and I wandered off in different directions.

The slightly longer version:
This is not a nice story. I should really change the names to protect the innocent. *Ha.* Like any of us are innocent, least of all me.

Love is a mystery and a puzzle. I loved, still love, my husband. That is immutable. It is a given in the way that you believe you will wake up with your heart still beating. Till death do us part, and all that . . .

What I had with Ben was something else, an apparently inescapable force.

We had no children, my husband and I, a fact that made it easier to drift our separate ways after he found out about Ben. We had no children not through choice, but because we couldn't. In the way of childless couples, we had a Labrador called Maisie. After our separation, Maisie went with Adam. I didn't think it was fair to take her away from him, being the guilty party in this relationship gone astray.

The trouble with marriage is that it makes no allowance for whirlwinds that strike your heart without warning. If you could just say, *sorry, darling, I'm in the grip of a tornado but I think it will pass*, there might be less heartbreak in this world. I'm not sure that humans are designed for monogamy, but then I have a stake in this opinion. Others would disagree.

Adam and I had been together for twenty years, married for fifteen. We were happy. Placid, but happy. It had been at least ten years since we'd had sex up against a wall or talked into the night trying to fathom the mysteries of each other's universe, but we were friends, companions. We had nice holidays together. I still found him attractive if not devastatingly so. We could have gone on for another twenty years in this way if not for Ben.

I have been thinking a lot about marriage in the year since we separated. I read in the paper recently that long-married couples actually know less about each other than those who have only just got together. It's a funny thing. People change. Twenty years down the track you find you're living with someone whose inner mind is . . . not so much a mystery, as that would imply mysteriousness and the reality is duller than that; it is more like a library you have explored so many times you think you know it. You haven't realised the collection has changed.

Ben. I hardly know how it happened.

I'd thought I was over all that, had left it behind, was surprised, shocked, bowled over by this thing I found. I plead insanity. He pulled me into a world of untamed emotions, raging hormones and wild craving. I was like a teenager again.

I hadn't even known there was a hole in my life until I met him. But then – there it was, suddenly spot-lit – a yawning chasm of need that must have been there all along. Had I been skating around it for years? It seemed I had.

Even now that the whirlwind has passed, leaving shattered roofs and broken hearts behind, I don't think I could have done things any differently. I mourn my marriage and wish it could be different, but I don't regret the decisions I made. What would be the point?

Since Adam and I separated over a year ago, he can now legally file for divorce. He does, however, need me to sign a paper saying I have received his application. I stand up and walk over to the wastepaper bin. In two seconds Adam's lawyer's letter is no more than confetti. Adam and I might not have seen each other for almost nine months, but it's going to take more than weasel words on paper to end our marriage.

Five

Lunch has come and gone. Haruko keeps looking over at me. I tap away on my iPad – a recent purchase – as if I am in the middle of something urgent. She is too proud to ask me. I am too scared to tell her. I know I should but I am afraid she will leave me. Go back to Japan. Start up her own trend-spotting business.

My Seven Lucky Gods eye me accusingly. *Just tell her*, says Benzaiten. *Tell her she's good. Tell her she doesn't need you anymore. Perhaps she will stay anyway.*

But perhaps she won't. And Haruko has come to mean more to me than just her ability. If I still had my power I would know what it is that she means. I would understand these garbled signals in my brain that tell me not to let her go. *Not yet. Not yet.* Not until I have my self back.

My self. My mojo. Like many things, you don't realise how much you need it until it is gone. Can this really be what life is like for most people? So grey? So two-dimensional? So lacking in possibilities? They say if you're born blind you never know what you're missing.

I can remember the moment I first discovered my power.

I was ten years old and skipping was huge at the time. Every break at school, out would come the ropes, and hey-diddle-diddle we'd be playing *rock the baby* and *high, low, dolly, pepper*. This went on for months. On the surface the enthusiasm never diminished, but I sensed something different. We'd been learning about the five senses at school. But this new sense had nothing to do with them. See, hear, feel, touch, smell – no, it was none of those. Although . . . now that I think about it, it was almost like a smell, a smell without odour. That sounds ridiculous, I know. But this sense wafted on the breeze too. It came in waves. As I moved my head in one direction it became stronger. Previously the air had been vibrant around the skipping rope. Now it was flatter, duller, almost, but not quite, stagnant.

One day as I was skipping I felt a stillness in the air. I kept jumping up and down. *Charlie over the water, Charlie over the sea, Charlie caught a blackbird but he can't catch me.* Up and down, up and down. I wondered what it was that we enjoyed about skipping. The up down thing reminded me of something. And for the first time it occurred to me that this skipping thing wouldn't last forever. Something else would take its place. What would it be? *Up down, up down.*

Yoyos. They had the fun of the up down, the freedom, the skill, the games. I didn't know the word zeitgeist at that stage, but I knew the time for yoyos had come. I found a dusty yoyo in the back of the toy shop and bought it for fifty cents. I still believe I started the 1982 yoyo craze that swept the country.

The yoyo is the second oldest toy in the world, after the doll, but while dolls never go away, yoyos – most appropriately – come and go. Toy manufacturers have tried to imitate the appeal of the yoyo with other, more expensive, toys, but they've never caught on. In 1965 there was the Swing Wing – a cap with a wing on top that you rotated by twirling your head. Unfortunately, it had to be recalled due to neck injuries in over-enthusiastic twirlers.

It's funny which toys catch on and which fall by the wayside. Monopoly, Twister, Mr Potato-head, Troll Dolls – all made their inventors into millionaires. But how many apparently similar inventions just disappeared? That, of course, is where the skill of the trend forecaster comes in. Kenny Rogers had it right when he said you've gotta know when to fold them. A good trend forecaster is like a water dowser – they can save a lot of wasted time and effort.

In modern times, there has been a yoyo craze every ten to fifteen years. Now that I think about it, there is one due right now.

The stillness which presaged my predictions became very familiar to me. I never took it for granted, but it never deserted me. *Until now.* I could walk down the street, thinking of nothing but what was for dinner, when suddenly it would happen. Maybe I would see a girl with wild hair and a torn dress, or maybe a boy gazing intently at a puddle on the road. And there I'd go . . .

It was like being an epileptic without the fits. A sensation of grace would descend, I'd hover between the conscious and the subconscious, and suddenly I would know – the next Big Thing was going to be *madness.*

The concept unfolded like a slide show: pale women curled up in padded white rooms, music that sang to you of worlds beyond worlds, couches suggestive of psychiatrists' offices, drinks with names like Schizo and Manic. I never saw it as anything mystical. It was just that I knew how to pay attention. I thought that anyone could have done it if they'd tried.

My trend forecasting was like being dealt a lucky hand, time after time after time. The trends were there, I just pulled them out of the pack.

Companies paid big money for my advice. They were never dissatisfied.

So what made my muse vanish?

Hmm, now there is a question that plumbs the depths of the psyche. I suspect the Ben thing rearranged my brain. Is it only coincidence that Ben was my seventh lover? I think not. Like I say, not only good things come in sevens. Though he seemed like a good thing at the time . . .

Falling in love was like falling off a cliff – the most thrilling and terrifying thing in the world. It seemed like a miracle. I was a married woman; I'd never expected to feel that way again. And you don't turn your back on miracles. I don't anyway. It's against my religion. My whole life has been based on acceptance of whatever the cosmos may throw at me.

Did he fall in love with me? It seemed that he did. While I held back, afraid to mention the l-word, he jumped right in. *I think I'm in love with you*, he said after the second time we met. Even before anything had happened between us. The words came out so easily. So confidently. Perhaps he meant it at the time.

Ben. Every time I saw him it was like his brain and mine connected at that innermost part – the part that was responsible for my predictions. While we were together I had an explosion of forecasting. The world was not just colour, it was Technicolor – saturated in significance. Trends wafted towards me on every breeze.

I came to depend on it, forgot that I used to be able to do it without him, forgot that I loved my husband. With Ben, I often lost all consciousness of my surroundings and after he left I'd feel this sense of utter calm, like I was in a trance. Then it would happen: *reptiles, glaciers, organics, angels* . . . The ideas gushed out of me like a fast-flowing spring. It was the most productive time of my life. It was also hugely addictive.

Oh, it is hard severing that kind of connection. I imagine withdrawing from heroin couldn't be much worse.

Especially when I realised he'd taken my mojo with him. It wasn't just the man I was losing; it was my livelihood. And not only my livelihood, but the thing that had been most essentially *me* for so long. It wasn't that the messages went away when he left; they were still out there, but I couldn't make sense of them. They were being delivered in another language now.

The thing that surprised me was how easily he let me go when his wife found out. It baffled me – hadn't he said he was in love? I felt like I'd had a limb amputated and he . . . it was more like he'd had to hand back a biscuit. There was regret – some – but not this raw, gaping disbelief and pain.

Pain. I don't think I'd known the meaning of the word until then. I hardly slept for weeks, woke constantly from dreams of him. Couldn't accept it. Wouldn't accept it. It was ugly. I humiliated myself dreadfully, pleading and begging. I would have been happy to drop the sex; just to be in his company from time to time would have been enough. But it was not to be.

I hardly noticed Adam's departure – didn't even get out of bed to wish him goodbye. I could feel him bleeding, but I was busy tending my own wounds. Yes, that is one thing I do regret.

'Better just to let it go, Arkie,' Ben said, in our last phone call.

'But . . .' *I love you? You love me?* 'You've stolen my mojo,' I said.

There was silence on the end of the line. 'I don't know what you're talking about,' he said.

There was a click. He'd hung up. That only made me more sure of it. That bastard had taken my mojo. He was using it himself.

Two broken hearts and Ben walks away with my mojo.

Six

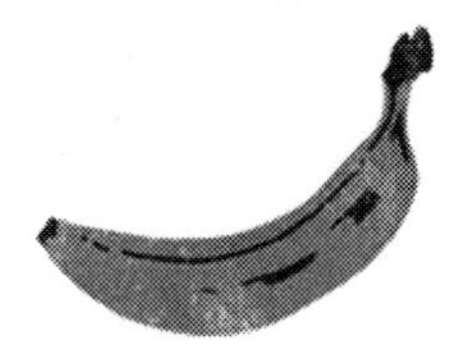

Haruko looks over at me. Her face is a question. Her brown eyes are magnified behind her glasses. I should set her mind at rest. She is resourceful, independent and smart and she deserves success. *Go back to Japan and start up your own business*, I should say. *You don't need me anymore.*

'Yoyos?' I say.

Haruko nods and I can see she totally gets it. 'Want me to put a concept together?'

I smile. 'Yes please.'

'Have you read the pilgrimage proposal?' A flush appears on her cheeks.

I can see how much this costs her. Haruko has a hard shell but it is only millimetres deep. 'Just about to.' I smile brightly.

Haruko turns away. Her pigtails droop.

I have an urge to cheer her up. 'What about shops made out of cardboard?' I say. This is a big effort on my part. I prefer not to use the c-word if I can help it. 'How do you think they would go?'

The effort is worth it. Her face transforms. It crinkles into laugh lines. Haruko is very pretty when she smiles. Her mouth is one of her best features. 'No way. Forget it, Misaki. Nice idea, but it never going to fly.'

If only I had known Haruko a year ago.

It was not too long after Ben and Adam both left me that I had a very good idea. That's what it seemed, anyway. I didn't realise when I took this idea on, when I turned it into a concept, a plan and then an action, quite how badly things had gone wrong in my head. The world had become very grey, but I thought I just needed to focus. I was going through a rough patch. As it turned out, that rough patch was a wilderness twice the size of Siberia and just as inhospitable. I haven't got to the end of it yet, or even sighted its boundary.

I knew I wasn't on form, but I didn't yet realise my mojo had totally left me. I was in denial. Reading *The Three Little Pigs* might have helped. You don't build your house out of straw. In retrospect, throwing all my money into a shop made of cardboard was a very bad idea.

I'd never put my own money into trends before. I was the forecaster. My clients were the ones who took the risk.

I'm not quite sure what made me do it this time. It could have been the impending divorce. Lawyers are expensive and I'd need a new house. My cardboard shop would be my little nest egg, my golden goose. Money can't buy happiness but it does help to insulate against despair.

My thinking went like this. We are heading towards an age of new simplicity. All the forecasters were saying so. Not just me – people who had their heads together as well. Consumers shop with their hearts, not their heads. A cardboard shop says environmentally responsible. It says affordable, but in a classy way. It says basic but new, both *now* and *then*, fashion forward, but harking back to old values. It offers an alternative to consumerism, while, of course, still selling things. What could be better?

And to top it off, I then remembered – in a flash – how, many years ago in Blossom Road, *The Enchanted Room* by Carlo Carra had dropped on my head as I was dusting. This painting of a jumble of cardboard boxes arranged around a fish was clearly auspicious. It was a sign I couldn't ignore – cardboard was my destiny. It didn't occur to me that the fish might be rotten.

The idea took place like a vision. It seemed the real deal – a true prophecy – *imagination, improvisation, dialogue, anticipation.* The vision was almost, but not quite, in Technicolor. I was so keen to believe I still had my mojo that I ignored the warning signs, the dullness around the edges, the way I had to coax the details out of myself. They didn't flow the way they used to. I should have known then that this wasn't the universe speaking, it was my desperation.

In my mind the cardboard shop was a thing of beauty, even glory. Everything would be made of cardboard – the counters, the shelving, the walls . . . I even looked into cardboard cash registers but that proved one step too far. My cash registers would be coated in cardboard! I whistled as I planned . . . *Cardboard hangers, cardboard shoes, cardboard hats and cardboard loos.*

One night I woke up with a brainstorm – portable cardboard privacy shelters! Don't we all feel like we sometimes need to build a little shelter and get inside – escape the herd, revitalise? My self-designed shelters folded up to the size of a small laptop. Unfolded, they covered the body from the head down to the waist like a cardboard burqa. If you sat cross-legged, you would be completely covered or, standing, you could at least maintain the feeling of being alone. I would have liked to trial my Revitashelter while waiting in the queue at the bus stop, but I wasn't quite that far gone. I was still keeping up appearances, still holding on to those vital constructs of clothing and manners that mark you as part of the herd, rather than an outcast.

One day though, perhaps, everyone would carry their Revitashelter, whip it out whenever they pleased, but until that day I tested it in the privacy of my own home. This produced modifications, a tiny interior light powered by a small solar cell on the top, just enough to read by, a flap that you could push to check up on progress outside and a choice of relaxing scents accessed through a scratchy pad on the inside of the box. Lavender and frankincense were my favourites.

I loved my Revitashelter. I got into the habit of climbing in at work – I had a private office – just to recuperate after a hard morning when the trends didn't flow. Business was tough. I had ten staff relying on me. They watched with dog-like eyes as I vanished into my office each morning. Every time I emerged their fingers hovered over their keyboards, waiting for my pronouncements – waiting in vain. It was enough to drive a woman to drink.

But there was something about being contained in that small cardboard space that instantly defused tension. It was like having your own private wilderness retreat. I was sure my cardboard shop and Revitashelter were going to be the Next Big Thing. I didn't tell my staff though. Something stopped me.

Oh yes, I had my doubts. I waited for the tingle in my fingertips that told me I was onto something, but it didn't come. I called on my muse but she had left me so I used my left brain, not my right. I signed a five-year lease on a space in a new shopping strip in Paddington. I built my straw house. I called it Arkie's Ark. I should have realised any enterprise involving a twee name like that could only end badly.

I got in an architect, from Japan of all places. But when you think about it they do a lot with paper over there, all those sliding screens and origami. Nori Fujimoto was even more enthusiastic about my vision than I was myself. He practically cried when he saw the finished product. 'So beautiful,' he said. Nori Fujimoto was rather beautiful himself. He had long, silky hair and high cheekbones. If I hadn't sworn off men for life . . .

And the shop *was* beautiful, in a totally hip, retro, funky downmarket way. The doors were cut into intricate patterns like lacework. I did a lot of it myself. It was what I needed – occupational therapy. Don't underestimate the calming effect of simple manual activities. Pre-school teachers know what they're doing.

Everything I stocked was in keeping with my theme – cardboard bookcases, toys, chairs, sculptures, bicycles and, also, coffins. That part was definitely a mistake. People who are into cardboard coffins are, well, unusual. They bring a certain tone to a shop that scares off other customers. I tried to define it, but could only come up with one thing – smell. I will say no more on this topic.

It turned out that people weren't as ready for cardboard as I'd thought. Not only that – the cardboard didn't wear well. It was a wet summer and even though the shop was indoors it started to smell damp. After one week it was like a school project gone wrong.

I had a sale in the hope of giving things a kick along. This worked, but the rush of customers pulled my shelves apart. Those Paddington blondes are surprisingly destructive once they've had their post-Zumba double-shot lattes. I put it down to too much adrenaline, caffeine and time on their hands. In retrospect, Newtown might have worked better. They understand downmarket chic on that side of town. I would have known that once.

The shop was my grand folly, my Taj Mahal, my pyramid. 'Look on my works ye mighty and despair,' I muttered as I slammed the cardboard doors forever. Like Ozymandias, I was left with a crumbling tribute to my pride.

My trend-spotting business folded just days after the shop. I could no longer afford the wages. It had been nine months since we'd signed a decent contract. I realised then that although the shop had been a folly it had been the only thing keeping me going. Without it I had nothing. And that's when my world turned to black and white.

I continue to pay the exorbitant lease on my folly, which is now nothing more than a mouldy eyesore. This rent takes all of my disposable income; I live like a pauper. The shopping precinct management sends me stern letters telling me I am bringing down the tone of the street. I'm not sure why they think I give a damn.

I know I should do something about it, but I haven't the heart. The idea makes me sick. I have developed a strong aversion to cardboard. Even the name makes me tense. I prefer to think of it as *Derived Paper Product*. Just the sight of it raises goose bumps on my arms and makes me feel like I've had one too many fairground rides.

The other week I was handed a box of fish and chips and had to run from the shop before throwing up. I now keep a pair of gloves in my handbag in case I am required to handle the stuff. I should see a counsellor, but I am too embarrassed. I am probably the only person in the world with this phobia.

Maybe one day when I can face Haruko's scorn we will get on a plane to Sydney. I will take her to my shop and we will design a new concept. One that works. Until that day, the c-word is better left unsaid.

Seven

It is almost five o'clock. Haruko's pilgrimage proposal is open on my table.

Her eyes flick in my direction and away again.

She has put a lot into it. The cover reads, *Journey to the Heart*. She has printed it on heavy paper – not cardboard, luckily – and bound it with a black binder. We don't have these facilities here in my unit, so she has had to make a special trip to an office supplies store. The proposal is for no-one's eyes but mine. I am flattered and touched that she cares so much about my opinion. Each page has an image, a stimulus word or phrase, an expansion of its meaning and associated trends. This is the way I have always done it. Trend proposals are deceptively simple. But a well-researched proposal is the tip of an iceberg; it is the thought and vision beneath that count.

The first picture is a row of deep orange archways painted with Japanese symbols. The arches are placed close together, almost touching, and a path runs up the middle. They curve around a corner and out of sight. The path beckons you in, towards another time and place, like a *Doctor Who* time tunnel.

Above the picture, Haruko has written, *Transition*. She has used a thick black pen and her handwriting is beautiful, like calligraphy. I learn new things about Haruko every day. The text below reads,

In the forest near Kyoto is a shrine for Inari, the fox goddess. Thousands of vermilion gates invite you to enter the spiritual realm. Tori gates separate the common world from the sacred. You emerge onto a hilltop with forest beneath you. The sound of shakuhachi flute drifts towards you.

The opposite page is scattered with images that suggest how this trend can translate into reality. Some are photographs, others are drawings that Haruko has done herself. Vermilion print designs, spiritual walking holidays, tables shaped like tori gates, bamboo flute CDs . . . Oh, Haruko is good. She is very good. The clients will eat this up. Not that we have any clients yet, but we will, we will.

I turn the pages. They get better and better. If this proposal had a button marked *buy now* I would press it immediately. On the last page is a Japanese Zen garden. No plants grow in this garden. It is just white gravel and jagged rocks. The gravel is raked into lines like water flowing around rocky islands. Over this image Haruko has written, *Liminal, subliminal, sublime*. And then below,

The garden of Ryoan-ji has fifteen rocks, but only fourteen can be seen at any one time. The meaning is something to ponder. Your subconscious recognises what your rational brain may not.

I gaze at the image. My heart rate slows. The picture draws me in. I feel a sense of longing, yearning, loss. If I could just be there, sit and look at those rocks, I could find my self again. I could find the part of me he stole away. It's in there somewhere.

Scattered around the picture of the stone garden are images of other parts of the garden, ponds, golden leaves, paths leading through mossy forest. They are beautiful but my eyes keep returning to the rock garden. Its simplicity draws me. It is like a puzzle I need to solve, an answer to a question I haven't yet asked.

My eyes move on. Next to the rock garden is a small image of a moss-covered stone bowl with Japanese writing around the outside. Beneath this Haruko has written,

Translation of writing – Everything you need, you already have.

Everything I need I already have . . . It's a nice idea, but is it true? If so, where is it? How do I find it? My eyes go back to the rock garden. *There. I'll find it there.* I rest my chin on my hand. I wonder what Haruko sees in the rocks. *Tangled trees? Braided rivers? Jagged mountains?*

I think the garden is like one of those Rorschach tests. Everyone sees something different. It depends on what you've known. On what you want. It is nothing but a stimulus for your mind to fly free. *Silver fish. Perching birds. Coiled snakes. A baby crawling.*

I blink to break the trance and direct my gaze at Haruko. 'This is exceptional. You don't need me, you can do this yourself.'

Her cheeks go pink. She runs her tongue over her front teeth. Haruko doesn't realise how cute that gap is.

And then I say something I didn't see coming. I didn't see it at all. It must have been there, a pebble, lying quietly in my mind ever since she said Shikoku. Unknown to me, pearl was accreting around it. It has come to fruition. And now, suddenly, the oyster shell opens.

'How would you feel about being my guide while we do some on-ground research on this pilgrimage concept?' I say. 'We can go to Shikoku.'

'Shikoku?' Haruko looks at me like I am soft in the head, then the side of her mouth curls up in a half-smile. 'Sure,' she says. 'I will be your pilgrimage guide.'

I smile back in relief. Maybe the problem of Haruko leaving me is solved. For now.

• • •

After Haruko goes home, I pace the streets again, high on a surge of enthusiasm. Haruko's proposal is in my handbag. Reaching the river, I pull it out and turn the pages slowly. It is perfect. Why haven't I realised before? This is the way to put it all behind me. A pilgrimage. I will repent, atone . . . transform. In my head I am already there. *Rock gardens, tori gates, stroll gardens, temples, Shinto Gods.* Oh, it is just what I need. The pilgrimage is a life raft. *Everything I need I already have.*

The mangroves that line the Brisbane River are covered in mud from the last time it flooded. The water is opaque and full of silt. Soon I will be gazing at the Sea of Japan, not this brown and sluggish river.

I jump on a bus back up the hill. Public transport is a novelty. In Sydney I walked to work and if we ever went anywhere else, Adam drove. Seeing no need for it, I let my driver's licence lapse. Buses are surprisingly soothing. They give you time to think of other things.

Drifting along on my happy high, I don't realise I have forgotten one minor but essential point. My life raft has left the river of reality and is floating down a tributary. The old Arkie has taken over, the one who sees no barriers.

After dinner for one and the sole glass of wine I permit myself – I indulged my addictive personality rather too much last year – I turn on my iPad. My life raft takes on water as I start my research.

The Shikoku pilgrimage takes sixty days. This is what a two-month pilgrimage to Japan with Haruko will cost me:

Airfares × two: $2000
Accommodation – sixty nights at $200/night: $12,000
Miscellaneous (passport, transport etc): $1000
Total: $15,000

I check my bank balance. Once I allow for this month's payment on Arkie's Ark, this is how much I have: $1368. I might be able to scrape up the airfares, but once I get there I'll be broke. Maybe we can camp? And beg for food. Isn't that what pilgrims do?

This sounds tough but possible until I realise it is winter in Japan. Camping is out of the question. It could be snowing. Besides, I'm not really a camping person, although I have glamped on a couple of occasions. Glamping is some marketer's term for glamour camping, which is nothing like camping in the traditional sense.

As I check the figures again, the Sea of Japan recedes into the reality of a hot and humid Brisbane night. A trickle of sweat runs down my neck and vanishes into the crevices of my singlet. The pilgrimage straw I have clutched at so desperately is no straw at all. I feel like an idiot. I turn off the tablet.

My phone goes *ting*. I have a text from Haruko. She is taking her role as guide seriously.

Dear Misaki,
Pilgrimage starts as soon as you are commitment. Now you must make your body, mind and heart to be ready.

I smile. *You are commitment.* I think she might be role-playing again. I imagine her wearing her Miss Iida clothes – the nerdy glasses and high-topped jeans. I wouldn't put it past her.

But I don't reply. I don't know how. How can I commit to a pilgrimage I can't afford?

On my bedside table is Haruko's proposal. Looking at it will make me feel worse, but I can't resist. I open it randomly at a page titled, *Sea – space between realms.* On the opposite page Haruko has scattered pictures of headlands, beaches, rocky outcrops with waves dashing against them.

Promontories into the sea mediate with other realms. One quarter of temples on the Shikoku pilgrimage are on the sea.

I turn the page: *Spirit mountains*, it reads.

Spirits congregate on mountains, making them ideal to explore border between common and divine. Ten of Shikoku temples are situated on mountains.

I sigh, close the book, pull my knees to my chest. I want it so much, the mountains, the sea, the rock gardens, my *self*. That is what I want more than anything. I thought I had the answer, but it is like my cardboard shop – no answer at all.

I flip over in bed. My window is open but no air moves through the room. Outside, a siren wails. Spring Hill, once a down and out part of Brisbane, is slowly being yuppified but a core group of druggies and minor crims ensures a restless sleep most nights.

My Lucky Gods are beside me on the table. Sitting up again, I touch them one by one. I need this pilgrimage so badly. I am tired, but wired – I feel like I will never sleep. In my drawer I keep Temazepam, begged off my doctor last year. Each one ensures five blessed hours of sleep but I only have ten left and I know she will not renew the prescription. My addictive nature mustn't be encouraged. Each night I struggle with the urge to take one. Tonight, I resist. There will be more urgent times.

As a flashing blue light illuminates my room I catch a glimpse of my reflection in the mirror on the opposite wall. For a moment I don't recognise myself. Can that person be me? I look deranged, bright eyed; my hair is ragged and badly in need of care. Is not recognising yourself the first sign of madness?

Ben would have had something to say about that. Ben had something to say about most things. That is one of the things I most valued about him – his insights. I bury my head in the pillow, trying not to think about him. It doesn't work. Oh God, I was so crazy about him. *You still are*, whispers a voice inside my head. *You'd go back to him in a flash if he'd have you.* I wish that ridiculous and unsavoury voice would go away. It's not true, it's not true. He is nothing to me. Nothing.

Somehow I find my phone in my hand with his number on the screen. I hold it to my ear and listen to it ring. Imagine it ringing beside his bed. Imagine his hand reaching out . . .

'Arkie?' His hushed voice is irritable. 'I told you not to ring me, Elaine –'

'Is not recognising yourself the first sign of madness?'

'No. Ringing someone at one-thirty in the morning to ask inane questions is.' He hangs up.

I check the time on my phone. He's right. I had no idea it was so late. For some reason this strikes me as very funny. I start to giggle but find myself crying. Great gulping sobs wrack my body. I feel like a boat being struck by a storm. I have no idea where all this sadness comes from. Just when I think I have exhausted my supply of tears the reservoir is restocked. Perhaps, if I cry long enough, the storm will pass.

Eight

My sheets are wet when I wake, whether with tears or sweat, I don't know. I am groggy, anticipating sadness, the return of disillusion, but wait . . . Something new is bubbling in my chest. It feels like . . . hope. At first this is inexplicable. I have nothing to hope for. I am not going to Japan.

As I listen to the sounds of the suburb waking up I remember a dream. This is unusual lately; apart from my dream about Haruko the first night I met her, my sleep is mainly dream-free. I used to dream a lot when I was happy, back when I had my mojo. I dreamt a lot when Ben dumped me too, but they weren't happy dreams and they stopped dead the day Adam left me. Dreaming gives me a warm feeling in my stomach. My subconscious is stirring. Not taking Temazepam was the right decision; in a drugged sleep you have no dreams. I close my eyes, let the dream come back to me.

I am walking along a beach, and up ahead is a temple. I am in Shikoku. The temple is pink, with a strange, pointy shape. As I get closer it looks even stranger. It is not a temple at all. It is a giant crustacean – a lobster. This does not surprise me. I have a sense as I approach this giant lobster that I am completing part of an important journey. The lobster has bulging black eyes. One of them winks at me and I wink back.

The dream lingers with me as I go through my morning routine. As I brush my teeth it strikes me that the lobster in my dream is the lobster from *Lobster Telephone*. In Blossom Road, a reproduction of Dali's *Lobster Telephone* sat on a table just inside the front door. Although it wasn't connected we used to pretend that it was, just for the slightly risqué pleasure of speaking into it. Also known as *Aphrodisiac Telephone*, its mouthpiece is formed by the lobster's genitals.

Lobster Telephone . . . It is mysterious, clearly symbolic. Does it have a message for me?

Walking is very good for contemplation. I follow my usual route along the city streets. Brisbane comes mainly in shades of grey. There are the buildings – greyish; the streets – greyish; and the river . . . Brisbane comes in shades of brown and grey.

But this morning is different. As I cross the road towards the Botanic Gardens, I see a splash of vivid pink. I keep my eye on it as I draw closer. How could I not have noticed this extravagant display of colour before? I come here every day.

I stop at the Garden's perimeter fence and peer through. It is a cherry tree. In full bloom. The sound of the cars behind me fades to nothing as I stare at the tree. It is at least four metres tall and its spreading branches are crowded with blossoms.

I feel like I have stepped from Kansas into Oz.

The Wizard of Oz movie made a big impression on me as a kid. I only saw it a couple of times at the local cinema but in my memory it seemed like much more. My mother gave me a record of the soundtrack for my tenth birthday and every time I listened to it I felt like I was watching the movie again.

My favourite scene was the moment after the tornado when Dorothy opens the door and steps outside. In that instant, the movie shifts from monochrome to saturated colour. And oh, what colours. Glinda the good witch appears in a phosphorescent pink bubble, the newly emancipated munchkins are as gaudy as parrots, the grass, the sky . . . It is like an acid trip. Not that I made that particular connection at the time. That came later.

Now, in the middle of Brisbane, I feel like I am reliving that moment – I'm not in Kansas anymore. I can't understand it. Yesterday – no tree. Today – tree in full bloom. Walking up to the gate, I keep my eye on it to make sure it doesn't vanish as quickly as it has appeared. Have I conjured it up from my imagination?

I walk briskly through the gate and back along the fence, half jogging, to the tree. As I get closer, I see the red tape surrounding it – not an apparition then. Someone else has noticed it, taped it off, this intruder from another hemisphere.

And then I see the security guard. He is leaning against a nearby post, chewing gum, bored. He eyes me with mild interest. I don't suppose I seem the vandal type. I glance from him back to the tree. Some of the flowers are quite low. If I reach up I can . . . I look back to the security guard. His eyes are still on me.

'Can I pick one?' I say.

He shakes his head. 'They're silk.'

'Silk?' I turn back to the flowers. 'They look real.'

'Well, they're not. Don't get cherry blossoms here, do we?'

I can't argue with that. 'So, why is it here?'

'Japanese beer commercial,' he says. 'Starts filming today.'

'Oh.' I study the tree in a state of rapture. It is so completely *other*, so clearly a message. At last, I notice the security guard's frown. He thinks I'm a nutter. Maybe I am. I take in one last glorious vision of the blossoms and move on.

My brain is fizzing – first the dream, now this. My subconscious is absolutely seething. I wish I knew what it was telling me. Once I would have known. *Lobster Telephone. Cherry Tree. Lobster Telephone. Cherry Tree.* There has to be a connection. The two go together, but I'm not yet sure how. Once I work that out, everything will fall into place.

If a tree full of cherry blossoms can appear in the middle of a Brisbane summer, then who knows what might happen next?

I am climbing the steep hill to my flat when it strikes me with the force of an electric shock. Laughing out loud, I run the last twenty metres with no effort at all.

This is it. This is it. This is it.

I hum to myself as I get ready for work. As I get older, maintaining my appearance requires more and more time. Lately, I have not bothered. Who cares what I look like? Possibly my clients would, but since I don't have any this hasn't seemed important enough to justify the effort.

My hair needs a cut. I should really get it coloured too, to cover the grey bits. My eyebrows need plucking; I probably have chin hairs, but I prefer not to notice. As I gaze in the mirror I see a woman who has Let Herself Go. *Letting go.* I smile. Not such a bad thing, surely?

Haruko climbs up the stairs at precisely nine o'clock. She is never late. Today she wears denim shorts, cut off at the top of her thighs. Underneath are fire-engine red tights, strategically ripped at the knees. She has left her glasses off and bright green contact lenses decorate her eyes. She could have stepped from the page of a manga comic.

I am a little nervous about sharing my new idea with Haruko, but it has to be done. Who knows how she will take it?

Once she has taken off her shoes and settled at her desk, I place the pilgrimage proposal down in front of her and tap it with my fingernails. Like my hair, my fingernails are not what they used to be. They are cut short and chipped red nail polish clings to them. *Splashes of blood. Flakes of rust.*

'This is really terrific,' I say, 'but I've been thinking . . . what we need for this concept is . . .' my throat constricts and I cough, 'an Australian pilgrimage.' The idea, which seemed exciting and bold in my head, comes out sounding about as plausible as a cardboard shop.

Haruko raises an eyebrow. 'Pardon?'

I think she has heard, but I clear my throat and repeat myself. 'An Australian pilgrimage.'

Haruko looks a little affronted. Perhaps she is thinking that ideas are her department. She studies me closely. Possibly she is wondering if my power is returning or if I am off on a wild caprice. She has a shine in her eyes I haven't seen before, but perhaps that is the green contact lenses.

'Why do you need to go to Japan to discover yourself?' I say. 'Can't we *Eat, Pray, Love* in Australia?' I should tell her I can't afford to go to Japan, but something stops me – a foolish pride.

'Well, sure, the concept needs to expand for everyday life, be made relevant. That is the next stage, right?' She flicks through the pages, her fingernails sparkling; they seem to be coated in gold glitter. She stops at my favourite, the Zen garden. 'But, Misaki, where do you find this sort of inspiration in Australia? In desert?'

'The desert's been done; there was that camel woman . . .'

Haruko cocks her head.

'You wouldn't have heard of her.'

'So?'

'There are plenty of places that are interesting. Places unique to Australia. Like . . .' My mind casts around. I open my mouth and say the first thing that comes into my head – something totally unexpected. 'The Big Prawn.'

Haruko's eyes widen, as if sensing danger.

The Big Prawn decorates the old highway in Ballina, the town I flew to on my ill-fated journey to Byron Bay. While it didn't make a major impression at the time, clearly it lodged in my subconscious.

I could have gone straight to Byron Bay from the airport, but I was on a determined quest for distraction, for adventure. It may not have occurred to many that Ballina was a place to find such things, but I didn't want to discount any possibilities. I told my taxi driver – a good-natured suntanned man in a white polo shirt – to show me the sights of Ballina first.

'The sights?' Apparently he had never been asked this question before.

'There must be some sights.' I gazed out the window at a forest of paperbark trees that bordered the airport. What I had thought was brown fruit in the top of the trees moved and flapped their wings. 'Are they bats?'

The man glanced at the trees. 'Yep. Flying foxes. They've had to schedule the flights around their flyout time. No flights at dusk.'

'That's nice.' I liked the idea that for once humans could accommodate an animal species, rather than the other way around. I wound down the window and sniffed the air. It was pungent, fertile. A bat gave a high-pitched squeal. I felt like I was already at a frontier, away from the skyscrapers and traffic jams.

'There's the Big Prawn,' said the taxi driver. 'Would you like to see that?'

'Aha. I knew there was something. Take me to the prawn.'

The Big Prawn was about ten minutes from the airport and easily viewed from the road. The cabbie drove past slowly, then turned at the roundabout and cruised past it again.

'Very pink,' I enthused.

'Should have seen it when it was new,' he said. 'You used to be able to climb up inside. And there was a souvenir shop underneath.'

The prawn was more than a little weird; there was something about it though, something stirring. We were halfway to Byron before I realised what it was. The Big Prawn was a dead ringer for the lobster in *Lobster Telephone*.

Nine

Haruko is eyeing me as if I am someone to be treated with caution. She runs her thumb along her keyboard and back again in a nervous action. Perhaps she thinks I have slipped over the boundary that divides the herd from the outcasts, the sane from the mad. For a moment, I wonder myself. How would I know?

'The Big Prawn?' she says finally.

I smile broadly, like the person I used to be. If I am mad, I don't much care anymore. My enthusiasm warms me from the inside. I am onto something. I know it. 'Did you see the Big Prawn? In Ballina, near Byron Bay.'

Haruko shakes her head. 'I did not go to Ballina.'

'The landscape of a pilgrimage is as much emotional as physical, right? The actual place is not as important as the place your mind takes you. Correct?'

Haruko looks bemused. She nods again.

'What do you think of when you think of the Big Prawn?' I say.

Haruko half-closes her eyes. She knows this game. 'Sunburn, summer, lunch . . .'

I sense that she is holding back, not taking me seriously, but I have never been more serious. 'Go deeper,' I say.

Haruko closes her eyes. She doesn't say anything. Seconds pass.

I touch her arm. 'Haruko?'

She opens her eyes and blinks. Drops of moisture glisten in her eyelashes. She gazes at my hand, as if wondering what it is doing there.

'Are you okay?'

She half-smiles. 'I am fine. Prawn is . . . creepy.'

Her voice warns me off. To me, the Big Prawn is just a metaphor for what I might find along the way, a symbol of discovery. But it seems to be more than a metaphor for Haruko. It means something.

She toys with her phone, then looks up at me. 'Too many leg.' She wiggles her fingers at me and smiles.

But I think there is more to it. I chew my lip, wondering if I should try to draw her out and what might emerge if I do. Yet another version of Haruko? Perhaps some other time. 'What do you think, Haruko? Will an Australian pilgrimage work? Will you still come with me and be my guide?'

Haruko gives me a long look. 'I will think about it.' She turns back to her computer and starts typing. Her neck is pale as she bends to her task. She pretends she doesn't know I'm still there.

I am dismissed. I watch her for a moment, wanting to touch her shoulder, tell her she can talk to me. What will she do now? Go back to Japan? My tender heart makes its presence felt as it does so often these days. Will I be like this for the rest of my life – so naked, so vulnerable? In some ways I don't mind. Feeling too much is better than not feeling at all.

I retreat to my desk, taking Haruko's proposal with me. While the idea of an Australian pilgrimage feels right, I am unsure how to bring it to fruition. My pilgrimage may not be exotic, but it still has to be meaningful. And what about Haruko? I'm not sure that I have the spirit for it without her.

I flick through the pilgrimage proposal. *Ten of the temples are in the mountains. One quarter are by the sea.* So, like the Shikoku pilgrimage, maybe I will have a combination of sea and mountains? That should be feasible. *What else?* Under a heading saying, *A pilgrim is removed from their normal life*, is a picture of pilgrims wearing white coats and pants and carrying staffs. *A special outfit is needed?* Yes, of course a special outfit is needed. All special occasions require a special outfit.

'Haruko?'

She looks up from her computer. She is back to her normal self, cool, unruffled.

I hold up the picture in the book. 'Are white clothes important for the pilgrimage?'

She cocks her head to one side, places a glittering fingernail against her cheek. 'The colour is symbolic.'

'Of what?'

'Of death. A burial shroud.'

I look at her, unsure what she means.

'The pilgrim is seen as close to death. A lot of them die. And if they did not, they were little bit reborn as result of pilgrimage, so it is like their old self die.'

'Reborn sounds good. Better than the alternative.' I make a note. *White clothes.* 'Am I being ridiculous, Haruko?'

Haruko smiles. She seems to have forgiven me. 'All best ideas are ridiculous at start. You are visionary, Misaki. Australian Pilgrimage will be big this year.'

'So you will come?'

Haruko fiddles with her phone. 'Maybe I will go back to Japan.' She sounds hesitant.

I don't push her. Haruko and I return to work, but my mind is still turning over. Haruko has given the idea her tentative endorsement. *Australian Pilgrimage – a pilgrimage as big as Australia.*

Excitement bubbles inside me but I tamp it down. I need Haruko's help with this – my instincts can no longer be trusted.

That night Adam rings. I haven't heard from him for months. We had no need to talk once the practical details of separation were finalised.

'Fabian says you haven't responded to the divorce papers.' His tone is restrained.

'Divorce papers? I don't think I've seen them.' Adam's lawyer is a mean-spirited toadie called Fabian Fernley. I know him well because he used to be my lawyer too. When Adam and I split I was happy to let him have Fabian. I never liked the man. I haven't engaged a lawyer myself. I refuse to participate in this game called divorce.

Adam sighs. 'I know you've seen them, Arkie. Why won't you sign them?'

We haven't discussed divorce before, but I know he assumed that once a year was up it would happen. I suppose I assumed that too, but now . . . I am almost surprised by the strength of my opposition. It is like I have never considered that divorce is the next logical step.

'I don't want a divorce,' I say.

'Why not?' Adam sounds baffled.

'I love you.'

The words fall into a pit of silence. The silence is full of the things he could say:

If you love me why did you have an affair with Ben?
If you love me why didn't you even get out of bed to say goodbye when I left you?
If you love me why didn't you see that I was hurting just as much as you?

But Adam is ever gracious. 'I'd like it sorted out, Arkie. Then we can both move on.'

'Is there . . .' I can hardly bring myself to say it, 'someone else?'

'No, Arkie. There's no-one else.'

I expel my breath in a sigh. I still have a chance.

'But that doesn't make any difference. I want a divorce.'

We are silent for some time.

You get more beautiful every day, Adam said on my fortieth birthday.

No-one says things like that, except in the movies, but Adam did. Daily. He loved me too much. I grew fat on his admiration, lazy and vain. His love was like air. I took it for granted, not realising it was essential to life.

'How's Maisie?' I ask. 'Have you taken her for her walk?'

'Yes. She's on a diet. She's not very happy about it.'

'Give her my love.'

'I dreamt about you last night,' Adam says.

My heart gives a tentative leap.

'I dreamt I flew out the window and left you behind, never saw you again, never thought of you.' His voice is quiet.

'Don't do that, Adam. Please.'

'Sign the papers, Arkie.'

'I shredded them.' I hang up before he can reply. In the silence that follows I realise I have made a tactical mistake. I should have played for time, pretended I was about to sign. Now Adam knows I have shredded the papers he will send Fabian after me.

I drum my fingers on the phone, then run to the computer. Research is required. The *do it yourself divorce* site tells me the divorce cannot proceed until I have been served the papers. *Good.* If I refuse to sign, Adam's representative – but not Adam himself – must deliver them to me personally and confirm I have received them. The divorce can then go ahead, with or without my signature. I turn off the computer. It is simple – if I can avoid Fabian, I can avoid getting divorced. At least for now. I need to disappear for a while. But where to?

I am sitting on the couch pondering my dilemma when there is a knock at the door. For a moment I think Fabian has teleported to my doorstep. I open the door a fraction then pull it wide.

It is Haruko. She is panting. She steps inside and pulls the door closed behind her. 'Misaki. Can we start pilgrimage tomorrow?'

'Yes,' I squeal and almost jump for joy. I still don't know where I'm going, but Haruko is coming with me. And we are going tomorrow – Fabian will never catch me. 'Hooray. I'm so happy.'

Haruko looks a little taken aback by my reaction. She smiles tentatively.

Suddenly my mind spins. I am starting a pilgrimage tomorrow and I have no idea what is involved. Or where I am going. Perhaps there is groundwork required? I can't just set off on a pilgrimage unprepared. 'Haruko, how do I get ready? What should I do?'

Haruko adjusts her glasses. 'Okay, Misaki, before you start pilgrimage you must know rules of being pilgrim.'

'Rules? Wait, I'll get a pen.'

Haruko shakes her head. 'You will remember. Only six rules, but very important.' Haruko counts them off on her fingers. 'One. You must not kill so no eat meat. Two. You must not be immoral, so no sex. Three. You must not drink alcohol. Four. You must not quarrel. Five. Do not have too much baggage. Six. You must not have a lot of money.'

'That sounds fairly easy.' *Apart from the alcohol.*

'Seem easy now,' says Haruko. 'Might get hard later.' She sounds like she is speaking from personal experience.

'I have so much to learn. You will have to help me.'

Haruko nods. 'I will help, but must go now.'

'Early start tomorrow, okay? I'll meet you at Roma Street Station at six-thirty?'

Haruko smiles. 'Early is good.' She opens the door, gives a quick glance up and down the street then runs down the hill.

'Haruko, where will we go?' I call after her. But she must not hear me as she doesn't stop.

I watch her knee-high white socks vanish into the night and wonder what made her decide to come. But perhaps it isn't important. Because, after all, there is already so much I don't know about Haruko and this is just one more little thing.

Part Two

'The road to the City of Emeralds is paved
with yellow brick,' said the Witch.
The Wonderful Wizard of Oz, *L. Frank Baum*

Ten

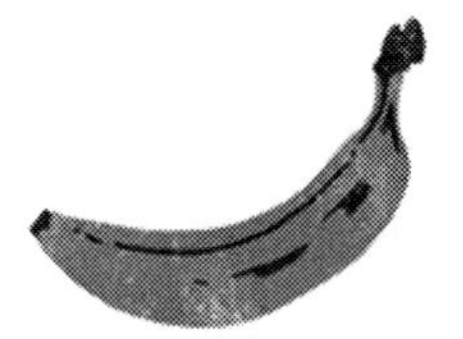

By six am, I am ready to go. I have packed my small wheelie suitcase and dressed in a white T-shirt and loose white pants. My white sunhat is in the daypack slung over my shoulder. I doubt that Fabian could be here this early, but as a precaution I pull out my sunhat, tuck my hair up into it and slide on a pair of Paris Hilton sunglasses before I go out the door.

As instructed by Haruko, I am travelling light. For me, that is. I am one of those people who likes to pack for every conceivable occasion. I would rather push the limits of my bag allowance than find myself invited to a function for which I have no suitable outfit. My small wheelie suitcase is usually just my cabin baggage, while my large wheelie suitcase travels below.

A virtuous glow fills me as I trundle out with my small suitcase. Technology-wise, I am taking only my smartphone and an iPad. My laptop and camera are left behind. This is a wrench, but I must be strong.

Searching for inspiration on what to pack, I trawled the web last night. Here, I discovered to my surprise that lightweight travelling is not just about packing your bag, it is a philosophy. Lightweight travellers have a 'never-ending commitment' to 'aggressively seek out' the lightest gear solutions. Unfortunately, I have failed to pre-stock with lightweight pants that zip off into shorts or quick-dry underwear. I don't have shoes that can take me from Everest Base Camp to a London night club. For some reason, my toiletries bag grows larger every year. A five-kilogram load is just not achievable.

However, down the rabbit hole of the Internet, I found an inspiring woman. Emma 'Grandma' Gatewood is known as the pioneer of lightweight hiking. Grandma's ascent to fame started in 1955 when, at the age of sixty-seven, she hiked the 3500-kilometre Appalachian Trail. An army blanket, a raincoat and a shower curtain were her only supplies. And on her feet – tennis shoes. This mother of eleven – *eleven!* – and grandmother of twenty-three did it all again at the age of seventy-five.

I try to imagine having eleven children. Fail abysmally. Would you get them mixed up? And then the grandchildren . . . imagine the noise when they all got together.

Without Grandma's inspiration, I probably would have weakened and taken my large suitcase. As it is, my wheelie bag is bulging with last-minute items I thought I might need. But still, I have much, much less than I would usually. It is hard to pack when you don't know where you're going. Hopefully Haruko will have some ideas.

Grandma's words are ringing in my ears as I walk down to the bus stop, my too-heavy suitcase trundling behind me. *Most people are pantywaists. Exercise is good for you.* I'm not sure what a pantywaist is, but I don't want to be one.

It is only five minutes before the bus pulls up. I hop in. As the bus goes down the street I see a grey BMW with New South Wales numberplates has parked outside my apartment. A man gets out of the driver's seat. He is large, more than six feet tall, with a soft white face and a stomach that spills over the belt of his grey business pants. Fabian. He must have driven all night. I pull my hat down, adjust my sunglasses and look the other way as I go past.

I wait out the front of the train station. Ten minutes later, Haruko steps down from a bus. Her glasses flash as the sun hits them. I take in her appearance in the moment before she sees me. She is so small, from a distance she seems like a child. She is wearing her Miss Iida outfit. Her jeans are still too high and her white polo shirt is tucked into them. She looks like a Girl Scout – a Girl Scout with a surfboard tucked under one arm and a briefcase held in the other. Haruko has mastered the art of lightweight packing.

'Where are we going?' she says as she sees me.

'I don't know. I was hoping you would have some suggestions,' I say.

She shakes her head.

We stand there, looking at each other.

'Well, here we are. Ready for our pilgrimage,' I say brightly. My eyes flicker up and down the street, alert for a grey BMW.

Haruko's eyes scan the street too. 'We have coffee?' she says.

'Good idea.' *When in doubt . . .*

Inside the station, she glances at the timetable information displayed overhead. 'Buses come soon. And trains.'

She is right, we have no shortage of options but this doesn't make it any easier. On the way to the coffee shop we pass a brochure rack. Haruko plucks one of each brochure out of its holder. 'Research.' She smiles.

But I'm pretty sure there's no brochure titled 'Pilgrimage Options'.

Haruko places her phone and the brochure stack on the laminex table of the cafe and raises her eyebrows at me. 'So . . .'

I eye the brochures. None of them look promising. Apart from the possible desirability of ten mountain temples and twenty-two sea temples, I have no idea of what constitutes a pilgrimage. I feel a pang of longing for the Zen rock garden. Where am I going to find something like that? 'We might not be going to Shikoku, Haruko, but I want the benefits, the feeling . . .'

'The vibe.' Haruko gazes hopefully out the window at the bay where the buses pull in as if she might be able to conjure up a temple out of thin air.

A cloud of exhaust smoke hangs in the air and it is hard to imagine a less alluring location to start a pilgrimage. 'How can we make it happen? We need to find the elements that will make it work.'

'So, we need eighty-eight temples, right?' Haruko inverts her fingers around the word temples.

I nod. 'Yes, like Shikoku.'

'And we walk between them? That is hard. Australia so big.'

'Perhaps we could catch a bus part of the way and then walk . . .'

Haruko nods. 'They do that in Japan. Bus pilgrimage. Some people think is better way.'

'Really? Why?'

'They have special bus guides. They tell you all about temples while you ride, so you learn more. But walkers think they are only ones doing proper pilgrimage.'

'I want to do something out of the ordinary. Something . . .' I hardly know what I mean. I want a pilgrimage that will restore me to myself. My mind returns to the Zen garden. *Everything you need, you already have.*

'Something of consequence,' says Haruko.

I smile. 'Yes.' Sometimes Haruko speaks better English than I do.

Haruko fans out her brochures on the table, like a magician spreading out a pack of cards. There are brochures for Lone Pine Koala Sanctuary, Sea World, Movie World, Australia Zoo, The Pet Porpoise Pool, Underwater

World, Glow-worm Tours, Surfing Safaris . . . They go on and on. Finally, there is the Big Banana.

My eyes rest on the last brochure. First, I dream of the *Lobster Telephone* and now a brochure of the Big Banana . . . *Lobster Telephone. Big Banana. Aphrodisiac Telephone. Big Banana. Big Prawn. Cherry Tree* . . . My mind flicks between them. There's a connection there of sorts – a loose one, but one Dali would understand.

It is like that game Adam and I used to play every now and then – *Exquisite Corpse.* The surrealists played it first. One of us would draw the beginning of a picture, then fold it over and pass it to the other, who would draw the next part and pass it back and so on . . . In the end when we opened up the paper we were left with a drawing made of parts which challenged our minds to make it whole. You could also play it with words. The name – Exquisite Corpse – was the result of such a game.

Haruko's eyes follow mine to the Big Banana brochure. She picks up her phone and types in a few words. Her finger scrolls and then taps. 'Did you know there are ninety-seven Big Things in just Queensland and New South Wales?'

Big Things . . . 'Give me a look at that.' I put out my hand. Haruko has a map open on her screen. My eyes run over it. *The Giant Mushroom, the Big Ant, the Big Beer Can, the Big Cheese, the Big Chook* . . . 'I had no idea there were so many.'

Haruko meets my eyes. She smiles.

I gaze at the screen. It's possible, it's definitely possible to put all these things together and make not an exquisite corpse, but a pilgrimage. A strange pilgrimage possibly, but one with its own logic. A surge of electricity races through me. *Yes.* A whiff of mojo makes my toes curl inside my white sandshoes. This is my Australian Pilgrimage, my body says so. But will Haruko agree? I look up at her, a question in my mind.

'We go to Big Things?' Haruko is silent for a few moments, letting the idea sink in. Then she nods slowly. 'Yes. I think so.'

'You do?'

She nods.

'You don't think it's stupid?'

She shrugs. 'Seems not stupid to me.'

'Yay.' I smile, putting up my hand. 'High five for the eighty-eight Big Things.'

Haruko meets my hand with a slap and a gap-toothed beam.

My hand tingles from the slap and I can feel it. Our pilgrimage to the Big Things is an idea whose time has come.

Outside the window, a bus to the Gold Coast pulls up, its door opening with a swoosh. I was thinking of going north first, into the heartland of Big Things, but I am impatient to begin my journey and there is the Fabian factor . . . It is possible he will look for me here when he finds me gone. The departures board says that the next bus north is an hour away.

'Let's go,' I say to Haruko, but she is already on her feet.

By the time I have paid for our coffee she is at the front of the line. She must be even keener to get out of Brisbane than I am. Haruko and I take our seats and I scroll the map southwards as the doors close. Our first destination will be a temple on the southern outskirts of Brisbane.

As the bus carries us down the motorway, I open Haruko's pilgrimage proposal to get me in the mood.

Somewhere near Kyoto, set in a forest of maple and beech, is shrine called Fushimi Inari . . .

I breathe deeply. Ah yes, the shakuhachi flute, the meditation, the monks . . . I want it all. I close my eyes, feel the throb of the bus. Temple number one, here we come.

'Where do we go first?' says Haruko.

I open my eyes.

She is gazing out the window expectantly.

'Surprise.'

Haruko smiles. 'I love surprise.'

Eleven

After twenty minutes or so it seems we are nearing the spot. Pulling out my phone, I check the GPS. A lonely bus stop sign marks the side of the highway ahead. Beckoning to Haruko, I make my way to the front. 'Can you stop here please?' I say to the driver.

He pulls over; his eyes move up and down, taking in my pristine white outfit, my wheelie suitcase. They swivel to Haruko, who, with her surfboard, looks like she should be on her way to the Waverider at Wet'n'Wild. 'You sure?'

I can see why he is doubtful; the landscape outside is inhospitable. On one side is a six-lane highway, on the other, a high chainmail fence. Beyond the fence appears to be an industrial wasteland. It is difficult to visualise a less inviting spot, short of a war zone. But, according to my GPS, the first temple is not far away. I nod, trying to act more decisive and rational than I feel, as if I have important business to conduct here. The bus driver shrugs and soon we are standing on the edge of the highway.

The bus takes off, blowing up a cloud of dry dust. I cough and pull on my sunglasses, ignoring the curious stares from the windows of passing cars. My GPS points us five hundred metres south.

It seems ten degrees hotter here than it was in Brisbane and it was already a warm day in Hades there. As I trundle down the road I can feel my face turning red. I flap my hand, trying to create a breeze. The almost unmeasurable cooling effect is offset by the effort required. Camping in the snow in Japan could have been a softer option.

Haruko is completely unruffled. She adds a blue bucket hat to her outfit, making her appear even more like a Girl Scout.

Ten minutes later I see our destination. The Big Redback Spider is perched on top of a disused weatherboard toilet. It is rusty, menacing and not as big as I thought it would be. A high fence still separates us from the object of my desire.

'The first temple?' says Haruko.

I nod.

Her mouth twitches, but to her credit she refrains from comment. I can't help imagining the contrast in her mind with the first temple in Shikoku.

There is no sign of a crossroads. Picking up my suitcase, I plunge into knee-high grass until I get to the fence.

Haruko follows. I have a vague idea that we will climb over, but once we are at its base I see how ridiculous that is. The fence is over three metres high. Grandma Gatewood would no doubt have vaulted over with her duffel bag in hand, but I am not an athletic person and I have a rather heavy suitcase. I am beginning to suspect that I may be a pantywaist.

Haruko gazes up at the fence. 'Many challenges face the pilgrim.' She sounds like she is addressing a bus tour about to climb the stairs to a temple.

Trudging through the grass with the fence on our right we at last come to a corner. We follow it around and find ourselves on a rough dirt road which leads to a gate. A chewed-up track heads towards the Big Redback. As I plod along it I wonder if the wheelie suitcase was the best choice of luggage. A backpack might have been more practical, or even a duffel bag. My white sandshoes are soon caked in red mud and my bag catches on every stray pebble.

Haruko takes the lead, making a surfboard and briefcase appear to be the ideal travelling accessories. I think Grandma Gatewood would have approved of her. She consults her phone as she walks. 'Big Redback Spider was built in 1996.'

1996. Over my years of trend-spotting, it proved valuable to remember trends from each year. This helped me to temper my visions with a reality check. If something was in fashion two years ago, then it was too early for it to cycle again. Twenty years ago, and it was almost certainly about to rise to the surface. Name any date in the past hundred years and I can tell you which fad was sweeping the world at that time.

'In 1996,' I say, 'I was twenty-four years old and the top song was "The Macarena" by Los Del Rio.'

'Bomber jackets in fashion.' Haruko throws this out casually.

I stop still and stare at her. 'What year were you born?'

'1993.'

'So how do you know that bomber jackets were in fashion in 1996?' She is right of course – 1996 was a huge year for bomber jackets; I just hadn't got around to mentioning them.

Haruko raises one eyebrow. 'I think you know what is trending when you are three, Misaki?'

'Yes, but –'

'Body piercings only just become trendy in 1996,' says Haruko.

'Honey soy chicken drumsticks were popular,' I add.

'Anything else?' says Haruko. 'I don't know any more.'

'John Howard became Prime Minister of Australia.'

'That is not trend.'

'No, but contemporary events influence fads and vice versa. It is always wise for a trend-spotter to keep an eye on what political events are saying about the mood of the country. If a country is electing a prime minister who is promoting 1950s values, then . . .'

Haruko gives an ironic bow. 'Yes, sensei. I understand.' She gives me a cheeky smile.

'So, Haruko, do you know trends from every year?'

She shrugs. 'I think so.'

'How far back?'

'Maybe fifty years. Maybe more.'

'How? Did you memorise them?'

She shakes her head. 'I am just interested. So I know.'

'I've never met anyone else who knows this stuff.'

Haruko smiles. 'I never met either.'

The sun beats down as we stare at each other, there on the dusty track. I feel like I did in the cafe, that first morning. There is something between us – something strange and unique. Haruko is the first to break away; she adjusts her bucket hat and continues down the track.

Haruko and I come to a halt in the car park. Our first temple is a garden centre, but not just any garden centre, The Big Redback Garden Centre.

My guide is on the job. 'Ryozenji temple is the first in pilgrimage. On arrival at temple, pilgrim will get their book stamped and pray,' says Haruko.

I feel an ache of yearning. None of that is going to happen here.

Haruko holds her phone towards me. 'Ryozenji temple,' she says.

The temple on the screen has sweeping golden eaves, which stretch upwards to a point. It has thick wooden beams and colourful murals depicting dragons on its walls. Beside the temple, trees blaze in orange, red and gold – it must be autumn. I can't see inside, but no doubt there are gold statues, perhaps incense is burning and monks are chanting. I pass the phone back to Haruko and gaze around me.

A tractor is moving piles of mulch nearby. I'm pretty sure the driver has never seen anyone like us here before but he looks away politely. We walk towards the mock outhouse on which the redback perches and peer inside. Its dark and dusty depths hold an actual toilet seat (disconnected), a bucket and some rags. I gaze up at the spider, which now looms above me, its bulging abdomen protruding over the back of the toilet.

That's a scary spider, Mummy.

Oh. The voice takes me by surprise. My water child has been quiet for some time. I realise I have missed her. I wonder what it means that she is back.

'You all right, Misaki?'

I nod. 'Just a bit hot. It's not much like the first temple, is it?'

Haruko shrugs. 'It is temple in the mind. Spider is quite exciting.'

She is right. While the location is uninviting, now I am close to the spider I find that it does have an almost charismatic allure. Its long legs reach down over the toilet as if to grab me and its bulging eyes follow me as I step back for a better look.

But, charismatic spider or not, we are in a dirt yard next to a highway. It is not Shikoku or even Japan. The tractor man is now tending to pot plants. He eyes us warily as Haruko takes a picture of me in front of the spider. My first temple and already I am struck by doubt. What am I doing here? If it wasn't for the spectre of Fabian Fernley, I would return to Brisbane. Perhaps the coast is clear now?

Haruko's phone rings. 'Trend-Spotters Brisbane?' She has diverted our business number to her mobile. 'Yes. You want to talk to her?'

'Who is it?' I mouth.

'Fabian Fernley,' says Haruko.

'Is that her?' His voice bellows from the phone.

'Hang up,' I say. *Ha. Just try and find me here, Fabian Fernley.* I gaze around at my surroundings. It doesn't seem like much, but maybe this is where I'm meant to be.

Haruko presses *end*. 'Who is he?'

'He's an arsehole.' I hesitate. 'He wants to serve divorce papers on me.'

Haruko regards me through her glasses. 'I am sorry, Misaki.' It seems like she might say more, but she doesn't. Instead, she wanders off towards the shop. After a few steps she crouches down, then beckons to me. I walk over to see what she has found. Perched on a stone among the pot plants is a statue. It is a wizard or gnome dressed in flowing robes, with a white beard and round face. He reminds me of something.

'Jurojin?' Haruko cocks her head at me.

I take off my daypack, unzip it, pull out my bag of Lucky Gods and tip them onto my hand. Jurojin tumbles out third. I look from my tiny statue to the garden gnome. Yes, they are an almost perfect match; the only difference is that my Jurojin is wearing an orange cap and holding a scroll with Japanese lettering.

'Jurojin is god of wisdom and longevity.' Haruko points at the scroll. 'Book of knowledge.' She eyes the shrubs around the statue. 'Jurojin is often found with plum tree, symbol of long life . . .'

But then I see something else. Perched among the shrubs is another statue, a shiny grey one. A Buddha. It seems incongruous here, in the urban wastelands of Brisbane. My fingers tingle. Byron Bay, of course, was full of Buddhas. I would have been surprised if it hadn't been, but here? Could a new spirituality be sweeping the outer suburbs? And if there are Buddhas, then . . . Surely the leap from putting a Buddha in your garden to taking a pilgrimage is not much of a leap at all. First you get the Buddha, then you start yoga or meditation and before you know it . . .

'Need any help?' says the garden man. He is in his mid-twenties, almost twice my size and wearing tight stubbies from which his muscular legs appear to have been squeezed like pink icing from a frosting bag. He pulls off his cap and runs his hand through his sweat-soaked blond hair.

Flustered, I point at the tree in a pot next to the gnome. It is less than a metre tall, stringy and unassuming. 'What sort of tree is that?'

'Plum.'

I had only asked for something to say but now I feel a pulse in the air, a tremor, a shiver. It feels like the merest whiff of my mojo returning.

Haruko gives me a triumphant smile.

Jurojin, the Buddha and now the plum tree . . . I must be on the right track. If this was a game of Exquisite Corpse it would be almost too easy. I smile. 'A plum tree?'

'You after stone fruits? We've got apricots, peaches, nectarines . . .' The man points around the garden shop. Even his arm is like a small sapling.

'No.'

'Shade trees?'

I shake my head. 'We're just here for the Big Redback.'

The man glances towards it, as if he had forgotten it was there. 'Oh. Yeah.'

'Do you get many coming just for the redback?'

'No. Can't say I've ever seen anyone do that before.'

Haruko points at the Buddha. 'Have you had that long?'

The man shakes his head. 'New range.' He sounds faintly embarrassed.

'What made you get Buddha?' Haruko sounds like she is conducting an interview.

'The owner's idea. She went to Thailand last year. Decided we needed to diversify. Used to just have garden gnomes and stuff before.'

'Are you selling many?' she asks.

'Yeah, we are. Bit surprised.'

'Do you think that sales of Buddhas are indicative of a new desire for spirituality in our everyday lives?' I say. This sentence just pops out. The old Arkie would never have tried to engage a man in tight stubbies in a discussion about Buddhism. This new Arkie seems to have forgotten the concept of boundaries.

Haruko and the garden man turn to me. Haruko has a slight frown on her forehead. Perhaps she thinks the interview is straying off-track.

The garden man thrusts his plate-sized hands in the pockets of his shorts. I'm surprised they can fit. He looks uncomfortable. Being quizzed about spirituality is not part of his usual routine. He seems to be considering the question, though. He gazes at the Buddha. 'I hadn't thought about it like that before, but now that you say that . . . It does make you think, doesn't it?'

I nod. 'I'm interested in Buddhism.'

The man's body language tells me that he has already said more than he meant to on that topic.

So the garden man, Haruko and I exchange small talk, comment on the heat, the possibility of rain. He is obviously bemused by our presence, our lack of car, lack of apparent purpose.

'Here's my card,' I say, handing it to him. 'I'd be interested to hear how you go with the Buddhas.' My new business cards are actually printed on plastic, due to my difficulties with derived paper products.

He takes the card reluctantly and I can feel his eyes on my back as I trundle away through the dust. I glance back as I get to the gate. He is standing with his hands in his pockets gazing at the Buddha as if he has never seen it before.

Twelve

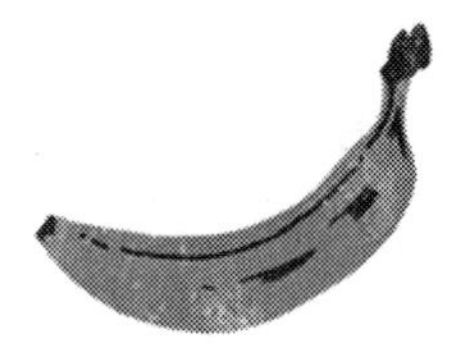

The journey away from the Big Redback seems much easier than the one in. I have a spring in my step that wasn't there before. Once we are out of sight in the long grass beside the fence I turn to Haruko. 'That was fantastic, wasn't it? I think I can feel my power returning already.'

'Great.' She is duly excited. 'And Buddha? In place like that? How strange. In Japan, they are everywhere. Big Buddha, small Buddha. Lots of Buddhas everywhere, but here? In garden shop?'

'It's a sign, Haruko. People are ready.'

'Ready for what?'

'Ready for . . .' I realise I have no idea. 'What is Buddhism actually about, Haruko?'

'Just be kind to each other. Live in the moment. That is Buddhism,' she says.

'Well. That doesn't sound too hard.'

'Seems easy at first. Might get harder later.'

'Like a pilgrimage?'

'Yes. So . . . we should start selling pilgrimage trend proposal?' She gives an eager skip.

'You go for it. It's your concept. Don't sell yourself short. Remember, you've got the goods. They need you. This is hot.'

'But what about Australian angle, Misaki? We need blog about journey. It would add marketing pizzazz.'

It's cute the way Haruko uses words like pizzazz. It's like she has been taught English by a 1980s American textbook. Maybe she has. I think about the blog. There is the Fabian factor to consider; I don't want to give too much away. But on the other hand, it can't hurt to talk about where we've been. He still won't know where we're going next . . . I smile. Let him chase me. I'll enjoy staying one step ahead. 'Okay. I'll work on the blog. You do the selling.'

My mind wanders as we make our way towards the highway. *A blog*. I will get fans. Maybe I will establish my own sect. In years to come people will follow in my footsteps. Perhaps they will wear clothes reminiscent of my style – white, chic, with a broad white sunhat. They will carry their worldly belongings in a cabin-baggage size white wheelie suitcase. Maybe one that converts to a backpack – that would be an improvement. I can sell my own range of pilgrimage wear . . .

'Where we going next?' Haruko interrupts my flight of fancy.

'It's a mystery tour, Haruko.'

'Oh, come on, Misaki. You can tell me.'

I glance at the map of the Big Things on my phone. 'What do you think of when I say . . . the Big Cow?'

Haruko's laugh gurgles as we trudge through the grass. 'Ice-cream, milkshakes, cold milk, cheese.'

I am happy to hear her laugh. After the prawn episode in the office I was worried she might have an adverse reaction to Big Things, but she is obviously fine with the Big Redback and the Big Cow. Apparently it is just the Big Prawn that bothers her. I'd like to ask her about her crustacean aversion, but it is not something we can talk about now.

'Can't wait to say moo to cow,' she says.

It is a hot walk back to the highway and even hotter walking along to an overpass that will take us to the northbound lanes. I am glad of my white hat. As the cars whoosh by I wonder where they are all rushing to. I feel a little exposed. Fabian could be in one of those cars.

Haruko carries her briefcase on her shoulder to shade her from the morning sun. Or is she hiding her face from the traffic? I wonder, again, why she was so keen to get out of Brisbane. But it is best to let her tell me in her own time. She can't be pushed.

Eventually we reach a bus stop. A bus comes and we get on. One change later, we are making our way towards the Sunshine Coast, north of Brisbane. The bus is half-empty, so Haruko takes the double seat opposite. She pulls out her little computer and starts to make contact with potential clients. The pilgrimage trend has been launched.

I should work on my blog but, gazing out at the cane fields, I start to feel sleepy. It was a big morning – the redback, the Buddha, the return of my water child . . . As the bus judders around me I fall asleep. My subconscious ushers my dream towards a place it knows too well.

Ben stays in my Spring Hill flat and makes a mess. He disappears when I'm not there, without leaving a note. His detritus clutters my lounge room . . .

The bus brakes and I wake with a start, my mind jangling, alarm bells ringing. I haven't dreamt of Ben for a long time. I'd thought that stage was over. Why is he back there now? Awake, I have almost managed to convince myself I'm over him, but my subconscious appears to know different.

I am still in the maelstrom.

A wallaby jumps across the road. The bus accelerates again as the wallaby bounds into the distance. My heart beats hard. The blood pulses in my veins. As it always did when I saw him.

Perhaps I should train myself not to think of him. But I need to make sense of it all, make sense of what happened between us. If I don't learn from it then what was the point? If I don't pay attention it might happen again.

I had no excuse for cheating. I wasn't neglected. I was loved, admired, constantly made aware of my value. Yes, I was bored, but only a little, such a small amount of boredom that I hadn't even registered it until Ben walked into my life. Suddenly I felt this great, yawning hole that only he could fill. Was the hole there, or did he create it? It's hard to know . . .

Ben is a political high-flyer, a back-door puppeteer. Like me, he forecasts trends, political ones. Ben is the one who tells politicians that the time has come to support same-sex marriage or a carbon tax. He too has some power in sensing the vibrations of the universe, the collective will. He thought we might be able to work together.

The first time he walked into my office I was struck by the way he carried himself. He is a tall man and he didn't so much walk as prowl, as if a pent-up energy might be released any minute. It made me think immediately of sex. I was surprised at myself. I'd never thought of a man in that way before. For me, sexual attraction had always come after affection, not in this lightning bolt to the groin way. Perhaps this is how men feel all the time.

So, yes, it was about sex, but it was more than that too. If I believed in past lives I would have thought we'd met before. I felt an instant connection. He'd come for a quick meeting but he stayed for two hours. We talked about work but soon moved on to art, music, poetry. It wasn't so much that our taste was identical; it was more that it fit together – two sides of a coin. He jolted me out of my comfortable mindset in an intensely pleasurable way. He talked to me as if he cared what I thought, as if my opinions were the most original he had ever heard. It was intoxicating.

As we talked we found ourselves leaning closer and closer together. And then something strange happened: I entered the familiar trance-like zone – powerfully, intensely. I had never done that before with another person, only by myself. And my vision took the form of an absolute certainty – this man was important to me. I knew it at the deepest part of me. I could no more reject that knowledge than I could turn off my power.

He touched my arm at one stage, to emphasise a point. My stomach contracted, my breath quickened and my mouth went dry. I felt like a hand had grasped hold of me and pulled me towards him. It was lucky the desk was between us or I might have embarrassed myself.

I hadn't felt a spark like that for half a lifetime – *no, never*. Not like that.

Later, when I looked in the mirror after he'd gone, I saw a small red mark just above my lip, like I'd bumped into something. I didn't connect it at the time with the odd feeling of anxiety and exhilaration swirling through me.

The second time we met – another two-hour meeting – I noticed afterwards a red mark on my arm, just above my wrist, about the size of a five cent coin. It was like a bruise, but looking closer I saw it was a little patch of burst blood vessels. It took a few days to fade. I realised then I was in trouble. It was as if my body was proclaiming its interest, desire, obsession ahead of my mind. He made my heart race so hard the blood had to find a way out through my skin. It was like a curse, a thumbprint, an enchantment. I was a marked woman.

The day after my mark vanished he rang and asked me to lunch. 'I think I'm in love with you,' he said.

I felt like I knew that already. I'd known it from the moment we met. A switch had been flicked from 'off' to 'on' and I couldn't find the will to flick it back.

Apart from those first two mornings in the office, almost our entire relationship took place in bed. I'd never seen myself as the type to cheat. It had never occurred to me. Oh, I know, I know, infidelity is rampant, everyone is at it, but I didn't set out to have an affair. I got bowled over by something stronger than my willpower. I was chosen.

I was guilty as hell, but I couldn't stop. It tore at me. I never knew how a secret could weigh you down. The effort it takes to hold it in. The way it bubbles to the surface and how you have to swallow hard to keep it inside. I felt that even if I'd dug a hole and whispered my secret into it, it would still have sung its way into the world. *Arkie is in love.*

I had no intention of leaving my marriage. Even in the grip of lust, longing and obsession I understood that there was value there, something worth hanging on to. Logic played no part in my thought processes. I needed Ben but I needed Adam too. I couldn't give up either. Not that Ben was asking me to.

I don't know what I'd expected. I knew he was married. I went half-crazy trying not to think of that and almost succeeded. If I'd thought about the other parties in this foursome, it would have destroyed me. Perhaps that's the only way adultery can work – you don't let your mind go to those places. You exist inside a bubble created by the two of you.

But it took my breath away, the way he cut me off when his wife found out. Surely love doesn't die from one moment to the next?

One day it was *you are the only person in the world who interests me*, the next it was cold silence – a pane of glass I could see through, but not penetrate. Attempts to do so left me wounded, haemorrhaging from the heart. I felt that even if I'd collapsed on the ground in front of him he would not have lifted a finger to save me.

I've tried and tried to understand but it still baffles me. The only explanation I've come up with is that the man I fell in love with never existed. I made him up out of desires and fantasies. This hard stranger was there all along, but I could not see him through the mirage I'd created.

In retrospect, the signs were there. He hinted at other relationships that had come to bad ends. He had flashes of anger. He always apologised. Until the day he didn't. Why did I think he'd be different with me? That I'd be the exception, tame the beast.

I blush at my vanity.

Oh, what an underrated virtue kindness is. Adam is the kindest man I know. I battered the storm of my emotions against his kindness so often I lost sight of it. Maybe I even – I hate to admit it to myself – saw this kindness as weakness. Now, I see it for what it was – unconditional love. No matter how unlovable I became, he still saw me as brilliant, beautiful. I believed him, thought I was too brilliant and beautiful to waste it all on him.

On a whim, as the bus rocks and sways, I pull out my phone and select Adam's number. Adam makes his living as a graphic designer. He paints in his spare time with only minor commercial success. He works from home, or at least he used to. I imagine the phone ringing and an almost unbearable yearning fills my chest. I don't even know where he lives now. Our apartment is on the market. Somewhere in Sydney, Adam is listening to that ring.

When I started my business in the city, we discussed where we would live. The Blossom Road terrace was fine for a while, but we'd only been renting and now we were grown-ups it was time to enter the property market. A high-rise apartment in the CBD seemed a natural choice. We'd be close to everything – work, restaurants, nightlife. Why would you live in the 'burbs? Adam was keen for something more homely, but he gave way to my insistence. Maybe once children came along, I said. But, as it turned out, they never did.

We lived on the seventy-second floor. At night the city lights sparkled below us – an inverted starry night; we couldn't see the stars in the sky. I'd wake up in the morning, lift my arm without getting out of bed and pull back the curtain. Below me street lights and neon signs flickered off as the day brightened. Cars streamed into the city while I smugly sat up in bed and drank the cup of tea Adam brought me.

Our surrealist prints had to go when we moved. They were too shabby and the decor in our new apartment was minimalist; there was only room for a few of Adam's own paintings. I packed the prints up and took them down to the local thrift shop. I only kept one – it seemed appropriate. *Seeing Is Believing* depicts a woman's head peering out of the clouds at the city below. Every morning as I peered down at the city, I felt like that woman. My office – *Arkie Douglas Trend Forecasts* – was only ten minutes' walk from our door. Life was good.

The phone rings and rings in Adam's new home. I wish I knew where it was.

Finally, he picks up. 'Hello, Adam Douglas.' I can hear him clearly but there is crackling in the background.

'Hi. It's me, Arkie.'

'Hello?'

'Yeah, it's me.'

'Hello?' He pauses, then puts the phone down.

I check my phone. There is only one bar of reception. I try again. We repeat the exercise. And again. On the third time he doesn't pick up. On the fourth he picks up just long enough to give an irritable *hello* and hang up again.

This failed attempt at communication leaves me frustrated and, more, longing. I replay his voice over and over in my head. That clipped but gentle tone I know so well. Even the irritation on the last call leaves me with a craving to hear more.

Without realising it, I had been rehearsing this call in my mind. I'd wanted to share the Redback Spider with him and the Jurojin garden gnome. I'd been looking forward to his humour. Adam always used to make me laugh. But now we are like two broken pieces of a jigsaw puzzle.

One year and twelve days ago exactly Adam left me. If I could replay that moment, I'd do it differently . . .

'I'm going now, Arkie.'

I registered his words, but didn't move. My head was too heavy on the pillow. We had been co-existing in our apartment for three weeks since he found out about Ben. I couldn't hide it from him – I had completely fallen apart. 'I've been seeing someone and he's broken my heart,' I wailed at last when the effort of trying to carry on became too much. I wasn't expecting sympathy; I just wanted to be left alone.

For three weeks Adam and I had barely talked. I had gone to work and come back again. We had moved in parallel worlds.

He hadn't gone yet.

I pulled the sheet over my shoulders. Did I really think he would leave me? Probably not. If he had said my name again, sat down on the bed, who knows? But the next sound I heard was the door closing.

Some hours later, the sound of fireworks woke me. I had forgotten it was New Year's Eve.

• • •

Adam and I were together for twenty years. It sounds like a long time. But now, it feels like not much more than a long conversation. We had our routines. They were pleasant ones. But we'd let things slide. Or was it just me? How long had it been since I'd really looked at him?

I watch the cane fields go past; outside the tinted glass the midday sun is intense, brilliant. Perhaps I was like Dorothy in Kansas, hungering for the wider world. But as soon as that twister came along and carried me away I realised there was no place like home.

Except that home isn't a place. Home is what I used to have with Adam. And now I can't find my way back.

Thirteen

We have been walking for an hour on weed-infested footpaths since the school bus dropped us off somewhere north of Nambour. We'd had to wait on the highway until school got out in order to catch it. This pilgrimage would all be much easier with a car.

Haruko is not in the mood for talking. She walks slightly ahead of me, her head nodding to the music coming through her headphones.

The scenery is dull – grassy paddocks with groups of cows sheltering under lonely trees – so as I walk, I flick through her proposal. It reminds me of what I am missing.

The Yamanobe-no-michi is the oldest road in Japan. It winds through fields of persimmons, past temples and burial mounds. Emperors were buried there and moats dug around their tombs. Today these mounds look like islands, rising from a green pond.

My T-shirt is sweat-soaked and there isn't the trace of a breeze. There are also no persimmons, temples or buried emperors here. I slide the proposal into my daypack before I stain it with my sweaty hands.

I would like to be enjoying the beauty of my surrounds, reaching a state of oneness with my spirit, discovering that everything I need I already have. In fact, what I am thinking about is my feet. I might have expected the bottom of my feet to hurt, that would be normal, but it is the top of my feet that are killing me. My white leather shoes, which were so right for coffee on the harbour on Sunday mornings, are apparently not the thing for a hot Queensland pilgrimage. I should have got some of those amazing lightweight shoes I saw on the Internet, the ones you could boulder hop down the Colorado River in, and then wear to dinner at the White House.

I think of Grandma Gatewood and her 3500-kilometre walk in tennis shoes and find that I dislike her intensely. *Pantywaist*, I hear her say.

'This pilgrimage is a ridiculous idea,' I say.

Haruko stops and looks at me. Even she has a bead of sweat running down her face. She removes one ear bud and cocks her head.

'Maybe if we were in Japan there would be some point to it. Maybe if we were in Spain. Maybe if we were somewhere where making a pilgrimage made sense. But on the side of a road north of Nambour, making a pilgrimage is just weird and sad.'

Haruko's mouth twitches. When she speaks, it is with her Miss Iida voice. 'After you become pilgrim, you must learn to deal with hardship. Without hardship you will not appreciate benefits.'

I smile. Bless her heart; at least one of us is enjoying herself. I have chosen my companion well. 'As soon as I finish this pilgrimage, I am going to have a big steak and a beer,' I say.

Haruko raises one eyebrow. 'And then?'

What other rules can I break? *Have sex*, is the obvious one, but who am I going to have sex with? 'Have a great, big . . . argument,' I say.

Haruko smiles.

We trudge on. As we reach the rise of the hill I see it – the Big Cow. It is impressive, in a strange way, and rather realistic.

'It looks like real cow,' says Haruko.

And it does, from a distance, but as we get closer we realise it really is very, very big.

The shop next to the Big Cow, which presumably used to sell cow-themed souvenirs, has a sign out the front advertising furniture. The only sign of life is two tattered Australian flags which fly from the roof. The cow itself is in a fenced-off yard next to the shop, as if to stop it running amuck. This is a scary thought.

Haruko is googling. She reads from her screen. 'Cow was built in 1976. It was part of Suncoast Dairy and they call it Ada. People came to see cow milked and butter and cheese making.' Her head comes up. 'That sounds nice.'

‘1976?’ I say.

‘Peasant look,’ Haruko jumps in.

‘Pumpkin scones.’

‘Pet rock.’

‘“Silly Love Songs” by Paul McCartney and Wings.’

Haruko shrugs as if to say she’s beaten.

I take a deep breath and imagine the smell of pumpkin scones drifting towards me. Quirky times, the mid-seventies.

Haruko gazes at the cow. ‘It looks friendly.’

The cow is maybe five times as tall as us. It has long, pointy horns and a hopeful expression. Possibly it is longing for the days when children would climb the stairs, open the flap and step inside its cavernous belly to discover the mystery of milk. It seems neglected, like a discarded child’s toy. ‘I’d like to climb the fence and get a bit closer,’ I say. The fence is only waist high, it wouldn’t be difficult.

Haruko points to a sign saying *Keep out – guard dogs patrol*.

While I can’t see any guard dogs, the quiet atmosphere is foreboding. It would not surprise me if a pack of barking hounds was lying in wait ready to attack at any attempt to set the Big Cow free.

A car arrives. Three children pile out, have their photos taken in front of the cow and disappear again.

‘The second temple.’ Haruko sounds doubtful. Perhaps this pilgrimage is not living up to her expectations. Perhaps she was expecting the Big Things to be more impressive.

I contemplate the cow. There is something magnetic about its sheer size and crazy eyes. In a way, it is a work of art. As much as any sculpture in a gallery, it forces you to think. It raises questions. I try to imagine what the second temple on Shikoku is like. Perhaps there is a giant Buddha, or fierce statues of Shinto Gods; perhaps a door leads into a hidden chamber . . .

'Why would you build Big Cow?' says Haruko.

It is obviously raising questions for her too.

'And why we looking at it?' she adds.

This is a rather philosophical question and I don't have an answer. The word *folly* comes to mind. The cow reminds me of my cardboard shop. I would like to meet the person who designed and built the cow. We might have a lot in common. I wonder if they developed a cow phobia in later life.

'Who builds Big Things?' Haruko asks.

'I don't know. Someone who thinks that bigger is better?'

'Men?' says Haruko.

'I think so.'

Haruko smiles. 'I think so too.'

I take a photo and wait for inspiration.

'Lucky Gods?' says Haruko. Perhaps she is hoping for a moment of kismet like that with the gnome at the Big Redback.

I pull out my Seven Lucky Gods and Haruko sorts through them. She pauses when she pulls out Daikokuten.

'God of farmers,' she says.

Daikokuten wears a hood and carries a mallet.

'When he strike mallet it give anything you desire,' says Haruko. She points at the sack he is standing on. 'This rice symbolise fertility and plenty of crops.' She turns back to the cow as if she is trying to draw a comparison.

The cow probably could stand as a symbol of abundance and fertility. Its bulging udders look full to the brim. *Fertility . . .*

There's nothing wrong with you, the doctors said after I had been probed and prodded to within an inch of my life. *Nothing wrong with either of you. Just relax and give it time.* That was over ten years ago. Ten years of timing intimacy for ovulation, eating the right foods, lying with my bottom propped up on pillows after sex. Ten years of peeing on plastic sticks and watching them come up negative.

I gaze up at the cow above me. The sun is shining around its head so brightly it creates a halo. Drops of last night's rain fall from its teats to the ground in a gentle rhythm.

Can we milk the cow, Mummy? Can we?

I turn my head, but of course there's no-one there. My heart constricts. After a year's leave of absence, my water child has definitely returned. I wonder where she's been in the meantime.

I'm not sure when it was that the water child came into my life. To begin with she was just an impression – a tinkling laugh, a shimmer in the corners of my mind. I called her the water child because that was the sensation she brought with her – she tugged at me like a fast-flowing stream. I can't remember when she first spoke to me, when it was that I replied.

'There is Big Bull in Rockhampton.' Haruko is looking at her phone.

'It's a pity they can't get together. Then they'd have some company.'

Haruko sinks to the ground in the shade of the cow and sips from her water bottle. Pulling out her phone, she inserts the buds in her ears again. Soon she is tapping away on her keyboard. Cars go past on the road but none pull off to view the cow.

'Sad cow with crazy eyes. What secrets have you got inside?' I murmur. I feel sorry for her. How would it feel, standing there day after day, wearing your bigness like a wedding gown, waiting like Miss Havisham for your prince to come? I blink as a tear comes to my eye. The heat must be getting to me. My eyes keep coming back to the entrance in the side of the cow.

Before I can think twice, I walk towards the fence and climb over. Haruko is oblivious. She is working hard on her pilgrimage sales.

I climb the stairs to the cow's belly, my eyes on the flap which guards its secret, its essence. It promises a fantasy journey – into Narnia perhaps. What is on the other side of that door? The magical world of milk? A paradise of ice-cream and milkshakes, of milky bars and cheese? Souvenirs maybe . . . Inflatable cows, cow snow-domes. As I touch the flap, my heart is beating hard –

'Oi. Can't you read? It says keep out.'

I peer over the edge of the railing.

A woman is standing on the shop side of the fence. She is wearing a blue sun-dress that displays her deeply tanned shoulders and her bleached blonde hair stands off her head in a way that suggests the over-use of hairspray.

'Oh. Sorry.' I try to think of an excuse. Fail. 'I just wanted to . . . see what's inside.'

'There's nothing inside.'

I don't believe her. In fact, the way she says it makes me think the opposite. There is something very, very good inside the cow. I am sure of it. I turn to the flap and lift it. There is a locked door behind it. I look back at the woman.

She shakes her head. 'You people.'

Beneath me, Haruko has taken the buds out of her ears. She gives me a little wave. I touch the door. Perhaps I am not ready for the journey inside the cow. I climb back down the stairs.

The woman watches me, hands on her hips, like she's seen it all before.

I slink back to the fence and climb over. Once I am there, I wave and smile to show how harmless I am.

'Mummy,' shrieks a toddler from inside the building. After a few moments, the woman goes back inside.

'Locked?' says Haruko.

I nod. I stare at the cow, at its inaccessible secret compartment. 'Anything could be in there.' The cow's interior hints at hidden depths. 'I'm going to blog now.'

Haruko smiles encouragingly.

Keeping the cow in view, I sit down on the grass and pull out my new iPad. Being a trend forecaster it behoves me to keep up to date. At the same time I feel slightly embarrassed about my purchase, like I have jumped on a bandwagon with no wheels.

I suspect that the iPad, in all of its various models, is an example of successful marketing of stuff that we never really needed. Apple is so good at that. It does turn on very quickly, however, and feels light and smooth in my hands. It is vaguely useful.

The Australian Pilgrimage . . . I brush away a fly that persists in buzzing around my face. I start to type.

> Shikoku, Camino, Lourdes, Nambour . . . the journey is the same.
>
> A Buddha. A man wearing tight stubbies. A crazy cow with a locked door that can only lead to a milky paradise. I have tramped many lonely miles on the back roads and highways of subtropical Queensland.
>
> I have learnt that a pilgrimage is what happens inside you. Nambour, Shikoku or Camino, the pilgrim must surmount problems and challenges in pursuit of wisdom.

The woman comes out of the enclosure and stares at me.

I am tempted to stick my tongue out, but I smile in a reassuring way.

She frowns and goes back inside.

I am meeting some interesting people along the way.

(And possibly making some enemies, but I won't mention that.)

Is slow the new fast? Travelling slowly, I rely on intuition, not information, to tell me what to do. I pay attention to the climate, the landscape.

(I swat another fly, wonder where we'll spend the night.)

Big Things and temples are an opportunity to reflect. Magnified to many times its normal size, a cow forces me to consider the essence of 'cowness'. Cows of course are sacred to Hindus and are often revered as a symbol of wealth and abundance in other religions too. Is building a Big Cow therefore a subconscious effort to call forth good fortune? It seems more than likely. As I continue, I will reflect on what Big Things reveal about the objects they represent, their makers and future trends.

I email my piece to Haruko.

Her notebook goes *ting* as it arrives. She scans it quickly. 'That so cool, Misaki. You sound like you are getting vibe, out on the street.'

I laugh. The street is the Holy Grail of trend forecasting. It is where trends come from. 'Out on the grass, you mean.'

'I'll seed it. See if it flies,' Haruko says. 'See if social networks pick it up.'

She sounds so enthusiastic, like I did twenty years ago when I thought this stuff mattered.

'I am making blog site for you now,' Haruko says. 'Send me picture too.'

I hold my phone up to take a photo of Haruko with the cow, but she shakes her head. 'Not me. Just cow.'

'People like to see a face . . .'

'Your face.' Haruko takes the phone from me. 'Cheezu.'

'Cheese,' I repeat.

She clicks and emails the photo to herself.

'You getting much interest in the pilgrimage stuff yet?'

'Yes, lots.'

Sometimes Haruko sounds like a little girl.

'Who's biting?'

'Big department store, furniture franchise and . . . mystery man.'

'Oo, a mystery man.' I waggle my eyebrows.

'He sound classy. We having phone meeting tomorrow.'

'Well, take care. Watch out for weirdos.'

Haruko laughs. 'Misaki, I know about take care more than you.'

'Yes. I suppose you do.' I wonder though. Haruko might go with men for money, yet she can still seem so innocent at times.

After Haruko closes her notebook it is time to move on. I have decided that we will stay the night in Tewantin.

Tewantin is to Big Things as Newcastle is to coal. This little town is home to the Big Stubby, the Big Shell and the Big Pelican. Getting there could be tricky, however, as we are off the main bus route. I pick up my bag and we start to plod along the road.

'Is it far?' says Haruko.

'I don't know.'

'Challenge is good for pilgrim.' She says this as if she is trying to convince herself.

Half an hour later a battered Holden with a surfboard on the roof beeps and pulls over on the road ahead of us.

'What do you think?' I say. Accepting lifts is probably against the pilgrimage rules.

'Pilgrim in Japan are often offered gifts and other help on pilgrimage,' says Haruko. 'You should accept. Then gift-giver has benefit from pilgrimage too.'

'A win-win situation.'

'Winwin?' Haruko frowns. She must not have encountered this expression before.

'Good for both of us.'

Haruko nods. 'Yes, winwin.'

A suntanned woman leans over and winds down her window as we reach the car. 'Want a lift?'

I eye our saviour. She has a kind face. I smile. 'Thank you.'

'You can slide your board inside,' she says to Haruko.

I jump in the back and Haruko climbs in the front.

As I do up my seatbelt, I notice a Buddha sticker on the dashboard. I touch Haruko on the shoulder and she nods slightly to indicate she has seen it. First, the Garden Centre and now this . . . I might not have my mojo, but I can spot a trend when it jumps out and hits me between the eyes. We are definitely on to something. *Be kind, live in the moment . . .*

We exchange small talk as we drive north. The woman says she works down near Nambour, but is on her way to Noosa for a surf. 'You too?' she says to Haruko.

Haruko smiles. 'I hope.'

As the car goes around a corner, a cardboard box that I hadn't noticed before slides across the floor and brushes my foot. I repress a scream, tuck my feet up under me and wind the window down to quell my nausea. This cardboard phobia is ridiculous. A cow phobia would be much more manageable.

The woman's eyes meet mine in the mirror. 'Bit carsick?'

I nod.

'Sorry, I'll slow down.' Her eyes flicker over us. 'On holidays?' She is probably wondering what we are doing, wandering down the Nambour road, me with my wheelie suitcase and Haruko with her briefcase. We are unusual holiday makers.

'Yes.' I nod. 'Just visited the Big Cow.'

Her eyebrow arches. 'Not many people do that.'

'It's pretty good.'

Her face lights up. 'It is, isn't it?' This seems to satisfy her and she doesn't ask any more questions.

Fourteen

Half an hour later I am holed up in my cabin in the Hibiscus Caravan Park in Tewantin. Haruko has the adjacent cabin. I turn on the TV as I settle in. The voices are a background hum as I test the mattress in the bunk bed. It is thin, and the boards underneath dig into my back.

Given the state of my budget, the standard of our accommodation can only go downhill from here. I hope Haruko is okay with that. I get up and slip a couple of complimentary teabags into my daypack as insurance against declining circumstances.

Suddenly I freeze. *That voice.* Turning to the television I see him. *Ben*.

I haven't seen him for over a year. He is exactly as I remember him. Or is he? Ben has made the jump to politician now, it seems – out from behind the curtain and into the spotlight. He is running as an Independent. *Of course.* This sums him up. He is a man who likes to keep his options open, who makes a virtue of fence-sitting. Although, as far as Ben is concerned, there is no fence. Climate change deniers or dark-green forest pole sitters, all would be welcome to his church. He has the gift of making everyone feel he is on their side.

There is a by-election coming up in Brisbane apparently, a fact that hasn't registered as important until now. He must have moved interstate just to run. As I look at Ben, I work out what it is that is different. *His aura.* He always did have tremendous charisma, but this is something more. He practically glows. It wouldn't matter what he was talking about, he'd have my vote. He has metamorphosed into a celebrity.

I am reminded of Dali's *Metamorphosis of Narcissus*, which used to hang in our Blossom Road lounge room. In the painting, Narcissus wastes away, unable to pull himself from his watery image in a pond. But as I gaze at the television, I realise it is not Narcissus who is wasting away here, it is me.

I often find myself wondering how I was so stupid as to wreck my marriage for a brief affair, but looking at Ben now my heart still beats faster. I feel a pull in my chest that can only be craving. His words wash over me like a song. Seeing him makes sense of the state of my life. Even knowing what I do, I'm not sure I could resist his charm. If he hadn't chosen politics he would have made a good cult leader.

Then suddenly, one word stands out. *Pilgrimage.* I put the kettle down and move towards the television. It is like he has put his hand out and pulled me closer. That's my word. Hands off.

'We are all in search of something intangible and sometimes the easy way is not the right way,' he says. 'In Mongolia pilgrims will travel hundreds of kilometres, measuring the distance of their body on the ground.'

The reporter, a blonde in a pink suit, looks perplexed. Perplexed but charmed. Her earrings bob as she nods her head. She wrinkles her nose at him in a cute way that reveals more about what is going on inside her head than she would like. 'I'm sorry, Mr Robinson, but how does this relate to the carbon tax?'

Ben smiles.

I feel sorry for the reporter. I know what it is like to be on the receiving end of that smile. A long sigh escapes me. I inch closer, fighting a ridiculous urge to lick the TV screen. I want to taste him, pull him out of there to rest on top of me, press my nose into his cheek, run my fingers through his thick though slightly greying hair. Only the increasingly high-pitched wail of the kettle reminds me of our physical separation. I give myself a mental slap around the face. *Stop it, Arkie.*

I sometimes wonder how technology has changed the human psyche, how it messes with our heads. Those tribes who think the camera steals our soul could be right. And if a mere camera can do that, what does Facebook do, or

Twitter? Are we distributing our precious essence willy-nilly to the winds of social media?

The kettle drowns out Ben's answer, but it doesn't matter. I can tell it is convincing. As we all know, only a small fraction of communication relies on the actual words spoken. The camera zooms in on the now rosy-cheeked reporter. Her earrings – tiny Buddhas – dance as she says a few words to camera. The news moves on.

Pilgrimage. Can this just be a coincidence? And suddenly I remember what Haruko said, *A mystery man . . . No, Haruko, not Ben.* I pick up my phone but then put it down again. I don't want to interrupt her in her cabin, outside work hours, as loose as those may be. Haruko and I are becoming close in some ways, but we are still oceans apart in others.

I don't even know where she was living in Brisbane. All I knew was that I was paying her enough to keep her off the streets. She murmured something about a flat in the city when I asked her. Haruko is like a wild creature. She needs her privacy, her secrets. I'd like to take care of her but she won't let me.

As I sip my tea I turn on my iPad, open Facebook and scroll through the faces of my friends. *My tribe.* Fortyish, successful, professional and mainly female. A few male faces are scattered among the lipsticked, smiling ranks. One of them is Ben. Adam is not there, he has unfriended me. Perhaps he would have stayed if I had removed Ben first.

My mouse hovers over Ben's face. I should, of course, unfriend him. I am surprised he didn't get in first. Perhaps, like all politicians, he needs all the friends he can get, even jilted lovers. On my part, I feel a mixture of inertia and curiosity. I still have a small window into his life. I can see who he chats to, where he is travelling. It is a bit stalker-ish, but he invites it.

A message appears on the screen. *Ben Robinson is now friends with Jasmine Harris*. Jasmine is the reporter. That was quick. My stomach clenches and I feel nauseous. This is not good for me. I must unfriend him at once. I go through the motions, but at the last hurdle click *cancel*. I can't do it.

Has Ben been talking to Haruko about the pilgrimage concept? Where else would he have got it from? And it fits – he is always trawling the Internet in search of the latest trends. Does he know that Haruko is working for me?

I search Haruko's name and her profile appears. Haruko updates her profile picture frequently. In today's picture she is looking over the top of her glasses straight at the camera. Her straight black hair is blowing across her face and she is holding it back. She is wearing her Miss Iida outfit. The photo was probably taken this morning before she left. I wonder who took it; it seems too far away to have been taken by her. The background is blurred but I get an impression of red bricks. Could this be her Brisbane home?

Looking at Haruko's profile is also a bit stalkerish. Haruko is not my Facebook friend. I haven't sent her a friend request, because I am not sure if our relationship encompasses Facebook friendship and I couldn't bear to be rejected.

I have a new friend request from someone called Patty. I don't know anyone called Patty. Patty's profile picture is a Labrador dog. This intrigues me. The dog is a lot like Maisie. I miss Maisie.

Patty's profile says that she is into ball sports, running and food. She is ten years old. I never accept friend invitations from people I don't know, let alone dogs, but what the hell. I click on *accept*. I am now friends with a Labrador called Patty. I can't wait to read her posts.

I update my status.

Today I was menaced by a giant redback and communed with a crazy-eyed cow. Onwards ho to the Big Shell, the Big Stubby and the Big Pelican.

I attach a picture of the Big Cow and post it.

There is a *ting*. I have an email. The sender's name is not familiar to me.

Dear Ms Douglas,

You and your friend seemed so interested in the Buddhas, I thought you might like to know that I sold five more today after you left. I remembered what you said about people wanting more spirituality in their lives. Maybe we should expand the range? Can you suggest any other garden products of a similar nature?

Yours sincerely,

Chris Campbell

PS. What is that picture on your business card? I like it.

It is the young man from the Big Redback. What a surprise. I reply.

Hello Chris,
You might want to check out some Shinto Gods. There are a lot of them, but if you look up 'Seven Lucky Gods' you will get the idea. If you look at the picture attached you will see that one of your garden gnomes is already a lot like a Lucky God, so I think this could work well for you.

Cheers,
Arkie Douglas

PS. The picture on my business card is *Meditation* by Magritte. It's a nice one, isn't it?

I snap a picture of my Lucky Gods, attach it to the email and press *send*.

In the absence of anything else to do, I am starting to think about going to bed when there is a knock at my door. Haruko is standing outside with a newspaper dangling from her hand. '*The Wizard of Oz* movie,' she says. 'Is it good?'

'You haven't seen it?'

She shakes her head. 'Is it Australian?'

'American.'

'Why is he Wizard of Oz, then?'

'Huh? Oh. Oz is a fantasy country. Not Australia. Is it on?'

Haruko holds out the newspaper. 'Eight o'clock.'

I snatch the program off her and inspect it. 'We have to watch it. I haven't seen it for years. I love it.'

We settle onto the vinyl couch together. The television is small and mounted on top of the cupboard, so it will be a fairly ordinary viewing experience. As we wait for the program to start, I take a deep breath. 'Haruko. You haven't run into someone called Ben Robinson, have you?'

'Yes, he one of my new clients, mystery caller. Why?'

My mind freezes. *Because he's dangerous. Because he stole my mojo. Because he dumped me and broke my heart.* 'I saw him on the TV just then. Talking about pilgrimages.'

'Oh, yes. I saw. It was great, wasn't it? He going to use pilgrimage idea as platform for his campaign. *Renewal* is word I give him. He is running with it. It is so great, Misaki. I love it. Furniture and fashion okay, but this big picture. Politics. Like you say, politics influence trend, trend influence politics.'

Did I say that? I suppose I did. 'Do you know much about his policies?'

Haruko nods. 'He into youth issues, environment, multi-culture . . .'

Ben would naturally be into youth issues and multi-culturalism when talking to Haruko. With a middle-aged farmer, he would be deeply into rural issues. When he was with me he professed a profound interest in surrealist art. He is entirely convincing. It is an uncanny power he has to be everything to everyone.

'You know him?' says Haruko.

Haruko doesn't know much about my past life. She knows I am separated from my husband, that is all. I can't bring myself to expose this raw part of me, but I want to warn her off. 'I've heard things . . .'

'What sort of thing?' Haruko sounds petulant.

'Just gossip, I guess. Just . . . be cautious.'

Haruko laughs. 'Misaki, you forget I am used to men. I am cautious as chicken in snake nest.'

I smile. That sounds like a Japanese saying, but perhaps Haruko just made it up herself. She has a very adventurous attitude towards English.

The soaring music of 'Over the Rainbow' starts up and it doesn't matter that I am perched on a vinyl couch in a tin cabin in Tewantin, in my mind I am ten years old and the lights have just dimmed in the cinema. The movie is as wonderful as I remember it – the colours so bright, the characters so heart-warming, the dangers so deliciously scary. The witch so delightfully evil.

Haruko seems entranced too. She hardly moves a muscle throughout the movie. 'Oh,' she sighs as it finishes. 'Dorothy does pilgrimage too.'

I hadn't seen it like that before, but . . . there it was. Dorothy was doing a pilgrimage to find her way home. Perhaps it could work for me too.

As Haruko walks the short distance to her cabin, 'Follow the Yellow Brick Road' drifts in through my window. She sounds a bit like Judy Garland.

Fifteen

Sun streaming through my cabin window wakes me in the morning. It is early, but the day is heating up already. My mind feels fuddled – like it needs a good clean out. I was dreaming of arms wrapped around me but I'm not sure whose they were – Adam's or Ben's? This is very bad, I should know, but I don't. Agitation bangs at the inside of my head. I long for calm, for the sweet untroubled sleep of the innocent. I sigh, sit up and pull on my clothes.

There is a *ting* from my iPad. I have a comment on my blog. It is rather bewildering.

> Hey Mukker!
> It is about time someone looked into this. There has been a travesty of justice for too long. I look forward to your next update.

See ye efter!
The Big Scotsman.

Is it just me, or is that message completely bizarre? I scan my blog again and try to add some context, but, no, it is still obscure. I reply.

Dear Big Scotsman,
Thank you for your comment, but I think perhaps you have replied to the wrong blog? Is that Scottish you're speaking?
Yours,
Arkie Douglas

I press *send* feeling like the day has got off to a bad start.

Haruko knocks on the door as I am making tea. 'I join you for breakfast?' She is wearing a long T-shirt which must be her nightie. It makes her look about twelve years old. She holds up two paper bags. 'Did you order continental breakfast?'

I take one of the bags and inspect it. It contains four pieces of white bread, four squares of butter and four packets of assorted spreads. I'm not sure which continent this breakfast hails from.

We sit down at my flimsy plastic table and I smear peanut butter on dry white toast and chew it slowly. 'If I was in Japan, what would I be having for breakfast?' I ask.

'Rice and pickled soybeans. *Natto*.' Haruko taps on her phone and shows me a picture. A pair of chopsticks pincers some brown lumps with stringy mucous-like strands hanging off them. 'Very good for you.'

They look somewhat unsavoury, so perhaps it is lucky I am not there after all.

Haruko correctly interprets the expression on my face. 'And maybe some salad or miso soup, or seaweed dipped in soy sauce.'

'I think I might like that.' I finish one piece of toast and eye the next one. Food does not hold the pleasure for me it used to. In Sydney we ate out or got takeaway most nights. Eating exotic food was a favourite pleasure. These days I eat as a means to keep my body moving, to stop my pants falling further off my hips. I have never been fat and now it scares me to see the way weight drops off me as soon as I lose concentration. I force down the second piece of toast with a cup of tea and think about the day ahead.

'Ebisu is god for today.' Haruko points towards the fake wood dresser beside my bunk where I have placed my Lucky Gods. 'Because we are near the sea.'

I peer into the glare coming through the window and seek out Ebisu, the god of fishermen. Ebisu holds a red fish to symbolise luck and congratulations. He has a gold cap and a white pack on his back. Like all the gods, he is round and fat.

'He is known also as laughing god,' says Haruko. She has commandeered all the Vegemite and is onto her fourth piece of toast. 'Or leech child. He is born with no bones.'

'Do you like Vegemite, Haruko?' I say, as she peels the wrapping off yet another Vegemite container.

She nods. 'It is little bit like miso.' She finishes a mouthful and continues. 'Ebisu's parents cast him into sea in boat of reeds. He washed ashore on Hokkaido and was brought up by Ainu.'

'Ainu?'

'Indigenous people of Japan. Only live in the north. Ebisu also watch over restaurant that serve *fugu*. Some people still die though.'

Fugu, I remember, is the poisonous puffer fish. 'Why do people eat a fish which could kill them? Is it really so delicious?'

Haruko shrugs. 'It is quite nice.'

'Or is it that they enjoy the risk?'

Haruko shakes her head. 'No. No-one expect to die. That is why Ebisu is there, looking over things.'

'Do many people die?'

'Not so many. Maybe six a year,' says Haruko casually.

That seems like quite a lot to me.

'So . . .' Haruko pushes her glasses up her nose and her voice changes. 'I hope you are enjoy your pilgrimage.' She has slipped into her Miss Iida guiding mode.

'Yes. Thank you. I am enjoying very much.'

'And keeping to pilgrimage rules.'

I think of my dream. I probably shouldn't be having dreams like that when I am on a pilgrimage. I nod anyway.

Haruko rests her chin on her fist and regards me intently. 'Many young women in Japan do pilgrimage when they have broken heart.'

Is she a mind-reader? I wonder if she is waiting for me to disclose, but no, she continues.

'Most famous was Takamure Itsue. She did Shikoku pilgrimage in 1918 when she was twenty-four year old. She have one man she love too much and one man who love her too much. Big problem. So she went away. She write many newspaper stories about her walk. Later she is very famous author and poet.'

Takamure sounds like the kind of woman Grandma Gatewood would have approved of. 'She must have been an unusual young woman to undertake a trip like that alone, in those times. And she wrote about it too?'

Haruko nods. 'Like old-day blog.'

I glance at my watch. It is nine am. 'I'm going to walk to the Big Pelican, the Big Stubby and the Big Shell now. Coming?'

Haruko yawns. 'I think I will go for surf, there is bus to Noosa. Then I will do more work selling concept.'

I'm disappointed, but I try not to let it show. Of course Haruko wants to go for a surf – the beautiful beaches of Noosa are just up the road.

Haruko goes back to her cabin and I pack up and organise a late check-out for her; we're the only guests in the caravan park so it's not a problem,

'You will take photos for blog?' Haruko says when I drop off my bag.

'Of course.' Closing her cabin door, I set forth.

My walk along the Noosa River to the Big Pelican takes me past boat and canoe hire shops. The road is busy with cars going to and from Noosa. I suspect that, out of all the travellers in this area, I am the only one who does not have my eyes set on the restaurants of Hastings Street or the Tea Tree Bay surf break. I am here for the pelican.

Tewantin turns out to be bigger and more confusing than I'd anticipated. Roundabouts send me this way and that, like a ball in a pinball machine. At one stage I seem to have the river on both sides, which is hard to make sense of. I almost feel like I'm under an enchantment, doomed to wander the streets forever. *Follow the yellow brick road.* At least I'm not towing my bag behind me.

Although early, it is already warm and humid. Dark clouds lurk on the horizon as I trudge along the footpath. Forty-five minutes later, with sweat trickling down my neck, I spy my destination. At exactly this moment, the clouds burst like a balloon, spilling out a drenching waterfall.

I run for the nearest shelter – the canvas awning of a boat hire shop. From this semi-dry location I survey my third temple. Rain might be coming down in sheets but it doesn't dim the happy smile of the Big Pelican. It is impressively big. It also has eyelashes to die for and a rather flirtatious look about it. I think it must be a girl.

The first day I met Ben he told me I had beautiful eyes. He said it as if he'd never said that to anyone else before and somehow it wasn't corny, coming from him. The memory makes my stomach clench.

'You admiring Pelican Pete?' says a voice behind me.

I turn.

A stocky old man in a bright yellow raincoat is opening up the doors of the boat hire shop. He stands beside me surveying the rain and the pelican. 'Did you ever see it in action?'

I shake my head. 'No. What sort of action?'

'It was built for a floating parade – 1977, I think it was.' He smiles. 'Its eyes, wings and beak used to move.' He flaps his elbows to demonstrate.

'I'd like to have seen that. It must have been quite a sight.'

He chuckles. 'Fell in the river one year.' He stares out at the rain in an accusing manner. 'Wasn't supposed to rain today.' He turns and retreats into his shop.

I gaze at the pelican. So it was built in 1977 . . .

The year I turned five,
'Tonight's the Night' by Rod Stewart was top of the pops,
Apple pizza was consumed by some foolish souls,
Tank tops were worn by many,
Blonde hair with a long fringe à la Blondie was rampant, and
The Queensland Government banned marches
and demonstrations.

Parades with pelicans were not banned though, I take it.

I have it on good authority that given the opportunity a pelican will eat anything that fits in its mouth. If I was a chihuahua I'd be worried. The Big Pelican may look friendly, but it could fit a whole mini or a small whale inside its beak.

Do you think it could gobble me up too, Mum?

No, it is way too friendly for that. I'm glad the man has gone inside the shop, as I think I may have spoken out loud.

Is it a girl?

Well, it's called Pelican Pete, but, yes, I think it's a girl, don't you?

But my water child has gone.

The rain is slowing now; fat drops slide off the edge of the canopy and land on my shoulders as I step onto the grass. It is peaceful here beside the river. Teatree-stained ripples wash languidly at the sand. Hire boats sit forlornly at their moorings. No-one is boating in this weather. I take a photo of the pelican in its riverside home to show Haruko.

I wonder what she would say if she were here. Would she tell me about the third temple – its glistening gold gates, its enormous Buddha, its spiritual meaning? Would she tell me more about Takamure Itsue? *One man who love her too much and one man she love too much.*

I remember last night's dream again. Like Takamure, I have two men on my mind, but I don't think either of them loves me too much. I take a long breath as I think of Ben on the TV. If I could shut off that crazy yearning, I would do it in an instant.

Out of the corner of my eye I imagine I see movement. I turn back to the pelican. I could have sworn it winked, but now of course its eyes are flirtatiously frozen. As I turn to go a ray of sunlight makes the river shimmer and for a moment it looks like a pool in a Japanese garden. I imagine boating slowly across it, dressed in a kimono, a bowl of green tea held to my lips. Perhaps one day I'll come back and do that.

As I trudge back towards Tewantin the sun emerges from behind the clouds in full force. Instantly, the temperature rockets. Steam rises off the footpath like a sauna. I stop halfway to rest near the river. Placing my daypack under my bottom I sit down on the damp grass and lean up against a tree, pulling my hat over my eyes. Through a small chink, I watch the cars go by. Red cars, blue cars, yellow cars, white cars, a grey car . . . A grey BMW. A grey BMW with a fat, pale-faced man at the wheel. *Fabian.*

I pull my hat down further, ostrich-like. If I can't see him, he won't see me. After about thirty seconds, I peer out. The car is gone. I wonder how Fabian knew where to look for me. Did he read my blog from the Big Cow and work out that I am likely to turn up in Tewantin, the home of no less than three Big Things? Perhaps it is good deduction, no more.

Unless . . . I remember my Facebook message to my friends, *Tomorrow I will encounter the Big Shell, the Big Stubby and the Big Pelican.* Is one of my friends passing information on to Fabian? Who could it be? And then I think of my new friend, Patty the dog. Is Patty Fabian? Or, more likely, Adam, who is passing messages on to Fabian?

Fabian is spying on me. I think of last night's movie and the Wicked Witch of the West – who needs a crystal ball to find their prey when you've got Facebook?

I pull out my iPad and trawl through the profile pictures of my friends. Not only does Patty *look* like Maisie, it now seems to me that she *is* Maisie. *Interesting. Patty is Maisie is Adam.* So Adam is following me on Facebook. This provides possibilities.

I post a status update. *Have seen all the Big Things Tewantin has to offer. Heading north to the Big Mango.* Hah. If my theory is correct, I will soon see a grey BMW heading back in the other direction towards the highway. I duck behind the tree and wait. It takes about fifteen minutes to prove me correct. As Fabian's car disappears towards the horizon where the mango beckons, I continue on my way back to town with a spring in my step.

Sixteen

Half an hour later, I am eagerly anticipating the Big Stubby. My reading tells me that you can climb up an internal staircase then slide down a slippery slide outside. It sounds like fun.

After another fifteen minutes, I am still wandering up and down a suburban street. According to my map, I should now be standing right next to the Big Stubby. But in actual fact it is no longer there. Or if it is, I can't find it. The Big Stubby sounds impressive and hard to overlook. I scan up and down the street. Perhaps it is more subtle than I imagined – just a normal house, but built out of bottles? I do another lap of the street, but, no, none of the houses here are built out of stubbies.

I double-check my map and decide to continue on to the Big Shell. I can make a detour to the information centre later for better directions to the Big Stubby.

Strangely, the Big Shell is also hard to find. I stroll down an attractive street, lined by big figs and neatly kept lawns. I am not looking hard because, after all, it is a Big Thing. It will be easy to see. I only realise I have gone too far when I see the river ahead of me. I turn around and retrace my steps. I never would have imagined that Big Things could be so secretive. Surely the point of being a Big Thing is that you stand out from the crowd? The street is deserted, or I would ask for directions.

The Big Shell, when I find it, is a study in camouflage. I was imagining a brightly painted, glossy shell, but the one I see is bleached almost white and overhung with poinciana branches. It is like a shell that has lain on a beach for at least ten years, battered by sun and tide.

The building behind it is low and white as well. The effect is monastic, pared back. Information regarding the Big Shell's debut is sadly vague, indicating only that it was built in the sixties. I take a stab in the dark. 1967 seems as good a year as any.

Five years before I was born,
Peace signs,
Afros,
'To Sir with Love' by Lulu,
Flower power, and
Frisbees were big.

The building behind the shell is a beach lifestyle shop. 'Open Thursday to Monday' says a sign on the door.

Unfortunately, today is Tuesday. My fourth temple is shut. This is somewhat disconcerting but still, the shell is here. I am the only person currently admiring it, which is unsurprising considering its low-key appearance.

I contemplate this vision in concrete. It is about four times my size and rather beautiful in its own faded way. It appears to be a conch, upended into the ground. I walk inside its curving walls and look up through the narrow gap at the top, placing my hands on the cool, concrete walls. Inside, sounds are muted, echoing. It is otherworldly, like entering a church. Or a temple.

I hear a tinkling laugh. My water child calls to me. She sounds older this time, about ten. *Listen, Mum, you can hear the sea.*

I close my eyes and listen. A low roaring noise fills the air, as it does when you hold a shell to your ear. It sounds like a white-capped wave sweeping towards me on a tropical beach. *Dolphins jump, turtles swim, fish dart across a glassy face . . .* The wave vibrates in my ears and my head swims. A tingling sensation makes my fingers curl.

On unsteady feet, I come out of the shell and lower myself to a nearby wall. *A conch. A Buddhist symbol. A horn to the faithful. A sound to awaken the ignorant.* I breathe slowly. I am grateful now that the shop is closed. I wouldn't want to be interrupted.

My phone rings. *A call, an awakening, a message from the other side.* I check the number before answering.

'How is it going out there on pilgrimage?' Haruko says.

'Amazing. The Big Shell is like a Zen garden. I can feel my mind opening just by being here.'

'Fantastic.' Her keyboard chatters in the background. 'Great copy.'

'How was the surf?'

'Beautiful. Only little, little waves, but they go forever. And dolphins.'

It sounds like my vision inside the shell. 'So, what are you doing now?'

'I have phone meeting. With Ben Robinson.' Haruko is guarded.

She is warning me off, so I keep my voice neutral. 'Let me know how it goes.'

'I will. So, what next?' says Haruko.

'I think we should start heading south again. I need to get away from Fabian.' I tell Haruko about my narrow escape.

'But what about blog? That talk about where you are. Maybe you should stop.'

'That's okay. Let him chase me. Right now, he's heading for the Big Mango at Bowen.'

'Where is Bowen?'

'No idea. A long way north, I think.'

Haruko giggles. 'You very sneaky, Misaki. So . . . where are we going next, or is it secret?'

'Hmm.' I open a map of the Big Things on my phone and study the area south of Tewantin. 'What do you think of when I say . . . Big Pineapple?'

Haruko giggles. 'Tough on outside, tender inside. Great hair.'

She sounds so young. I fight off an urge to rush back to the cabin, protect her from Ben, build a wall around her so he can't find her. 'That's where we're going.'

I touch the walls of the shell again before I leave. It whispers as the air rushes through it – *come back and paint me, come back and care for me.* But I can't stay here all day. I have the Big Stubby to find.

I walk back up to the main street and climb the stairs to the information centre, which is inside a tiny wood-panelled hut. The white-haired woman behind the counter asks where I am from. I am temporarily flummoxed. 'Brisbane,' I say tentatively. She makes a note in her book. 'Can you tell me where the Big Stubby is?' I ask.

She shakes her head. 'Not there anymore. They demolished it to build a housing estate. Big Things just aren't as popular these days.'

'Oh. I was looking forward to it.' The Big Stubby sounded impressive, a labour of love. 'Who built it?'

'Old George, used to run the tours to coloured sands.' There is a fond note in the woman's voice. Her deeply tanned face crinkles up into lines above her crisp, white polo shirt. 'He'd pick up bottles on the sand, then when his doctor told him he had to quit the tours, he decided to build a house out of bottles – 17,000 of 'em. 1966, it was. You wouldn't have been born then, would you?'

I shake my head, thinking of George, picking up his bottles, building his bottle house. 'I'm sorry I missed it.' *1966 . . .*

Six years before I was born,
'The Ballad of the Green Berets' by Sergeant Barry Sadler was the number one song,
Twiggy was the style icon,
Batman-inspired hairstyles were all the rage,
People were known to eat something called Hearty Har Crab, and
Anti Vietnam War protests swept Australia.

'There was the House of Bottles too,' says the woman. 'Had a bottle from Ancient Egypt, over 2000 years old.'

'Really? What happened to that?'

'Not too sure.' The woman tidies her brochures on the counter. 'Tewantin's not what it used to be,' she adds.

For some reason this remark strikes me as incredibly profound. 'Is anywhere?'

The woman rearranges the brochures on her counter. 'No. You never know what's around the corner, do you?'

Again, this seems very profound. I feel a stillness in my chest, a shiver in the air, as if there is something here just out of reach. I used to know what was around the corner. It was how I made my living.

'You okay?' says the woman.

I notice her name badge for the first time. 'I'm fine thanks, Bertie.' The moment is gone, but something still lingers, a wisp of mojo thin as mist.

'They used to put Tewantin on the map.'

'The Big Things?'

She nods. 'They've all been let go now.'

'Have you been to the Big Shell lately?' I say on an impulse.

'I walk past it most days.'

'What do you think of it?'

'Needs a coat of paint. I remember when it was as fresh as a live shell. Looks like it's been left on the beach too long now.'

'Have you been inside?'

'Not for a while.'

I am unsure whether to trust her with my revelation. 'Do you have an interest in spirituality?'

Bertie's eyes dart to the door. I think she is looking for an escape, but then she nods. 'Some. Most people get that at my age. Not long left in this world.'

'It's a conch, you know,' I say.

'Is it? I never really thought too much about what sort of shell it is.'

'Conches are very auspicious.'

Bertie appears mildly startled at the turn this conversation is taking. 'Auspicious? How do you mean?'

'Quetzalcoatl, the Aztec god, created life with a conch and the Mayans used them to summon their ancestors.'

She half-smiles and cocks her head to one side. 'That's very interesting.'

'Triton used one to calm or raise storms,' I add. I think she is probably just waiting for me to leave so I hand her one of my business cards. 'It was nice talking to you. You might like to read my blog. Keep in touch.'

'I've never read a blog before.'

'First time for everything.' I smile and turn to leave.

'In England, we would have called them follies.'

I notice her faint English accent for the first time. 'Pardon?'

'The Big Things. They're like the fake castles you get in the grounds of English mansions. There's one called the Dunmore Pineapple which has a pineapple on top. Don't see that kind of thing so much here.'

'Follies – that's a good comparison. It's exactly what I thought.'

Bertie watches me as I leave, turning the card in her liver-spotted hands. I look back and see her gazing intently at the picture on the front of the card.

'It's called *Meditation* by Magritte,' I say.

She smiles. 'Kind of mesmerising, isn't it?'

I nod. Magritte's painting of three snake-like candles on a soft-focus beach used to hang above my desk in Blossom Road. Every time I looked at it my pulse rate slowed. 'It's one of my favourites,' I say.

As I step outside, a jogger in a Buddha T-shirt almost runs me over. He glares at me and shakes his head.

'Be kind. Stay in the moment,' I want to call after him. But I don't.

Seventeen

The door of Haruko's cabin is open. I tap on it, but she doesn't answer, so I step inside.

Haruko is at her table with her back to me. She has headphones in her ears and is gazing at her computer screen as if contemplating an artwork. Today she is like a Japanese version of Frida Kahlo. Her hair is looped up on top of her head and secured with a pink bandana. She is wearing a tight blue satin top and numerous necklaces. I can't see her bottom half, but I anticipate a flouncy Mexican-style skirt.

As I watch, she begins to type rapidly, her fingers flying across the keys like a pianist at the climax of a symphony. Instead of music, words flow from her fingertips.

I don't mean to stand here watching her like this, but she is so engrossed, and having not declared my presence yet I am now unsure when to do so. I don't want to startle her, to interrupt the flow of her thoughts. It has been a while since my words have flowed so freely. It is beautiful to watch.

Her phone rings. Haruko pulls a bud from one ear and picks it up. 'Trend-Spotters Brisbane.' Her voice goes up and down like a melody. She giggles, twirls a stray strand of hair around her finger. 'Hi, Ben.' She swings to and fro on her chair. I was right about the Mexican skirt. It is purple, with embroidered flowers. Haruko looks like a painting by Monet. A butterfly would get dizzy contemplating her. 'Mmm,' she says. 'Just working on it. Want me to read you what I got? Okay.' Haruko scrolls her screen up and reads. 'Traditionally pilgrims walk in search of enlightenment in this lifetime . . .'

She pauses, obviously listening to his response. 'What does it mean for you? Okay.' Haruko leans back in her chair, half-closes her eyes. When she speaks her tone is softer, dreamy. 'People are ready for extreme change, ready to break convention, explore new terrain, run free. They want old but new, modern but ancient. That is pilgrimage. People are sick of digital landscape, they want reality. A wanderer spirit drive us towards future. We return to nomad roots. People are scared our earth is fragile, they want strength in a leader.'

Haruko is in her element. I have never seen her so confident, so in control. I gaze at her, seeing her through Ben's eyes. Haruko's skin is soft and pale. It blooms with youth. Her hands are smooth, her lips are full. An image of Haruko in Ben's arms comes to me. I will it to go away.

Bile rises to my throat. I am unsure why this upsets me so much. Is it because I want to be there in her place?

Haruko swings her legs. 'You need to be seen in right places, with right people, spiritual people. Seeing you will make people feel they have started something new, become bigger than themself. Make them feel you know the way to next temple, you are going to take them there. Your clothes should be white. Everything should be white –' Haruko stops suddenly. A soft blush touches her cheeks. 'Yes, I would like to have dinner. I will see if I can.' She twirls in her chair, her skirt billowing out. Her eyes register me as she spins around. 'Got to go now.' She puts down the phone.

'Hi.' Haruko's face is radiant, but I don't think it's for me. She is still on a high from her phone call.

I pull my mouth up into a smile. 'Hi.' A bitter taste lingers in my throat.

Haruko hesitates. 'Are we back in Brisbane tonight?'

'We could be.'

'Just one night?'

'Yes, I don't want to hang around too long or Fabian might catch up with me. Why?'

'Just wondering.'

I don't believe her, but there is no point in pursuing it. *Haruko and Ben.* I don't like it at all, but it's not my place to object. I need to collect my thoughts, calm down.

'I'll just go wash my face,' I say. 'It was a long walk. I'm all sweaty.'

Inside the tiny, plastic-lined bathroom, I drink some water, then press my face to the mirror. My breath fogs the glass. When I open my eyes my image is blurry, soft focus. I look like a girl again. I wipe away the fog and the lines under my eyes reappear, the grey hairs are visible among the red. I feel like the wicked queen in *Snow White*. I was never aware that my looks were fading until I took up with Ben. Adam always told me I was as beautiful as the day we first met. I think he believed it.

Now, I try to unravel what it is I feel when I think about Ben and Haruko. I dissect my feelings, try to be honest with myself.

But no, what I feel when I think about them is not jealousy. It is a fierce need to protect her. I'm not sure where it comes from, this feeling. I am like the mother of a teenage daughter, powerless to protect her from injury. But I have no rights here, I am not a mother and it is most unlikely I ever will be. I am forty-one years old.

Standing, I splash cold water on my face, pat it dry. When I walk back out to the office Haruko is typing again.

I saunter over, sit on the table. 'You're having dinner with Ben? In Brisbane?'

Haruko nods.

'He's got a reputation.'

Haruko eyes me quizzically. 'It is just dinner. He is a client.' She sounds defensive.

I wonder if I should tell Haruko about Ben and me, but I sense that the time is not right. Haruko is friendly, but she keeps her distance. Deep and meaningful is not our modus operandi. 'How is it all going?' I say instead.

Haruko smiles. 'This pilgrimage thing going so well, Misaki.'

She chats on, while I sit on the end of her table, enjoying seeing her so animated, so sure of herself. It was a good idea to put her in charge of this project. She has come into her own.

'Isn't Ben based in Sydney?' I try to sound naive.

Haruko twirls slightly in her chair. 'He is campaigning. For a seat in Queensland.'

I expel a breath. 'Shall we make a move?'

After checking out of Haruko's cabin we walk into town and eventually board a bus going south. I watch the highway go by and ponder my situation. I am on the run from my husband's divorce lawyer, my husband is posing as a dog to entrap me, my mojo is still missing in action and my demon ex-lover is lurking near Haruko . . . But, all things considered, my pilgrimage is going well. Being out on the road is freeing. I can feel my mind loosening, expanding.

We have to change buses on the highway to one that takes the back road. This involves another lengthy wait, but at last we are on the right path and after about half an hour, the Big Pineapple comes into sight. At first it is just an orange shape on the horizon. It could almost be a golden pagoda, but then the orange blip grows and grows into a plus-size fruit. It is impressive, though it appears almost deserted. A single car sits in the car park. As the bus drops us off, the wind blows an ice-cream wrapper against my legs. It clings for a moment then swirls off into the air as a mini-tornado grasps it.

'Why aren't more people here?' Haruko cranes her neck to see the top of the pineapple. 'It is amazing. Look how big it is.'

It's a good question. But then, all the Big Things have been notable for their unpopularity. Were they perhaps a phenomenon for a pre-Internet age? Maybe kids these days expect more from their attractions.

'Our fifth temple.' Haruko sounds like she is making a favourable comparison with the temple in her mind. She examines her phone. 'It was built in 1971.'

'The year before I was born.' I survey its peeling paintwork and dusty looking spines. 'Is that what I look like?' I'd like to think I hold my age better than the pineapple.

Haruko smiles. 'No. You are not dusty at all, Misaki.' She touches my hair with her finger. 'And your hair is much more orange.'

'1971 . . .' I say. 'Hot pants.'

'Disco,' says Haruko.

'Pineapple cheese ball.'

Haruko frowns. 'I give up.'

'"Joy to the World" by Three Dog Night was the top hit. I win.'

Haruko doesn't look happy about this. She taps her screen. 'There is Big Macadamia near here too. Can we go there? I like to eat macadamia nuts.'

'I didn't know about that one. It's not on my map. Where?'

'It does not say. Only near Big Pineapple.'

'Makes it a bit hard to find, then.'

As we walk towards the pineapple, it becomes apparent that, despite the plethora of signs welcoming us, it is, in fact, closed. A notice on the locked gate says *No entry* and *Patrolled by security*. The single car in the car park must belong to staff.

I stop at the signs. 'Why didn't the bus driver say anything?'

'Perhaps he did not know,' says Haruko.

'Perhaps he isn't paid enough to offer free advice.'

A large sign advertises train rides, gift shop, kangaroos, koalas, snakes and the Parfait Cafe.

'It would be nice to take a train ride through pineapple plantation.' Haruko sounds wistful.

'Yes, we could see all the little pineapple heads poking up through the dirt.' I sigh, but the thing that really makes me wish it was open is the parfaits.

'What are parfates?' Haruko is reading the sign.

'Ice-cream and pineapple.' Just imagining a cold ice-cream and pineapple concoction slipping down my throat makes me salivate. I can almost taste the sweet fruit on my tongue, hear my spoon chink against the frosted glass . . . I take a sip of lukewarm water from my bottle. It is no compensation.

'Maybe parfates are still there?' Haruko gathers up her Frida Kahlo skirt. 'We take a closer look?' She leans down and crawls through the fence.

I follow.

Up close, the pineapple is even larger. At the top, where the spikes come out, there seems to be a viewing platform.

'I would like to climb inside,' says Haruko.

'We could look out over the pineapple plantation.'

'We would hide in spines. Like insect.'

Can we climb up and play beetles in the spines, Mum?

'It would be like we'd gone through a magical shrinking machine.' I'm not sure if I am talking to Haruko or the child. It doesn't seem to matter.

I hear a rumble and turn.

A small tractor comes to a stop in front of me, a woman dressed in khaki at the wheel. Her smile is apologetic. 'Sorry. I'll have to ask you to leave. The pineapple is closed.'

We recognise each other at the same time. It is the woman who gave us a lift to Tewantin yesterday.

'Hello again,' she says.

'Sorry. We just wanted to have a closer look.'

'Yes. I can understand that. I can't let you stay though. Insurance, you know.'

'Yes, I know,' I say.

'We will go now.' Haruko hesitates. 'Do you have parfates left?'

'Parfates? Oh, parfaits.' The woman smiles. 'Mmm, I love the parfaits too. No, I'm afraid they're all gone. We shut at three-thirty.'

I glance at my watch. It is three thirty-five, but the pineapple looks like it has been shut for longer than that. It has the deserted air of a lonely outback roadhouse.

Haruko is despondent.

We wave goodbye, crawl back through the fence and make our way to the bus stop. I gaze back at the pineapple and its seductive viewing platform. I feel thwarted. Now I'll never know what's inside; it is like the Big Cow all over again. So near, and yet so far.

An occasional car passes as we wait on the side of the road. Haruko plugs in her headphones and taps her feet. She chews her lip and gazes at the over-promising and under-delivering sign. She must be still thinking about parfaits.

My hand drops into my handbag and I pull out my Shinto Gods. Benzaiten, the only woman, draws my attention this time. I notice for the first time that she looks a little like Haruko. I am yet to see Haruko in a pink kimono with her hair in a bun, but I'm sure she would carry it off with panache.

I hear a yap. A small white dog runs across the road. It is peculiar-looking – probably a mixture of breeds – with a fox-like nose and black button eyes. Its hair is rough and it has a fluffy tail that curls up in the air. It is not wearing a collar and is thin and unkempt. The dog approaches me, pushing its nose into the hand which holds my Shinto Gods. It wags its tail as its pink tongue emerges and licks Benzaiten.

'Benzaiten rides on magic white fox, Inari.' Haruko has taken out her ear buds and is examining the dog. 'Inari can take shape of human too. She is tricker but can also be good friend. Naughty Inari possesses people through fingernails.'

I note that my current companion is a girl dog – a girl dog with a very foxy face. The dog's wet nose sniffs along my fingernails. I curl them back out of reach. What happens if you are possessed by Inari? I don't want to take any chances. There is a roar in the distance – our bus is coming.

As I hail the bus I notice a shape rising above the trees that line the road. It is almost completely hidden, but it looks like a roof. The top of the roof is curved, brown, and comes to a point. Could it be . . .? The bus pulls up and the door opens. I glance from the bus to the roof.

Haruko follows my gaze. Her mouth opens. 'Big Macadamia?'

Eighteen

'Getting on?' The bus driver gives us a hard glare.

The dog presses its nose into my hand and, catching me by surprise, licks my fingernails.

I hesitate.

The dog wags its tail, walks towards the long grass on the side of the road and looks back at us. It yaps twice. Imperiously.

I look over at it. 'Sorry, I . . . we'll get the next bus.'

'Make up your mind.' The driver rolls his eyes, presses a button and the door closes with a whoosh.

Haruko smiles. 'I knew it was near here. Maybe they have parfaits?' She taps her phone. 'Big Macadamia was built in 1978. Platform shoes.' She gets in first.

'That was an easy one. Curly perms. For men.'

'Really?' Haruko raises her eyebrows. 'Not in Japan, I think. Strawberry Shortcake Doll.'

'*Watership Down*. Rabbits were big.'

'*Dallas* on TV.'

'The year I turned six.'

'Sony Walkman,' says Haruko.

'The Bee Gees,' I say.

'See-through plastic pants with leotards.'

I shudder. I'd forgotten that one. 'And Hummingbird Cake.' 1978 was a bad year. With the possible exception of Hummingbird Cake, I never want to see any of those things again. 'I'm out.'

'Me too.'

We both gaze towards the trees.

'Well, how about that?' I say. 'A surprise Big Thing.'

The dog wags its tail, gives another short sharp bark. It is definitely a command.

'You want to go down there?' I say.

Haruko seems doubtful. 'It is quite bushy.'

It does look like a bit of a bush bash. 'But it's a Big Thing and we're right here.'

Haruko nods. 'Yes, we must go. Sometimes pilgrimage is tough.'

The dog runs into the grass and is immediately swallowed up. Only a ripple in the seed heads shows its progress.

'Hey. Wait for us.' The grass comes almost up to our waists. I think about snakes as I push my way through it, following the rustling that indicates the dog's path. It is hard going, carrying my wheelie suitcase. I can't drag it through the dense grass. Haruko is doing much better with her briefcase and surfboard, even with her quite inappropriate billowing skirt. Maybe I should be travelling lighter, but I don't know what I could leave behind. *Pantywaist*, I hear Grandma Gatewood say.

The roof of the Big Macadamia seems to recede as we advance. It looks like a lost temple rising out of the jungle or a forest fruit that has run amuck.

'In Shikoku, people often get lost,' says Haruko. 'Never seen again.'

'That's not going to happen to us.'

Haruko sniffs.

Eventually we burst out of the long grass to find a muddy pond in front of us. The dog makes a slurping noise as it laps water at its edge. A turtle pokes its head up among the lilies, its bulging eyes expectant. Perhaps it is fed when people come here to picnic. A dilapidated picnic table nearby testifies to this possibility.

The Big Macadamia protrudes above the trees on the other side of the pond, its curved roof reflected in the water. 'I feel like I'm at Angkor Wat, or an Inca temple,' I say. The wind rustles the trees behind us, sounding like a slow breath through a conch.

Haruko cocks her head to one side, regarding the nut. 'We fight jungle and find lost civilisation.'

There is a splash in the pond as the turtle dives beneath the water. Haruko looks over at it. 'At one temple in Shikoku,' she says, 'there is a place called pond of blood.'

The pond does have a reddish tinge about it.

'It is where warriors clean their swords after battle.'

For a moment I feel like I am there, but then the sun goes behind a cloud and the pond changes from red to brown.

I shiver, suddenly cold, as I gaze at the Big Macadamia.

It's a bit spooky, Mum.

'What is the difference between a lost Big Thing and a ruined temple?' I say. It comes out sounding like a riddle.

'Big Thing is more spooky,' says Haruko.

I look at her and smile. She and my water child are on the same wavelength. But I'd expect that now.

For a moment we are quiet. I start to walk towards the lake, then stumble as I step on something hard underfoot. 'What was that?' The dog trots towards me, picks up the object and pushes it into my hand.

'Good dog.' It is a nut. I peer up. I am standing beneath a macadamia tree.

The dog wags its tail and barks.

'You want me to eat it?'

It barks again.

Haruko steps closer. 'It is well protected.'

The nut is enclosed in a woody capsule, half open to expose a shiny, harder wood inside. I pull at the outer capsule and eventually prise out the hard, round inner ball. The nut itself is still well secured inside this formidable armour. 'Now what?' I hold it up to the dog. 'Any suggestions?' My stomach growls. I haven't eaten since my frugal breakfast this morning and now, small as it is, the macadamia is tempting me.

Haruko leans down, picks up a rock and hands it to me.

Placing the macadamia on the table, I hit it hard. It breaks and the nut rolls out, perfect and whole.

'Miracle,' says Haruko.

I hold it out to her, but she shakes her head. 'It is yours.'

So I pop it in my mouth and chew. It seems like one of the best things I've ever eaten.

I am contemplating how best to tackle the final approach to the Big Macadamia when the dog barks. It is not the friendly yap I'm now used to. Its fur stands up along the back of its neck.

The grass rustles behind us.

Haruko's eyes widen, but then as a man appears relief passes over her face.

Was she expecting someone else? But I don't have time to think about that now. *Fabian.* He is about five metres away and holding a large white envelope. How close does he need to get to serve the papers? Can he throw them at me?

Haruko glances from him to me. 'Lawyer?'

I nod. 'Let's go.' Fabian is blocking our return to the road so we strike out through the long grass towards the Big Macadamia, the dog trotting behind. Perhaps we can find a place to hide in there?

'Hoi!' Fabian breaks into a run. 'Just stop and talk, Arkie. This is silly.'

Fat chance. I run faster. It isn't easy, lugging my suitcase. Stumbling through the grass. Fabian is gaining on me. A mental inventory of what is in my suitcase flashes before me – toiletries, clothes, spare shoes, a book . . . Can I live without it?

Pantywaist. All y'need is a shower curtain, a blanket and a raincoat. And that's for rough camping.

I drop the suitcase in Fabian's path and sprint away.

As we near the macadamia we pass a billboard overgrown with vines. *Rainforest Creatures of the Night*, it reads. An owl, a frog and a gecko cavort across a jungle backdrop and a fibreglass python slithers through the rampant vegetation on top of the billboard. It is like a setting from an Indiana Jones movie. I'd like to take a photo, but there's no time for that.

Pushing our way through overgrown palm trees and clinging vines we arrive, panting, at the door of the Big Macadamia. A faded sign on the railing says *Cafe Open*. Haruko's eyes light up and for a fleeting moment I believe that inside this deserted macadamia an optimistic soul waits for passing custom, parfaits at the ready. I try the door. It opens at my push and we step inside, the dog close behind.

Inside, it is dark and dusty. The cafe is definitely not open. A shaft of light enters through a high window, illuminating the dust particles. I have a soft spot for dust particles. Our house was always dusty when I was young. *Are you going to wish you cleaned more on your deathbed?*

my mother would say. I didn't mind. I loved how when the sun poured through the window the air sparkled and shone. Even though I knew what they were, the dust motes still seemed magical.

There is plenty of magic dust here, inside the deserted Big Macadamia. Benches, which once must have displayed souvenirs, or perhaps night creatures, run along one curving wall. We crouch behind one. It is pathetic, like hiding our heads in the sand, but it is all I can think of. The dog sits beside us, waving her tail slowly through the dust. 'Shh.' I put my finger to my lips.

She lies down and curls up, licking her fluffy tail. For a few moments it is quiet. The air is heavy, humid and smells of decaying wood. Something scuttles in the darkness – a rainforest creature?

The door opens. Floorboards creak and my heart accelerates. I now know how it feels to be hunted – a rabbit at the end of a shotgun, a fish on the end of a line. I am not yet in the crosshairs, but how long can it take?

'Arkie?' Fabian sounds nervous. This is not how he's used to meeting clients. Usually he doesn't have to get up out of his comfy leather chair. I hate to think how much this is costing, but perhaps Adam got a special deal – payment on successful serving of papers. Considering that our assets still need to be split I should just give up now and save myself some money. Fabian coughs. 'Arkie.' This time he has the correct legal imperiousness. 'I know you're in here. I have papers to serve on you.'

The dog's ears prick up. Hairs rise on the back of her neck. She gives a low growl.

'No,' I mouth at her, shaking my head. I put my finger to my lips again.

Fabian's steps come closer.

Damn. Why did we come in here? Why, why, why? Fabian is going to find me. He will serve the papers and my marriage will be over. I sigh. I am never going to find my way back home. I am about to stand up and admit defeat when there is a loud creak behind me. Sunlight floods the room as a door opens. A hand reaches in and grabs my wrist, pulls me out into the sunshine. Haruko and the dog race after me.

Nineteen

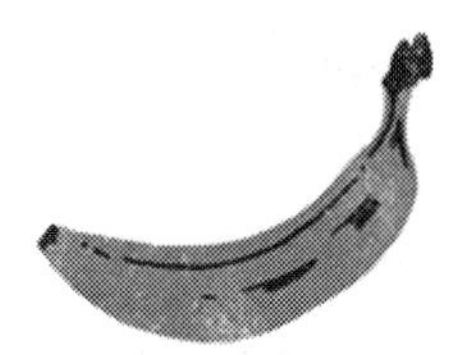

The tractor driver pushes the door to the macadamia shut, leans against it. Behind her, the handle turns. A banging comes from within. She braces her shoulders against the door. 'Need a ride?' Her voice is deadpan.

'Open up.' A muffled command comes from behind the door.

Haruko giggles and leans against the door as well. 'I don't think so,' she sings.

I giggle too with nervous tension. 'You're our saviour.'

The woman smiles. 'Jump on. I can't lock the door, so be ready to go. Anything you need to tell me first? You're not murderers, are you?'

I shake my head. 'He's my husband's lawyer.'

The woman meets my eyes. 'Sounds messy.'

'Yeah.'

She gestures with her chin towards the tractor.

I run and jump on. The dog leaps up beside me. We seem to be a team now. Haruko joins us next, still clutching her surfboard and briefcase. I feel very light with just my daypack, very virtuously free of encumbrances. Already, I have almost forgotten what was in my deserted suitcase.

The woman lets go of the door, sprints over and takes the wheel. The tractor is already running and we take off with a jolt along a bumpy, weed-infested path.

Looking back, I see Fabian burst out of the macadamia like a pale, round nut. He starts running after us, but we leave him behind in a cloud of dust. He actually shakes his fist at us. I've never seen anyone do that before. He yells something. It sounds like, *I'm going to get you, Arkie, and your little dog, too*, but that can't be right.

'Yee-hah!' I yell over the roar of the tractor, holding on to a bar in front of me as we accelerate over a pothole.

Haruko laughs as she bounces into the air. 'No parfaits, but we do the nut ride.'

The dog yaps, the woman smiles, the wind blows my hair out and I feel carefree, like Thelma and Louise on the run – in the early days before things turned bad. Before long we are up on the main road. Fabian's car is parked near the gate.

'Now what?' says the tractor woman.

We glance back over our shoulders. There is no sign of Fabian, but he can't be all that far away.

The tractor woman points at a small white weatherboard house a couple of hundred metres down the road. 'Cup of tea?' she says.

Haruko and I nod. We have to hide out somewhere until Fabian goes away.

A couple of minutes later we are at her house. She drives the tractor around the back, out of sight and switches off the engine. The silence is startling. Climbing down from her seat, she stretches her back before walking towards the house. Haruko and I follow, the dog trotting behind us.

The woman fills the kettle. Her movements are economical; she seems sure in her skin. Taking three cups from the cupboard, she places them on the wooden table, finds a bowl and fills it with water, lowers it to the ground.

The dog laps at it eagerly.

It is only then, with her eyes on the dog, that she speaks. 'What's her name?'

'Inari.' The name springs from Haruko and my lips at the same time.

We smile at each other. What else would you call a foxy white dog with an authoritative air?

'Unusual name.' She raises one eyebrow.

It's funny, I don't know this woman at all, but yet I feel at home with her. There is something very solid, very good about her. 'We just named her then.' I smile. 'She's not really our dog at all. She's adopted us.'

'Inari is Japanese fox goddess,' says Haruko.

The woman looks at the dog. 'Inari.'

The dog wags her tail.

'It suits,' she says.

'Have you ever seen her before? Maybe we should take her home,' I say.

The woman surveys the dog. 'She's not from around here. A bit underfed too. I'd say she's yours now.'

The kettle boils and she pours the water into a crockery teapot. 'And your names?' she says.

'Arkie.'

'I am Haruko.'

'I'm Maxine, Max.' She smiles. 'Nice to meet you, Arkie and Haruko.'

Inari yaps. She has found a red ball.

'Where did you find that old thing?' says Max. 'I used to have a dog. A long time ago.'

Inari places the ball on Haruko's lap. Yaps again.

Haruko picks up the ball. 'You want me to throw for you?'

Inari wags her tail.

'You can do it in the backyard,' says Max. 'You won't be seen out there.'

'Come on.' Haruko stands up. 'We go.' She and Inari go out the back door.

I walk to the window. Down the road, Fabian is at his car. I stand back so I can't be seen.

Max walks over and hands me a mug of tea. 'Want to tell me about it?'

I wrap my hands around the mug, take a deep breath and out it all comes, Fabian, Adam, Ben . . .

At some stage Max takes my arm, leads me to the table. Outside, a car roars by. It sounds like Fabian's but I don't look up to check. I talk and talk. I feel like I have never talked so much in my life. At last I stop for breath. I have no idea how much time has passed. 'I'm sorry. I don't usually talk about myself so much.'

'I like to listen.' Max gazes over my shoulder towards the window. 'Love is a strange thing, isn't it?'

I sense she has more to say. I wait.

'My partner, Cecilia, left me five years ago. She went on a painting course in Italy and never came back.' She pauses. 'Happens a lot, I've since found out.'

I am unsure whether she is referring to the partner leaving, Italy, or the painting course.

'Once people start going on courses, so I've heard, that's it,' she says.

'You must miss her.'

'Yes. She took up with her painting teacher. Antonia.'

Max seems such a nice woman. I can imagine how life here next to the Big Pineapple might become a little dull though. How broader shores might beckon. How a painting teacher called Antonia might be more temptation than a woman can withstand. 'Is she still with her?'

'I don't know.'

I think of Ben. 'Sometimes these things pass. It doesn't mean she doesn't love you. Not necessarily. You should get in touch.'

Max half-smiles. 'Perhaps. Cecilia used to run the nutmobile tours. You and Haruko would have enjoyed that.' Max's face grows dreamy. 'It was such fun, in the heyday of the pineapple. It's not quite the same now.'

'How long have you worked here?'

'Thirty years, on and off. I mean, I have done other things too.'

Max's face is weather-beaten, but she can't be too much more than fifty. 'You started pretty young, then. You must be an expert on Big Things.' I sense a mine of untapped information here. 'Is it just Australia that has them? Do you know?'

Max shakes her head. 'America had the first Big Things.'

'Of course.'

'They started building them in California in the 1920s but they didn't make it over to Australia until the sixties. The Big Banana was the first –' She stops, as if someone had interrupted her. 'Well, Cecilia always used to say it was the Scotsman. We had a lot of arguments about it.'

'The Scotsman?'

'Mmm, the Big Scotsman.' Max grimaces. 'It's on the side of a motel, in Adelaide. Apparently. It was built in 1963, one year before the Big Banana.'

I remember my blogger – The Big Scotsman. *Thank goodness someone is finally looking into this* . . . Very strange.

Max reaches over to her bookshelf and pulls out a glossy tome titled *Australia's Big Things*. 'See.' She flicks through the pages and shows me a picture of the Scotsman. 'It's not very big at all. I don't think it counts. Do you? And besides, Big Things are supposed to be about agricultural products. That was how they originated.'

I study the picture. The Scotsman seems quite big to me. But I'm new to this game. 'How big does it have to be? To qualify as a Big Thing, I mean.'

Max frowns and I sense I have stirred a hotbed of debate. 'There isn't a recognised standard. There really should be. I've tried to get an association together to work on guidelines. It was going well for a while there, but . . . interest has waned. Cecilia used to say at least twice as big as the object it represents and at least twice human size. She wanted to make that the national standard.' She eyes the Scotsman sceptically. 'Suppose he just about is, but . . .' She turns her head slightly on one side.

'He's not very generously proportioned,' I say.

'Exactly.'

'Not like the Big Pineapple.'

Max smiles. 'That's what I used to say. Cecilia's guidelines were less stringent than mine. I think a Big Thing needs to be really . . .'

'Mind-blowingly big?'

'Exactly.' Max looks out the window. The spines of the pineapple are clearly visible. 'It's heritage listed, you know.'

'Really?'

'Yep.' She pulls a slim document from her bookcase and opens it. 'This is the heritage report. *The Big Pineapple reflects the growth of the Big Thing phenomenon. It was important in demonstrating the development of agri-tourism and roadside attractions. It is a north coast landmark, providing sweeping views of the landscape.*'

'Goodness, it's like the Taj Mahal. More people should know about that.'

'Yes.' Max ponders this. 'We should put up a sign, really.'

'You should.'

She holds the document towards me, but the cover is made of cardboard, so I shake my head. 'I can see it from here.'

Max seems a little taken aback, but she continues. 'The idea was for travellers to see how country folk live. It's a bit strange really, when you think about it – a farming theme park. It's not as if I don't realise how lame and kitsch it is . . . But, I just think there's something about them – something . . .' Her face colours slightly.

'Weird and sweet,' I say.

She smiles. 'Yes. There used to be another Big Pineapple, you know.'

'Really? Where?'

'Just up the road, about an hour's drive away – Gympie. It got demolished a few years ago. They were both erected in the same year. Can you believe it?'

'How did that happen? Surely there wasn't enough interest around here for two Big Pineapples.'

'No, there wasn't. Some people say that this Big Pineapple,' she looks out the window, 'got wind of that one going up and decided to trump them. This one was finished just a few months before the other.'

'Which one was bigger?'

'They were both exactly the same height. Strange, huh?' She raises one eyebrow. 'Caused a bit of bad feeling between them, I think. Conspiracy theories abound, leaked plans, a mole in council, that kind of thing.'

'Duelling pineapples,' I murmur. I had no idea that the world of Big Things was so cut-throat.

Max shows me her Big Things stamps. 'They did a special collection.' And photos of people admiring the view from the top of the pineapple. 'I can take you up there if you like,' she says.

Haruko and Inari come back in at that moment. They both seem energised by their ball throwing.

'Oh, yes, Misaki,' says Haruko. 'We should go.'

Out the window, the viewing platform beckons. 'I'd like to, but . . . we've got to get to Brisbane.' I think I am safe from Fabian for now.

Max checks her watch. 'There's a bus in twenty minutes. Time for a quick look.'

Haruko smiles.

Max plucks a key off her wall and we walk across the road to the Big Pineapple, ducking under the fence. The door at the base of the pineapple creaks as Max opens it. 'The power's off for the day.' She turns on a torch, shining it up a curved staircase. 'Up we go.'

The torchlight flickers on black and white photos of pineapple plantations that decorate the walls and a display of pineapple tins. We climb up the stairs. It is too dark to see much detail.

'History of pineapple farming.' Max gestures at the wall with her torch.

I blink as we step out into the sunlight. We are on top of the pineapple, just underneath the spines.

'It is like being in a lighthouse,' says Haruko. 'I can see the sea.'

The view stretches across the green stubble of a pineapple plantation, framed by low hills.

'Magnificent, isn't it?' says Max. 'Cecilia and I used to come up here, just to watch the sunset.'

I nod, picturing the two of them, possibly drinking beer, watching the sun set over the hills – a simple life, maybe too simple for Cecilia. Perhaps she longed to see sunsets from the Eiffel Tower or the Pyramids, not just the Sunshine Coast version of the Taj Mahal. We climb down and Max locks the door behind us.

Max walks us to the bus stop. She doesn't talk the whole way there. 'I might do that,' she says, eventually, as the bus rounds the corner.

'What?' I have no idea what she is talking about.

'Call her.'

I smile. It is as if the rest of our conversation never took place. 'Yes. Call her. She might be sick of Antonia by now. Perhaps she doesn't know how to tell you.' I pull a card out of my wallet and give it to her. 'Let me know how it goes?'

Twenty

'What are we going to do with Inari?' I say as we wait for the bus.

The dog pricks her ears at her name.

'We are a team now,' says Haruko. 'We cannot leave her behind. She does not have a home, Max said.'

'I don't suppose dogs are allowed on public transport.'

Inari, as if sensing our dilemma, places her front paws on top of my daypack, which is lying next to my feet. She wags her tail.

'You want to go in there?'

She dances with excitement.

'You do?' I eye her, yes, she is small enough. I unzip the bag. There is not much in it – just some water and my iPad. I take out the iPad and Inari jumps inside. She turns herself around so her head pokes out the top. As the bus comes around the corner, I push her head down and zip the bag up with just a small hole at the top. 'Just for a moment.' Inari seems to understand. She doesn't object.

'Where is your other bag?' says Haruko.

'I left it behind. When we were being chased.'

'Good.' Haruko nods. 'Now you are more like pilgrim. Do you remember all the rules?'

'No meat, alcohol or arguments and not too much baggage or money.'

'And sex,' says Haruko.

'That's right, no sex. Easy.'

'Maybe,' says Haruko.

I think about her appointment with Ben and wonder if she is talking about herself or me.

The bus is almost empty so Haruko sits opposite. I place my daypack on the window seat and unzip the top so Inari can poke her head out. We pass Max on the road. She is walking swiftly. I hold my hand up to the window and she gives a brief wave before jogging up to the house.

I have only just got settled when my phone rings. I check the number. Adam. Even though I suspect the call won't be pleasant, a warm feeling fills my chest at the sight of his name on my screen.

'So you gave Fabian the slip again. He's pretty irate,' he says.

'Yes.' I try, but fail, to keep the smugness from my voice. 'It was funny really. You remember that painting that we used to have above the couch?'

'*The Hunter*.'

'Yes, that's what I felt like when Fabian was –'

Adam sighs. 'Why do you have to make it so difficult? What are you doing, anyway? He said you were at a big macadamia. Is that right? I couldn't make sense of it.'

'Yes. No. Not *a* big macadamia, *the* Big Macadamia. It was fantastic, Adam. You would have loved it. It reminded me of one of those temples near Angkor Wat. You remember the one that had all those trees growing over it?' We had been to Cambodia about ten years ago.

There is a long silence. 'Only you could compare a run-down theme park nut to Angkor Wat,' he says at last.

'But it was, Adam. You should have seen . . .'

'What will it take to get you to stop fighting this divorce, Arkie?' He sounds like he is coaxing me back from a high ledge. 'We both need to move on.'

What would it take? I haven't seen Adam for so long. Surely, if we could just talk . . . 'I want to meet. Just you and me. No Fabian.'

'And then you'll sign the papers? We can put in an application together? It's so much easier if it's a co-application.'

I hesitate. Inari pricks her ears. 'Yes, I'll sign the papers.' If that's what it takes to see Adam again.

'Jesus. Okay then. Where can we meet? Soon. I don't want to drag this out any more. It's driving me around the twist.'

'I'll be in Brisbane tonight.'

'Brisbane?'

'Yes.'

'Tonight?'

'Yes.'

'Arkie, it's already six o'clock.'

'Is it?' I glance at my watch. 'Only five o'clock here.'

'All right.' Adam's voice is flat. 'I'll catch a flight to Brisbane. I'll give you a call when I get there. Don't muck me around, Arkie.' He hangs up.

My stomach skips as I gaze out the window. I am seeing Adam soon. I smile. Signing the divorce papers seems like a minor cost to pay to see his face again.

Although I would rather go straight to Brisbane, there is one more Big Thing to visit on the way. We can't start shirking so early in the piece. I touch Haruko on the shoulder. She pulls out her ear buds and raises an eyebrow. 'We're getting out here. Let's go, Inari,' I murmur as I stand up and make my way to the front.

The bus drops us on the side of the highway. My GPS tells me that we are still quite a few kilometres from our next destination. The countryside is flat, and the road dusty. The only good thing about the walk is that I no longer have my wheelie suitcase. *Y'see,* I can hear Grandma Gatewood say, *y'didn't need all that stuff, y'only thought y'did.* I am starting to see where she is coming from. Less really *is* more.

One hour later, after emerging from a pine plantation onto a busy road, I can see our seventh temple, the Big Mower. I am sweat soaked, dusty and sorely in need of inspiration. I pause and cross my eyes to put it in soft focus. Mmm, perhaps it looks a little like a samurai statue on top of a gateway.

As we arrive at our destination Haruko gives me a blank stare.

She is right – up close there is no resemblance to a samurai. It doesn't seem worth the effort. 'The journey is more important than the destination?' I say. My aching feet protest this trite justification. The journey and its destination are both exceedingly lacklustre.

The Big Mower is a shop which sells, obviously, lawn mowers. The Big Mower itself is perched on top of a platform at the side of the shop. Despite the late hour, ride-on mowers are still lined up on the grass beneath it, giving the impression that they have just hatched.

Beside the Big Mower is a large illustration of a girl in a bikini riding a mower. It is very retro, very seventies. Her nipples poke through her blue bikini top, her mouth is half-open, an expression of rapture on her face.

Haruko puts her head to one side. 'Riding a mower is sexy?' she says.

I nod. 'Thrilling. That's what they'd like us to think, anyway.'

'I didn't know. In Japan, we don't do it like that. Not very much grass.'

I wonder why products aimed at women never show a man amorously clutching a vacuum cleaner or draped seductively over a washing machine. No-one would believe it, but women clutch power tools, fondle cars and apparently orgasm on lawn mowers. Why? Male appliances clearly function as penis substitutes, while women's appliances . . . I think of vacuum cleaners and washing machines – well, things do go *in* them. *Interesting.* I sense a whole new area of research opening up. Inari presses her nose against my leg, drawing me back to the present. This is probably lucky, as I might be in danger of over-thinking myself into oblivion.

'She is beautiful though.' Haruko gazes at the ecstatic mower girl.

Pretty, agrees my water child.

The girl on the mower does have a classical fifties film-star glamour. She has bouncy blonde hair and rosy cheeks. I'm sure she could do much better than that lawn mower.

The Big Mower looms over us, the sun shining around its red body, which also functions as a face. It has a bit of a nudge-nudge, wink-wink look about it. A sly smile spreads beneath its square eyes. I think the Big Mower might be a playboy, albeit a fairly nerdy one. *Yeah baby, I'm coming to mow your lawn.*

'How old do you think it is?' says Haruko.

I eye the faded bikini girl sign; that sort of thing has gone out of style. 'Mid-seventies?' I say. A truck pulls up and a man dressed in khaki unloads another mower. I decide to seek confirmation.

'Excuse me.' I point at the Big Mower. 'Do you know how old it is?'

'Built in seventy-five,' says the man. He tips his sunhat at us and pushes his mower into the shop.

Bingo.

'You were right,' says Haruko.

'One year younger than the Big Cow.'

'Wrinkled look.' Haruko sounds despondent.

I don't reply. I don't think either of us is in the mood for the trend competition. Cars whiz past as we stand on the side of the road.

Haruko gazes up at the Big Mower. 'It was long walk to get here.' There is a note of reproach in her voice.

'It may have been a mistake. Not all Big Things are created equal.' I take a photo anyway. As I put my phone away, my hand brushes against my Lucky Gods. I pull them out and open the drawstring bag. My eyes fall on Hotei, the laughing Buddha. There is something about his smile . . . I stare up at the Big Mower. 'Look, Haruko.' I hold him up.

'Same smile.' Haruko sounds delighted. 'Something else is the same too . . . Hotei is often on wheels like toy. He is called rolling monk.'

Suddenly the smile of the Big Mower takes on new meaning. Hotei is the god of good luck. I hold the statue out to Inari. 'What do you think? Does it look like Hotei?'

Inari wags her tail and barks.

'Yes, that's what I thought.' I slide the Lucky Gods back in my bag. The madness of our expedition suddenly strikes me. 'Haruko, you and I are definitely the only people in the world who would notice the resemblance between the Big Mower and a Shinto God.'

'We are visionary?' says Haruko.

'Either that, or mad. Who decides if you are a visionary or a lunatic? How do you know?'

'Maybe doesn't matter.' Haruko seems quite unfazed by the possibility of madness.

I am not quite so serene. Staying on the right side of sanity has always seemed important to me. If only because it feels like it could be so easy to stray.

Inari touches my hand with her nose and, before I can curl my fingernails out of the way, she licks them.

We start our long walk back to the highway. At least it is a little cooler now. The sun is dropping towards the horizon and the shadows are long. About twenty minutes later, I step to the side of the road to avoid a car and my foot strikes something hard. A rusty teapot pokes out between the blades of grass. The parts that aren't rusty are blue enamel with a faint white flower pattern. I stare at it.

Tanuki. For a moment I think the voice is in my head.

'Tanuki teapot,' Haruko repeats. She bends down, picks up the teapot and croons in a sing-song chant. *'Tan, tan, Tanuki's testicles. There isn't even any wind. But they still go swing, swing, swing.'*

I stare at her, bemused. 'Are you all right, Haruko?' Has one of us already skipped over into madness?

Haruko holds up the teapot and smiles. 'Naughty Tanuki turns himself into teapot. Don't look at me like that, Misaki.' She giggles. 'I am not crazy. Tanuki is racoon-dog. He is Hotei's friend. Tanuki is not very clever, but very mischievous.'

'And he turns himself into a teapot?' It seems a strange thing to do, but then the Japanese do have a complex relationship with tea.

'Sometimes. Or sometimes he turns leaves into money, to pay for his drinking. Soon as he is out of sight, they turn back into leaves.'

Like goblin gold. 'And the song?'

Haruko purses her lips. 'It is schoolyard song. Tanuki's testicles are very big – sometimes as big as 1000 tatami mats.'

I try to visualise this and fail.

'They can be used as parachute. Or drum.'

I smile. The Japanese are very quirky people.

Inari barks. She jumps up and puts her paws on Haruko's stomach, presses her nose to the teapot, wags her tail.

'Tanuki,' says Haruko, holding the teapot out to her.

Haruko hands the teapot to me and I put it in my daypack. It is almost weightless.

'Would you like a lift?' The voice comes from nowhere.

We turn, startled.

A mini-bus with *Australia Zoo* on the side has pulled over on the other side of the road. I didn't hear it coming. A man in a khaki shirt with an Akubra hat pulled low leans out the window. 'Where are you off to?'

'Brisbane,' says Haruko.

'Not going that far, but I can take you to the highway,' he says.

Haruko and I look at each other and exchange the faintest of nods. I know she is thinking what I am – it's a long walk back when your feet are already aching. And the logo on the bus inspires confidence.

The bus is empty, so Haruko sits up the front, opposite the driver, while I take the seat behind. Thick brown hair pokes out from beneath his hat and strong suntanned hands grip the wheel. 'Crikey, bit hot for walking, isn't it?' he says.

'Crikey it is,' says Haruko.

I've never heard anyone say crikey before, let alone Haruko. No doubt she is filing it away for later use.

'On holidays?' says the man.

'Yes,' I say.

'No,' says Haruko at the same time.

'Working holiday, eh? Like me. I love my work. Don't need a holiday – love every minute of it. No point in doing anything you don't love, is there? That's what we're put on earth for, I reckon – to find what we're passionate about and chase it down.' He takes one hand off the wheel and makes an action as if catching a ball.

His enthusiasm is infectious. Haruko nods eagerly. 'That is very true.'

'Wouldn't be dead for quids, ay?' says the man.

'Crikey, no,' says Haruko.

The journey to the highway, which took so long to walk, only takes a few minutes in the bus. Before long we are standing at a bus stop. It is twilight now; the rushing cars have turned on their lights. The man beeps and waves a suntanned arm as he drives off.

Soon after, a Brisbane-bound bus comes along. My purse has slid down to the bottom of my daypack, beneath the rusty teapot. When I hand the bus driver our fare, the money rustles like leaves. *Tan, tan, Tanuki . . .*

As we start off down the highway the bus's headlights pick out a large billboard advertising Australia Zoo.

'That is him.' Haruko points at the man on the sign. 'The man in the bus.'

'It can't be. Steve Irwin is dead. He got killed by a sting-ray.'

'Oh.' Haruko cranes her neck, but the sign is gone. 'Looked like him.'

I rest my head against the seat rest, running my thumb along my fingernails where Inari licked them. I hadn't had a good look at the man – the twilight, the Akubra hat pulled low . . . *Crikey* – he acted like him though. I give myself a mental slap around the face – that is one strange step too far. 'All men in khaki seem the same,' I say.

Haruko gives me a long look, shrugs and gazes out the window again.

I can sense her disappointment in me.

As the sun sets behind the hills, a full moon rises over the flat lands to our east. Dark orange at first, it turns white as it climbs higher. And then it shimmers and I see something I've never seen before . . . I nudge Haruko and point.

'Look, a moonbow.' The illuminated sea mist has formed a white rainbow.

Haruko nods. 'Takamure Itsue saw white rainbow too. Quite rare, I think.' She sounds matter of fact. As if this is exactly what you would expect at this point in the pilgrimage.

The road turns and we head directly towards the shining arc of light.

'Now we are going somewhere under the moonbow,' Haruko says dreamily.

Why not? So many strange things have been happening lately that going under the moonbow seems like just one more. As the bus nears the beam of light, the moon climbs higher; the moonbow fades, and then disappears altogether.

Haruko presses her nose to the window, her breath fogging the glass.

The noise of the bus and the darkness outside encloses us. My breathing slows and my mind wanders . . . A fox-dog, a magic teapot, a ghost bus, a moonbow . . . Maybe we really are in the Land of Oz.

One hour later, we are on the outskirts of Brisbane; a jumble of fast food outlets and car yards flash by outside. Haruko is dozing against the window. A low-flying plane cruises overhead and my stomach clenches. Adam could be on that plane. It seems improbable – a form of magic almost – that I can conjure him up like that. I gnaw my already well-gnawed fingernails, chew on the ends of my hair. What will it be like, after all this time? While I long to see him, my body is a mass of nerves.

This is my last chance.

In search of diversion, I decide it is time to update my blog. I pull out my iPad. Though my mind is a whirl, once I start, the words flow easily.

A Pilgrim's Life

Japan has a long tradition of travellers who kept diaries and composed poems as they roamed. One of these was Takamure Itsue. Tonight, like Takamure, we saw a moonbow – a white rainbow. It wasn't there for long and we might so easily have missed it. How many such splendours do we miss each day because we are focused on what has happened or what is to come? The moonbow reminds me to stay in the moment.

Pilgrimages can be tough. Every day raises new questions. You are forced to examine yourself.

I had thought of a pilgrimage as a solitary undertaking – a lone traveller, walking the long roads in search of enlightenment. In fact, it has been nothing like that.

I have a companion and am pursued by a hunter. I have met several people along the way and been joined by a dog. I have lost a suitcase, but picked up a teapot. I am lighter than I was, both physically and mentally.

I wonder if I might be in reach of a point of perfect equilibrium.

I press *publish* and stretch, my mind calmed by the distraction.

Soon after, the bus drops us off at Roma Street Station. Inari is sound asleep in my daypack, like a possum in its hollow. She has had a big day.

Haruko and I stand at the bus stop. I have been trying not to think about Haruko and Ben, but here we are in Brisbane . . .

Haruko's gorgeous Frida Kahlo outfit is crumpled from the day. In the headlights of a passing car she looks like a butterfly which has just emerged from its cocoon. She stretches as if getting ready to fly away.

I'd like to wrap her in a blanket and keep her somewhere safe. Put her back in her cocoon out of sight. 'So, you are having dinner with Ben?' I try to keep my voice light.

Haruko nods, smoothing some wayward wisps of hair off her face, then gives me an exasperated glare. 'What?'

My disapproval must be showing. I smile. 'Nothing. Have fun. Take care.'

Haruko rolls her eyes. 'I can look after myself.'

'I know you can.' I glance at my watch. Adam's plane has probably touched down. And it occurs to me that Haruko can most likely take care of herself much better than I can.

Twenty-one

Our divorce papers rest on the table between us.

Signed.

In triplicate.

It is a co-application – we are supposedly in agreement on this matter. We have no children to muddy the water and our property will be divided amicably. Our divorce will sail through the court like a yacht with a full spinnaker.

In the end I felt nothing as I signed. The papers seem meaningless, my efforts to avoid them ridiculous. Married, divorced, it makes no difference. Either we are two people who love each other or we are not. Pen on paper won't change anything.

Adam has booked into a one-bedroom apartment in a river-front high rise. Perhaps he thought we needed more space than a motel room to conclude our married lives.

I appreciate the thought, but can't help noting the marked contrast between beginning and ending.

There is a distinct lack of ceremony – no flowers, no champagne, no bridesmaids, no confetti. Adam and I didn't kiss or hug when we met tonight. We were subdued, businesslike. He offered me tea. I accepted. We were like two representatives of warring parties meeting in a neutral zone to sign a treaty.

I am surprised at how well I am behaving. How well we are both behaving. It is as if we have sent along emotionless clones of ourselves. The real Arkie and Adam wouldn't have been able to cope with this.

This is not how I imagined it when I agreed to meet.

Adam has finished his tea. He is sitting with his arms resting on the kitchen table; his eyes, which at first were distant, now focus on me.

I study his face. That is why I came here, after all. I've paid the price, so I should claim my reward.

His hair has got longer since I last saw him. I like it like this, almost brushing his shoulders. He has a few grey hairs I've never seen before among the black. Did I cause them? The thought makes me cringe. I want to touch his hair, wipe the grey away. Wipe away my guilt.

My daypack rests beside me on the floor. Inari lies with her head on my feet. The idea of my pilgrimage was to let go, but instead I seem to be collecting. Or does the dog replace the suitcase, leaving no net gain? Perhaps – but then there is the teapot. *Tan, tan, Tanuki's testicles* . . .

The flat did not come with a teapot, so I offered Adam my Tanuki teapot to make the tea – he had bought tea leaves rather than bags. Adam and I always used to drink cup after cup of tea out of a pot in bed in the mornings. One hand to drink tea, one hand to hold hands . . . I haven't had tea from a pot since he left me.

He washed the dirty teapot in the sink and it came out completely different – nothing like the rusty piece of junk we found on the road. Now, it is a pretty blue teapot with white flowers.

As I sip my tea I look out the window and notice that the small verandah has not escaped the obligatory Buddha statue. Once I would have shared this observation with Adam, but I haven't the heart for it now.

'Thanks for meeting me, Arkie.'

The words are formal, but his voice is soft. Now that he has what he wants he can afford to return to his natural mode – kindness. His long hands wrap around his empty cup. I know those hands both by sight and feel almost as well as I know my own.

I drain my teacup and place it down on the table, take a deep breath, examine his hands. It comes suddenly, surprisingly – a tug in my breast, in my groin. It is as hard to ignore as a blowtorch to the belly. I want him. I want his hands on me. Where did that come from?

His eyes flicker away from mine now. He feels it too. He gazes over my shoulder towards the window, towards the sluggish river and high-rise buildings. He chews his lip from the inside as he always does when he is thinking. His hands still toy with his teacup.

I breathe deeply. I should go now. But I don't. My stomach knots. I can feel my cheeks flush, heat radiating out from my stomach, down my limbs. Was there something in the tea? I haven't had this feeling for some time.

Not since Ben.

It has been a long, long time since I've felt this urgency, this desire, this hunger for Adam. Has signing the divorce papers given him the allure of illicit love? My pulse thumps in my neck.

I should go now.

Adam's hands release his cup. 'Are you hungry?'

My stomach growls out loud at the question. I am hungry in more ways than one. Except for one macadamia nut, I haven't eaten since breakfast.

We laugh, which defuses the tension.

'Maybe I should have asked you that question before.' He gets up from the table, opens the small fridge and pulls out bread, ham, cheese, tomato. 'I went shopping.'

This is so like Adam. He flies up from Sydney to divorce me, but he is still nurturing, still feeding me.

I blink back tears. I don't think he notices.

He places the food on the table in front of me.

I watch him as he takes out a few slices of ham and places them on a plate in front of Inari. He has lost weight too. He was never fat, but now his jeans hang loosely off his hips. If it wasn't for the grey hairs he would be like the boy I met all those years ago.

He sits down again. Leans his head on one hand and looks at me.

I don't realise how hungry I am until I start eating. All politeness and propriety is lost as I devour two ham sandwiches. *No meat.* It only hits me as I finish them. Never mind, Haruko will never know.

When I pause, Adam is smiling.

I smile back.

We don't say anything, but I know we are both remembering all the times he has fed me before.

And then, because I am warm and fed, because the man opposite me is smiling, because I haven't been touched for a long time and because it seems like the natural thing to do I slip off my shoe and place my foot upon his knee.

His face changes, becomes more serious. He sucks in his breath. 'I wasn't expecting that.' His hand touches my foot, wraps around it. He meets my eyes.

'It's nice to see you,' I say.

He hesitates. 'It's nice to see you too . . .' He sounds like he is going to say more, but he doesn't.

No meat, no sex. I slip off my other shoe, place my second foot beside the first. There is no rule against foot contact, however. 'But?'

He closes his eyes for a moment, his hands lie warm on my feet; he is neither accepting nor rejecting my advance. He opens his eyes again and cuts to the chase. 'I think that undressing you and making love to you would be about the best thing I can imagine doing right now, but . . .'

I hold my breath. He has seen straight through my *it's only foot-touching* defence. 'But?' I've already eaten the meat, after all. I have nothing to lose.

'Are you sure it's what you want?' His eyes glance towards the divorce papers. 'It won't change anything.'

'It's just sex. I know that.' I am such a good liar, I even believe myself.

He presses his hands around my toes. 'It's never *just* sex, is it?'

There is a lot hidden in that sentence – my betrayal, for one thing. I exhale slowly. 'No. But . . . I'd like to touch you again.'

'It won't make things any easier. For either of us.' His body is still, but it is a contained stillness; I can feel the energy humming beneath my feet.

I look into his eyes and they seem darker than I remember them. This strange similarity and yet difference to the man I thought I knew makes my breath run fast, my pulse race. I curl my feet against his hands, willing him to want me enough to disregard his judgement. 'It might.' The way I'm feeling right now convinces me that it will. *It will, Adam, it will.*

His eyes flicker away from me. 'It won't, Arkie. And what about after?' The way he says this makes me know that he has fallen into the moment as I have.

'After?' The longing between us is tangible, a magnet pulling us together. I feel a flash of triumph until he speaks.

'After, we will pretend it never happened. We will go our own ways. It's broken. Making love won't put it back together. You need to know that, Arkie.'

I slide my feet to the ground. 'Sounds fine to me.' I am lying. I don't believe that making love won't put things back together. In actual fact, I am scarcely thinking at all. I am following the commands of my body, which is telling me I want to hold, be held. I want to be held by Adam. For barely a moment I remember again the no-sex rule of the pilgrimage, but I am beyond caring. And I have already eaten the ham.

I long for him with the intensity of new love. His so-familiar body beneath my fingertips, his chest against mine, his eyes on me like I'm the most astonishing thing he's ever seen. Even after twenty years he still used to look at me like that.

Adam stands up as I walk around the table to him. He puts his arms around me. He looks at me like that.

He looks at me. Like that.

And I feel astonishing. In his gaze. It is as if last year never happened. We stand there, holding each other for a moment. Several moments. My forehead rests on his shoulder. His heart beats against my chest. He feels unfamiliar. I haven't held him for so long.

He kisses my neck and I pull my hair aside to make it easier for him. His lips are warm; they send a shiver through my whole body. I undo one button on his shirt, slide my hand inside, pull gently at the hairs on his stomach.

His tongue rasps down my neck, leaving a cool patch behind it. He bends and kisses my throat, undoes my top button. His fingers run lightly over my breast, through my shirt. They feel like the hands of a stranger. My stomach flips.

Our eyes meet. He smiles. He smiles at me like he's in love. 'Okay?' he says.

I expel my breath in a long sigh. 'Okay,' I confirm. We sound like two scuba divers about to descend, which in a way we are, because after this point, there's no turning back.

Adam unbuttons my shirt, runs the back of his hand across my stomach. He takes my fingers, leads me towards the bedroom. Inari stands up and trots after us, but he stops her with his foot. 'Two's company.' He shuts the door gently in her face.

I lean against the door, taking in a neatly made double bed, a book, a sketchbook on the dressing table. Suddenly I want to know much more about him, about what he's been doing since we separated, but now isn't the time.

He stands close, close enough for me to feel his breath, and places his hands on my shoulders. 'How do you want this?'

'You've never asked me that before.'

'Well, I'm asking now.' He stares into my eyes so intently I have to turn away.

And I know why he's asking. Because it's the last time. Tears spring to my eyes. I blink them away, look over his shoulder. It might be the last time, but I'm going to pretend it's the first. I wipe my cheeks, meet his gaze. *This is the first time . . .*

The first time I made love to Adam, I was twenty. He was twenty-one. He wasn't my first; I'd had five encounters before him. You couldn't call them boyfriends; the term implies friendship and there was none of that. None of the boys I'd met did anything to dispel my notion that males and females were natural enemies. Adam was different. He made me laugh. He treated me like a person. If it was a tactic, it worked.

'How many surrealists does it take to change a lightbulb?'

I turned from the painting to see a boy with dark hair that fell over his eyes standing next to me. His threadbare T-shirt had the name of an obscure heavy metal band emblazoned across it.

I smiled. 'I don't know. How many?'

'Two. One to hold the giraffe, and the other to fill the bathtub with brightly coloured machine tools.'

He told me later that he'd been working up to using that pick-up line for over ten minutes.

Adam and I made love in some strange places in those early days. It wasn't that we had nowhere to go. When we first met we were both living in share-houses while we studied at Sydney Uni. It wasn't long before we moved in together in Blossom Road. But even that didn't stop our erotic excursions. We got a kick out of it. Cars, libraries, beaches, parks, bus shelters . . . Sydney offered endless opportunities for playing that game we call sex. It was exciting and loving, but what I mainly remember is how much we laughed.

Adam touches my cheek. 'Arkie?'

I think of all the ways it could be for us, this first time which is also the last – slow, fast, rough, gentle, athletic, traditional . . . 'Hmm,' I say. I pull his shirt out of his pants, run my hands around his waist. 'Gee, I don't know.' Sliding out from under his hands I walk towards the bed, pulling off my shirt as I go, undoing my bra. I turn, holding the shirt in front of me, coquettishly. I raise one eyebrow, throw the shirt in the air. It catches on the blade of the ceiling fan, hangs like a flying fox.

Adam laughs. He takes off his shirt, throws it in the air too. In two quick strides he is beside me. He lowers his mouth to my shoulder, gives me a nip with his teeth. 'Like that, huh?'

'Mmm,' I reply.

I wake to the sound of clatter from the kitchen. Inari is lying across my feet. Outside, cars are roaring past on the road. Sun comes through the window. I feel like I'm a teenager again, which is ridiculous. Good sex can do that to you, though. I stretch my toes and Inari raises her head with a grumbling moan.

It's never just sex, Adam said. I wonder if that's true. It was never *just sex* for him and me, it was always a conversation, a communication. And this is why he can't forgive me. He knows that what I had with Ben was not *just sex* and he is right. It was a betrayal of the deepest kind. But surely . . . I roll over, pressing my nose into the pillow, breathing in deep, breathing in Adam's smell. But surely, a man can't make love with a woman the way Adam did last night unless he loves her. I feel it in my bones, in my breasts, in my limp and languid legs. *He loves me.*

Then Adam's sketchbook catches my eye on the dressing table across the room. I slide out of bed, wrap a soft blanket around me and pad towards it. I probably shouldn't be doing this, but I can't resist. I open it, turning to the most recent drawing.

The sketch is more abstract than Adam's normal style. It shows a woman with two faces, joined at the back of the head. One face is smiling, happy, open, the other wears a seductive smirk. She is winking at the shadowy, indistinct outline of a man. It is me. She is me. The sketch is dated with yesterday's date.

'I call it *Two faces*.' Adam is standing at the door. He is holding two mugs of tea in his hands. He is wearing a threadbare T-shirt and jeans. He has barely changed in twenty years.

I look from him to the sketch and back again. The irrepressible sense that all is well drains out of me. I close the sketchbook, pick up my clothes off the floor and dress silently, holding back tears. Holding back a howl of despair.

Adam hands me my tea, as he has done so many times before. 'I used your teapot again.' He avoids my eyes.

We sit on the bed together and drink our tea – a parody of a happy couple. Not a word passes between us. If last night was the last fuck, then this feels like the last supper.

After I have drunk my tea, I get out of bed. I search his face, seeking forgiveness, love, a chink in his armour. 'I love you.' My words are almost whispered.

Adam looks over my shoulder as if there is something very interesting there. 'Don't forget to take your copy of the papers,' he says in reply.

'Okay.' I bite my lip hard to stop myself crying. 'Goodbye.'

Something passes over Adam's face, a quiver. The corner of his mouth twitches. 'Goodbye.' He still doesn't meet my eyes. He picks up his sketchbook.

Out in the lounge room, I pick up my copy of the divorce papers from the table and slide them into my day-pack. My hands shake as I zip it back up. Then I see my Tanuki teapot. Adam has washed it and left it draining on the sink. I open my daypack and place it on top of the divorce papers. They rustle, and for some reason my heart beats faster.

I am almost at the door when I hesitate. Adam is still in the bedroom; he can't see me from there. Retracing my steps, I snatch up the other two copies of the papers and let myself out. *Tan, tan, Tanuki's testicles*, I hum as I run down the stairs.

Twenty-two

I have the divorce papers in my hand. I peruse them again while I wait for Haruko at the Roma Street Train Station. I am bruised with love after my evening with Adam, my thin skin even thinner, emotions that were half-repressed stirred up again, set free. I could laugh or cry in an instant.

Even though Adam told me that the sex wouldn't change anything, I can't believe that it hasn't. I felt it, he loves me. He may not trust me, but he loves me. He is still my husband. And while he is my husband, the situation is reparable.

I study the papers. They seem faintly ludicrous, their legal language ridiculous. How can you cut a marriage in two with Acts and Statutes? A pagan ritual might work – a bonfire and a magic spell – but not this. It is laughable. You might as well issue a speeding fine to a comet.

It is after ten o'clock and I have been pacing up and down with the papers in my hands for twenty minutes when my phone goes *ting*. I have a text from Haruko.

Sorry I am late. I am coming.
Haruko.

A second *ting* – another email from Chris at the Big Redback. I scan it.

Hello Arkie,
I have been reading on the Internet about those Lucky Gods you told me about. They do look like garden gnomes, don't they? The gnome in the garden here is like the one called Jurojin. Is that what you thought? I might see if there are any books on Shintoism in the library here. It would make a change. I have suggested to my boss that she order in some Lucky God statues. Yesterday I sold eight Buddhas!
Bye,
Chris Campbell

I reply.

Hi Chris,
It is nice to hear from you. Yes, I thought your garden gnome looked a lot like Jurojin. My favourite Lucky God is Benzaiten. She is the woman in pink. Make

sure you get a few of her. I think she would be popular with women. Goodness, eight Buddhas – what is going on?

Best,

Arkie.

I stuff the divorce papers in my daypack as Haruko approaches. She is walking briskly and wearing a big hat with big sunglasses – like an incognito film star. She smiles shyly at me and I am suddenly delighted to see her. I give her a quick hug. She hugs me back, awkwardly. Inari jumps at her legs.

'Inari, no.' I pull at her lead.

This morning on the way to the station I passed a pet shop and, on a whim, popped in and bought Inari a matching collar and lead. 'She's an unusual-looking dog,' the woman in the shop said. 'Very foxy, isn't she?' A small boy had tried to pat her, but his mother pulled him away. Being approached by children was one of the things I used to like about walking Maisie.

Haruko glances around, then removes her hat and sunglasses. Her narrow face is half-shadowed in the morning light, her fine eyebrows rising upwards. She looks a little foxy herself. Like someone with a secret. 'So you are still possessed by Inari,' she says.

I am not sure if she is joking. Inari pricks up her ears as if she is following the conversation. 'What happens if you are possessed by Inari?'

'You go a little mad,' says Haruko. 'Possession by fox is most common diagnosis for lunatic in old times.' She doesn't sound perturbed by the possibility.

'Oh.' Am I a little mad? Probably. Going to bed with your estranged husband and then running off with the divorce papers may not be the actions of a rational person. As if prompted by this thought, my phone rings. My heart gives a happy skip at the sight of Adam's name. 'Hello?'

'For fuck's sake, Arkie,' he says.

'Excuse me,' I say to Haruko.

She smiles and retreats a few steps.

'Sorry,' I say to Adam. 'I changed my mind.'

'You can't just change your mind. That's not how it works. We had an agreement.'

'Well, perhaps you should have thought of that first.'

Adam knows what I mean. 'I told you it wouldn't change anything.'

'But it did.'

Adam sighs.

'It did, didn't it? I know it did.'

'You're making this so hard for me, Arkie. So hard for us both. I can't believe how frustrating you are.'

'Well you shouldn't have slept with me then, should you?'

He sighs again.

'I know you love me.'

'That wasn't love, it was sex.'

'So you say.'

'Yes, I do say. God, you're so . . . exasperating. It was just sex. I wish we hadn't done it. You started it. I knew it was a bad idea. I had no intention . . .'

'It takes two to tango.'

'Well, it was a stupid thing to do.'

'So you don't love me?'

Adam is silent for some time.

I wait.

'I don't love you.' The words drop like pebbles.

'I don't believe you.' I hang up on him.

Haruko smiles at me apologetically. 'You are okay?'

I smile back. 'Fine.' And I am. Right now, I don't feel like there is anything wrong with my life that I can't solve with a bit of willpower. I am clearly possessed by Inari.

'You are not quarrelling I hope?' she says.

I'd forgotten that one. *Meat, sex, now quarrelling.* I may as well get pissed and have done with it. 'Not really,' I say.

'Sound like quarrel.'

'No. Just a conversation.'

Haruko frowns, but says no more on the subject. 'Where do we go now?' she asks as I guide her towards the train.

'Ballina.'

'Ballina?'

'Near Byron Bay.'

'Good. I still have surfboard.' She holds up her board.

'Yes, I saw that.'

Haruko falls asleep on the train; she can't have got much sleep last night. Inari, in contrast, is bright and alert.

She pokes her head out of my daypack and watches the world go by with great interest.

So, here I am on a train. I am reminded of my first meeting with Haruko. The possibility of throwing myself under a train seems to have receded for now. I no longer feel like that woman on the platform. My life is not yet in Technicolor, but it does have shades of pastel like a touched-up sepia print.

Haruko murmurs in her sleep. I gaze at her and wonder what happened with her and Ben. I can't ask though; I will have to wait for her to raise the subject. Slumped against the window, her briefcase on her lap, she is like a child on her way home from an exhausting school excursion. She looks so young.

Another memory surfaces . . .

Once when I was with Ben, shortly before the end of our affair, we went to a cafe. Our waitress was young, early twenties perhaps, and wearing way too much makeup for the daytime. Her long bottle-blonde hair was tied up in a ponytail. She had an abrupt, almost condescending, manner. I thought no more about her.

Later, as Ben and I were strolling along the road, I commented on the food, something bland about enjoying the quiche.

Ben was silent for a moment, then he said, 'She was a bit of a cutie, that waitress.'

I hardly even knew what it was about this statement that hit me so hard. On one level it was such an innocuous thing to say, but on another level, I felt dismissed and somehow demeaned. What was I – just the warty toad next to him? In retrospect, it was a sign. A man in love doesn't comment on other women.

'I didn't notice that,' I said. 'What I noticed was that she was wearing way too much makeup.' I sounded like a middle-aged sourpuss.

I suppose that was when I realised that while Ben might have been my erotic fantasy, I was not necessarily his. I had been naive to think that all my hard-won wisdom, wit and humour were a match for youthful skin. In retrospect I felt foolish. I knew the power of beauty, the way everything else falls in behind.

It's not like I'd never been beautiful. I had – or something close to it. Is there a woman who doesn't know precisely the value of her own attractiveness? You see it in male faces, in their reaction to you. It's like money in your pocket.

I had mixed feelings about losing my looks. On one level, they had never really brought me joy. They say that money can't buy happiness and beauty is the same. What it brings you is power, status and a level of attention not afforded to those who don't have it.

This attention can feel like affection, love even, and maybe it is. But it is only now as I learn to do without it that I realise how it eroded my confidence. Beautiful women know that their achievements are not valued. It sounds pathetic, like a millionaire complaining he has no real friends. But the fact is, he probably doesn't.

So, when Ben commented on the waitress's appearance it was a watershed moment. I went home and inspected myself in the mirror. I noticed for the first time the lines radiating from the corners of my eyes. I noticed how my neck seemed loose. I stretched the skin around my eyes and it took ten years off my face.

For weeks I contemplated having *some work done*. If it was done well I might lose a few wrinkles. If it was done badly I might end up looking a fright. But that wasn't what stopped me. Having poison injected into my face was never going to make me look like the waitress. This was a race I couldn't win.

Ben. I have made him sound like a monster. Which he wasn't, or why would I have fallen in love with him?

But the man knew how to keep me destabilised. At the very moment when I might have decided it was all too hard, my heart too wrung out, he would turn incredibly sweet and gentle. There would be that spark between us – those insights, that conversation. That falling into each other that only happened with him. It seemed vital that I hold on to him or risk losing my mojo and my mind.

All my resolutions to end it were rendered void each time he smiled at me again.

I wonder if he knew how he kept me so agonisingly tied to him with his hot and cold. If I had been either sure of his love or sure of not having it my mind would have been my own. I became addicted to the highs and lows. It felt like love. It is only now that it occurs to me – love shouldn't make you ricochet from elation to despair in the course of a few hours. Love should be kind.

Even with her face half-squashed against the window and her glasses sliding down her nose, Haruko is beautiful. Even in sleep, she clutches her briefcase. I remember the noodles and presents she had in there when I first met her. I wonder what she has this time.

As if she has heard my thoughts, Haruko sits up with a start and looks at me. She blinks and opens her briefcase. 'I forgot. I have present for you.' She rummages around and brings out a carefully wrapped parcel.

'Thank you. I wasn't expecting that.'

Haruko smiles. 'Open.'

I tear off the wrapping. Inside is a simple cloth doll. Its face and hair are drawn on with a black pen and it is wrapped in a plain blue kimono. I look at Haruko for an explanation.

She smiles. 'It is almost time for Hina Matsuri, doll festival. This doll, you throw in the water, it takes bad luck with it. I make it for you.'

'Thank you, Haruko.' I am touched.

She shrugs and glances out the window. 'It is nothing.'

I study the doll. It is going to have a heavy burden to carry – my marriage problems, my lack of mojo . . .

Haruko's eyes flicker over my face. 'You want more dolls?' She pulls two more from her briefcase and holds them towards me.

'No, no, those must be yours . . . Do you have bad luck, too?'

Haruko sighs and takes off her glasses. 'I did not tell you before, but . . .' She rubs the bridge of her nose. 'I am running away too.'

Perhaps that explains the big hat and sunglasses. 'From Ben?' I say.

Haruko laughs. 'No. From Yakuza.'

'Yakuza?'

'Japanese mafia.'

I stare at her.

'Last night. I am having dinner with Ben. He took me to Japanese restaurant. That was a mistake. There was a man there. Japanese man. He stared at me. Later, I walked past his table to go to bathroom and I see tattoo, just a little bit. And he was missing fingertip. That means he is Yakuza. I think it will not be long now until they come to find me.'

'Why do the Yakuza want you?'

Haruko looks out the window, then back at me. 'In Japan, Yakuza run English conversation class. I join class, but I don't have enough money to pay. No problem, they say, I just have to go with men who they tell me to. So I do, but I take some money from men to save for trip to Australia. I only give Yakuza some. When they find out, I run away. They have been chasing me all the time, I think. I am a little bit scared to go back to Japan.'

'Is that why you decided to stay in Australia?' I remember the text she got in the cafe. 'Did someone send you a warning?'

Haruko nods. 'My friend told me to stay away. And then, the night before pilgrimage, she told me they know I am in Brisbane. So I need to leave quickly.'

'But surely they haven't followed you all the way over here?'

Haruko shrugs. 'There are many Yakuza here already on Gold Coast,' she says. 'They have holiday house. Big mansions. Geisha parties. They don't need to come just for me.'

'Really? I had no idea.'

Haruko nods. 'Many, many Yakuza. It is okay, they won't find me now.' She turns and smiles at me. 'You should have told me about you and Ben.'

I open and shut my mouth. 'Did he tell you we . . .?'

'No. I told him I work for you.' She looks at me. 'Did you think I . . .?' She raises her eyebrows meaningfully.

'Maybe.'

'It was just work,' she says. 'Pilgrimage consultation. He is interesting man. Sexy too.' She gazes at me over the top of her glasses. 'But perhaps not a nice man?'

'What did he say about me?'

'He did not say much. Just you were a friend. But I knew.'

'What did you know?'

She meets my eyes. 'He has your power. I could feel it.'

I stare at Haruko. She surprises me every day. 'You could feel it?'

She nods firmly. 'He has it.'

'How did you know?'

She rolls her eyes. 'It was very obvious. You need to take it back.'

'But how can I do that?'

'Just take.' She makes a gesture as if pulling something from my chest. 'Stop loving him.' She clicks her fingers and smiles. 'Just like that.'

Up until now, I hadn't really believed that Ben stole my mojo. There was a power transference, but that is what happens in relationships if you let it. I thought my loss of mojo was due to sadness. I just needed to cheer up and it would come back.

'Do you really think that's how it works?' I say. 'I stop loving him and I get my power back?'

Haruko laughs. 'Perhaps, Misaki.' She taps my head. 'It is in here. In Japan we say there are eight million kami. They are divine power of universe, like gods. Kami talk to me. Give me power. I think you have let your kami go away. I think they have gone to him.'

'So, how do I get them back?'

'Everything you need, you already have,' says Haruko. 'You know yourself, what to do.'

I am considering this when my phone goes *ting*. I have a text from Max at the Big Pineapple.

I have contacted Cecilia. We are going to meet (Antonia leaves fingernail clippings in bed).

At least someone seems to be getting her love life in order. I smile and show Haruko the text.

She nods casually, as if this is exactly what she expected.

Inari presses her nose against my fingers. Her pink tongue comes out and she licks them.

Twenty-three

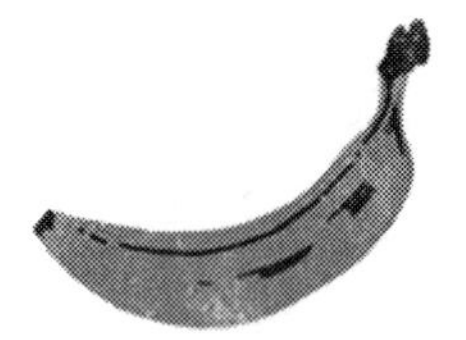

I look out the window as the train pulls into a station. *Yatala*. The name strikes a chord. I stand up. 'Let's get off.'

'What do we do here?' says Haruko.

'We have lunch. At the Big Pie.' I open my daypack and click my fingers. Inari, who has been sitting on my lap, jumps in. We are old hands at this now.

'Big Pie?' Haruko follows me off the train, her nose crinkled up in amusement.

As we cross the highway I see it, set back a little from the road. It is like a flying saucer on a stick. The car park in front of the pie shop is full. We stop at the base of the Big Pie before we go in.

'The eighth temple,' I say.

Haruko looks doubtful. She cranes her neck to peer up. 'There is nothing like this in Japan.' It is unclear whether she thinks this is a good thing or not. 'Australians like to joke, I think?' she says.

'Yes, you're right. It is kind of a joke, but also, perhaps, kind of serious.'

'Both?' says Haruko.

I nod.

Haruko and I study the pie for some time. Perhaps each of us is hoping that the other is finding meaning there in the car park. Maybe neither of us wants to admit that the earth isn't moving for them.

'Shall we get pie?' says Haruko eventually.

Inside, the queue is about twenty deep at the counter. It is a change to see a Big Thing thriving. But then the Big Pie itself is almost superfluous; they are here for the pies.

The selection is overwhelming. I have never seen such a wide array, both savoury and sweet. I never eat pies and have no idea what I want. *Beef? Chunky beef? Curry, chicken, lentil, spinach, lamb, pork, steak and potato, steak and peas* . . . And then I remember the *no meat* rule.

Haruko looks like she is inspecting a museum display about other cultures. She wanders up and down the cabinet, peering around the bodies in front of her. She studies the labels and listens carefully to each person's selection. Eventually she adjusts her glasses and turns to me. 'I have what you have.'

'Vegetarian?'

She nods. 'Of course.'

Despite the crowd, the front of the queue appears way too soon. 'What'll it be?' says the plump woman behind the counter.

I point at the pies with a golden shiny crust that are exactly like miniature versions of the Big Pie which hovers in the window. A small label in front of them says *Vegetable Pie*. 'Two of them, please.'

Haruko and I sit down at a wooden table and eat our vegetable pies with knives and forks, as seems to be the custom here. As the pies are rather large, this probably makes good sense. I hold my daypack on my lap and slip Inari morsels of pastry when no-one is watching.

The clientele is staunchly working class, mainly tradies, and very enthusiastic about their tucker. Pies with peas are particularly popular. A pile of *Big Rig* magazines – a truck fancier's delight – sits on the table near the door.

A sign on the wall reads, *Yatala, land of the flooded plains . . . From the convict timber cutters harvesting Cedar and Yellow Wood to a flourishing township of Cane Plantations, Blacksmith, Pub and Bakery . . .*

Photos testify to a time when Yatala was not the hectic offshoot of the Pacific Highway that it is today. Horse-drawn carts and open paddocks have given way to car-choked streets and rows of brick houses.

'Pokémon.' Haruko is pointing at the sign.

My eyes follow her finger. For a moment I am baffled, but then I get it. While Yatala Pies might have a long history of feeding travellers, the Big Pie itself, it turns out, was only erected in 1999 . . . Haruko has struck the first blow in the game.

'The Y2K panic,' I say quickly.

'White jeans.'

'I turned twenty-seven.'

'I turn six.'

'Cheddar and Pepper Scones,' I say.

'"Believe" by Cher.'

I strain my memory, but can't think of anything else. 'You win.'

'Yes!' Haruko swallows her last mouthful of pie.

I continue to read the sign. As it turns out, the Big Pie was actually *re*-erected in 1999, following the store's move to its current location. *But never mind* . . .

Haruko is admiring the stained-glass images of native wildlife in the windows. 'What bird is that?' She points.

'Rosella, cockatoo, platypus, koala.' I point at each window in turn.

'I would like to hold koala,' says Haruko.

'I thought you went to Lone Pine that first day in Brisbane. After you left me in the cafe. Didn't you get to hold a koala there?'

Haruko looks embarrassed. 'Oh. I forget. No. I didn't go to Lone Pine. I just want to . . .'

I remember how she rushed away. 'Get away from me?'

She smiles apologetically and shrugs. 'I didn't know . . .'

'If I was crazy?'

'But now I know you . . .'

'You're sure that I am.'

Haruko giggles. 'Maybe we both a bit crazy, Misaki.'

'Maybe.' I think of the divorce papers in my bag, alongside my Tanuki teapot.

I suppose Fabian is chasing me again now. Even though I now have the divorce papers, in legal terms they have still not officially been served. This is a technical point. The papers I have are a joint application which must be signed by both Adam and me to proceed. Without a copy of these, Fabian still needs to serve me the papers for a sole applicant. He must feel sorry for Adam, having such a crazy wife.

'But that's what a pilgrimage is about, isn't it, Haruko? Opening yourself up to possibilities beyond the normal?'

'And no sex, meat or alcohol.' She gives me a cheeky grin.

I feel my cheeks flush.

Haruko studies my face as if she knows exactly what I'm thinking.

I cough and try to sound innocent. 'Why aren't you allowed to have sex?'

'Must keep your mind on spiritual things.'

I am about to confess my night with Adam, but then a muscular, tattooed man asks if we have finished with the table and the moment is gone.

Adam lingers in my head as Haruko and I go back outside. Our conversation that morning replays in my mind. Even though he said he doesn't love me, my body still tells me the opposite. What do I believe – my head or my senses? I hardly need to ask – intuition has always trumped logic as far as I am concerned.

We take pictures of each other in front of the Big Pie.

Why is that pie up on a stick, Mummy?

So that people can see it from a long way away.

But it doesn't even look like a pie. It's more like a flying saucer.

'Looks like flying saucer.' Haruko gazes up at the pie with rapt attention. 'Pie in the sky.'

Again, she echoes the voice in my head. I wonder if she hears the water child too. I wouldn't be surprised if she does, but I don't want to risk asking her, don't want to risk sounding crazy. 'Not my favourite Big Thing, I don't think,' I say. The Big Pie has none of the scary charisma of the Big Redback, the poignancy of the cow or the mysticism of the shell. It is just a very large bakery item. And I don't even like pies much.

'I like it,' says Haruko. 'Nice pie too.'

Inari yaps in confirmation.

There doesn't seem to be any more to wrest from this encounter, so we move on.

Inari trots in front, leading the way, as Haruko and I walk back to the highway. The train terminates just a couple of stations down the road, so we catch a south-bound bus from the train station instead.

'Ballina now?' says Haruko.

I shake my head. 'Not yet. We have the Big Avocado first.'

Haruko smiles. 'So many, many Big Things. Very big pilgrimage.'

I gaze out the window as we drive down the six-lane highway. We are passing Dreamworld now; this part of the road between Brisbane and the Gold Coast is theme park heaven. A small red cloud hovers over the Tower of Terror. The horizon is otherwise clear and it seems out of place, as if it has come out of a chimney. But there is no chimney.

It reminds me of something, but I can't think what.

The wind must be blowing from the north, as the lonely cloud is still keeping pace with us at Coolangatta Airport. Every time I look out the window it is right there – a little, lost cloud in a clear, blue sky.

Twenty-four

One hour later, the bus drops us off on the side of the highway. We are still some distance from our destination, Tropical Fruit World. It sounds like the booby prize of theme parks. I imagine a mother teasing. *Where shall we go today, sweetie? Dreamworld, Sea World, Movie World, or . . . Tropical Fruit World?*

We three proceed in our usual order. First, Inari, who instinctively seems to know where to go. She has her tail in the air and her bright eyes focused on the road ahead, as if she can smell out the next Big Thing. Perhaps Inari is a trend-spotting dog.

Haruko strides ahead of me, briefcase in one hand, surf-board under her other arm. I follow, slowly. I realise I am becoming slower and slower with each Big Thing I visit. I plod steadily, one foot after another. Perhaps I am getting in the swing of it at last – becoming a pilgrim. Who knows where this will lead? Maybe like Grandma Gatewood I will set off and walk the Appalachian Trail at seventy-five. I have over thirty years to toughen up, after all. That should be long enough to overcome my pantywaist tendencies. My little daypack bounces on my back; I feel much freer without my wheelie suitcase. At least I have mastered the art of lightweight packing.

The walking becomes more enjoyable once we are off the highway. Grassy paddocks and large trees line the road. We are only just over the border from Queensland, but somehow it is different – greener for one thing. Blue-tinged mountains, which must attract the rain, rise in the distance. Could I do this for months on end? Could my life really become so simple, so free of needs? A piece of newspaper flutters by in the wind. I pick it up, registering some minor scandal involving a politician. Do I need to know this? No. The world beyond seems ephemeral, unimportant. I crumple the paper and stuff it in my pocket.

'Haruko.'

She stops and looks back at me.

'I think I am becoming a pilgrim.'

Haruko smiles slowly. 'That is quick. Only third day on pilgrimage. Do you feel like your mind is little bit blank?'

'Yes.'

'Like you just want simple things?'

'Yes. That's amazing. You know exactly what I mean.' I wait for Haruko to congratulate me on my pilgrimage progress.

'We have name for it, in Japan. Little bit hard to translate.' She frowns. 'Senility?'

'Senility? Are you sure?' I frown.

Haruko nods. 'Yes. That is the word. Senility. You have pilgrimage senility.'

'I don't like the sound of it.'

Haruko shrugs. 'It happen to most people.' She turns and strides away.

Senility. And here I was, thinking I was on the verge of enlightenment. But perhaps something was lost in translation.

After about forty-five minutes, Inari yaps and breaks into a rapid trot. At first I think she has scented an animal but then I see it some way down the road, the Big Avocado. At a distance it looks like one of those carefully pruned oval-shaped trees that you find in Japanese gardens. This resemblance vanishes as we get closer.

Perched on top of a pole, it is mottled, whole, and its bright green colour suggests that were it a real avocado, it would take a good three days to ripen. It is also not nearly as big as I thought it would be. I obviously need to lower my expectations or I will keep being let down by these under-achieving Big Things.

Behind the avocado is a cafe and souvenir shop. A small group of Japanese tourists gathers at a wooden table, a platter of multicoloured tropical fruit in front of them. I wonder what made them choose Tropical Fruit World over the more obvious delights of the Gold Coast. Their guide, a young Japanese man in a tight white T-shirt, glances up. His gaze lingers on Haruko.

'Refreshments?' I say.

'Yes, please,' says Haruko.

In the cafe, I ask the woman behind the counter when the Big Avocado was built.

'1983,' she says.

The year I turned eleven . . .

'Pedal pushers,' murmurs Haruko from behind my shoulder. She doesn't miss a trick.

I smile at the woman apologetically and turn to face Haruko. 'Rubik's Cube.'

'"Every Breath You Take" by The Police.'

'French nuclear tests at Mururoa Island.'

'Shrimp and avocado cocktail.'

'I give up.' I turn back and survey the menu. 'What's the avocado milkshake like?' I ask.

The woman leans forward. 'Between you and me,' she lowers her voice, 'a little too rich for my taste, but good if you're hungry. It's a meal in a cup.'

I glance at Haruko. She is gazing at a fruit that has been sliced in half; its flesh is the colour of rubies, dotted with small specks of black.

'That one?'

She nods.

I buy half a dragon fruit and ask for two spoons. The woman hands me the fruit and comments on the beauty of the day. Her deep brown and wrinkled face suggests she has enjoyed many such sunny days. She pushes a couple of cardboard plates towards me, but I hold up my hands. 'No, thanks.'

Haruko and I sit down at a picnic table where we can admire the Big Avocado. Inari has made herself scarce, but I know she won't be far away. She is a mysterious little dog.

'Look, Haruko. That cloud has followed us all the way from the highway.' My small red cloud hovers above the avocado, cheerful and plump, like a tour guide about to make an announcement. It looks a little larger than it did when I first spotted it, swelled up with importance. And I suddenly remember. *Landscape with Red Cloud . . .*

'Where shall we put this one, Arkie?' Adam holds up the print. The painting shows a lonely landscape, but the cloud is bright and full of purpose. He hangs it and stands back from the picture. 'That is one determined cloud,' he says.

We are lucky we are under an awning as suddenly the cloud bursts, encasing the avocado in a silvery haze of rain. Immediately, the earth emits a rich, damp smell. I breathe in deep. Frogs start to croak. The downpour is very localised – down the road the sun is still shining. It is like Tropical Fruit World has its own climate.

Haruko and I scoop out the vivid crimson fruit and watch the rain. The dragon fruit's taste is bland but the texture and colour so gorgeous it convinces me otherwise. Perception is everything. 'The ninth temple,' I say.

Haruko nods. 'In Shikoku there is lucky temple. You visit to ward off bad luck in unlucky year.'

'That sounds like a good one. Do you think this one is like that?'

Haruko stares out at the rain. She shakes her head. 'No, maybe not.' She slides a spoonful of brilliant red fruit onto her tongue and chews thoughtfully. 'Taste like soap.'

Haruko is not as easily fooled as I am.

Shadowed by the rain, the Big Avocado takes on an aura of mystery, almost spirituality. As I gaze at it, it strikes me that the shape is not quite right. It is too symmetrical – like a Dali egg. Eggs are big in surrealism. If the Big Avocado were to feature in a surrealist painting, it would be a symbol for hope and love.

As I finish my dragon fruit, a cart pulled by a tractor discharges a load of dripping wet but still hearty-looking tourists. They have just returned from a tropical fruit safari. I wonder what drives people to come here – to be pulled by a tractor through a plantation of fruit. It seems a strange desire, but who am I to judge – I'm here too. And sitting with Haruko, watching the rain pouring down from a little red cloud and feeling dragon fruit slip down my throat, I feel something very close to contentment. I hold on to that feeling; it's been in short supply lately.

At the table in front of us a Japanese girl in short shorts and black tights holds a blue mirror to her face and checks her makeup. It strikes me that she is in my country, doing the same pilgrimage as me, while I am here, wishing I was in hers. There is probably a message there for me.

As suddenly as it started, the rain stops. The cloud, deflated, hovers over the avocado for a moment, then an invisible puff of wind blows my small red cloud away. I raise my hand in farewell as it vanishes over the trees, like a friendly face swallowed up in a crowd.

In the gift shop we sample avocado jams, buy some avocados and rub a little avocado body lotion on our skin. The atmosphere is slightly new-agey. Dream catchers and fairy wands mingle with books on improving immunity by eating tropical fruits. They also have a selection of Buddhas, ranging from key-ring attachments to mantelpiece ornaments and garden sculptures.

Haruko stops still in front of them. 'Why so many Buddhas? I thought Australia was Christian country.'

'Mmm. Kind of. People here are interested in Buddhism.'

'So they study Buddhism?'

'Maybe. Or maybe just get the statue.'

'Oh.' Haruko smiles. 'Now I understand. It is like souvenir. You like something from different country. In Japan we like to wear T-shirts with English language. Maybe it is like that?'

'Yes. I suppose it is a bit like that.'

Haruko and I decide to attempt a fruit quiz on a computer. The quiz is introduced by the owner of Tropical Fruit World, a broad-shouldered, middle-aged man. His screen image assures us that soon we will know as much about tropical fruit as he does. I find that highly unlikely.

The quiz asks you to drag a range of fruit and place them on a map of the world, indicating which country they come from. I give up after trying to place an avocado on Australia, Africa, Brazil and the Pacific without success. Haruko takes over and I discover something new about her – she is an incredibly competitive game player.

Haruko's brow furrows as she tries to find a home for something called a black sapote. Her whole body emanates concentration. Each time she finally completes the quiz, she immediately resets it with a new range of fruit. She is trying to beat the previous record for the fastest fruit quiz time. I imagine that she takes no prisoners in Tokyo pinball parlours.

As Haruko correctly places the lilli pilli on Australia, a prickling sensation runs up the back of my neck. I look up and see the Japanese guide peering through the shop windows, his phone to his ear. He turns away as I catch his eye. Inari is back; she stares at the man and makes a rumbling noise, which is not quite a growl.

'Rambutan,' says Haruko.

'Thailand?' When I look back up, the man is gone. I don't tell Haruko. I am probably nervous for no reason.

'Yes.' Haruko punches her hand in the air. 'I am the fastest fruit quiz ever.'

Out on the verandah, Haruko points at a model of a smiling avocado with a hole cut out in its belly. 'Take photo?' She leans down and pokes her head through. Now the avocado has a smiling Japanese girl for a stone.

That girl looks funny, doesn't she, Mummy?

I smile as I take her photo. *Yes, she does.*

I like her.

I like her too.

Inari appears from behind the Big Avocado as we are just about to go. She yaps and leads us back to the highway.

On our way to Ballina I check my emails. I have two new comments on my blog. The first is from Bertie at the Tewantin Visitor Centre.

Dear Ms Douglas,

I'm a bit new to this blogging, so I don't know if you will get this comment. I am on the computer at the information centre in Tewantin.

I took a walk past the Big Shell today and I thought about what you said. I was a bit taken aback at the time, but the fact is, I have always thought there was something about it too. So I just wanted to tell you that.

I liked what you had to say about pilgrimages. My husband died last year after forty years of marriage. I would have liked to travel with him, but he never wanted to. We holidayed at the same motel in Coffs Harbour every year. Reading your blog makes me think that I might like to do a pilgrimage one day.

Yours sincerely,

Bertie Webster

I smile and reply.

Hello Bertie,

I did get your comment, so well done. I think you may be a natural at this blogging thing. I'm sorry to hear about your husband, it must be hard to be alone after so many years. Thank you for telling me about the Big Shell. It's good to know I'm not the only one who feels something there. Have you stood inside so you can hear the sea? A pilgrimage is an excellent idea. I think everyone should do one. Please keep in touch and let me know your plans.

Yours, Arkie.

My other comment is from the Big Scotsman again. Now that I know there actually is a Big Thing called the Big Scotsman, I read this in a different light.

Hou ar ye?

Stop beating around the bush, lassie. Rise up and strike down the forces of oppression. We Scots must stick together to defeat the propaganda wars.

Guid cheerio the nou!

The Big Scotsman

THE ORIGINAL AND THE BEST

His comment has a *sent from my iPhone* message at the bottom. I visualise a ruddy-cheeked, bearded man with muscular calves striding over the moors, iPhone in hand. He is still strange, but perhaps he has a point. I reply.

> Hello Big Scotsman,
>
> Och, I will look into this matter. Be strong. Maintain the rage. Wear your kilt with pride.
>
> Yours,
>
> Arkie Douglas (from the Douglas clan by marriage)

The bus is now passing what appears to be another Big Thing, or at least a tourist attraction of some kind. An immaculate green lawn and precision-clipped hedge surrounds a large white-washed building topped by a clock tower. Cone-shaped trees are arrayed in front of the building. It is all very Disney-esque. Edward Scissorhands would be right at home here.

Haruko and I are near the front of the bus, so I lean forward to talk to the driver. 'What's that?' I point. 'Is it worth a visit?'

The bus driver cackles. 'Not while you're breathing. It's a crematorium.'

'Oh.' As the bus goes past I see *Crematorium* in big letters on the roof. It still looks like a theme park though.

'Used to be a tourist attraction – Melaleuca Station. A place for train buffs, y'know. They had a big steam train. You could go for a ride.'

A big train.

As I crane my neck, I see a grey BMW pull in. There is a familiar face at the wheel. Fabian. He must be using out-of-date tourist information. I smile. I hope he enjoys the crematorium. I wonder how many train-spotters still turn up there searching for the railway.

What kind of person would think to redevelop a railway theme park as a crematorium? They must be a lateral thinker. I'd quite like to meet them. As the immaculate hedges vanish from view I think that sometimes real life is quite surreal enough.

Twenty-five

As the bus pulls into Ballina, I am wondering how Haruko feels about visiting the Big Prawn. She reacted so strangely the first time I mentioned it, I haven't felt game to discuss it with her again. She seems cheerful, however, as we walk down the street looking for a motel.

Ballina has many motels. It is obviously a popular holiday spot, although right now it is hard to see why. Red-brick houses adjoin red-brick motels. I assume there is a beach somewhere nearby, but at the moment we could be in western Sydney.

'Which hotel should we choose?' says Haruko.

I scan up and down, hoping to see one that looks right for two people on a pilgrimage. Two people on a tight budget.

'That one,' says Haruko.

The motel Haruko is pointing at seems indistinguishable from the others in the street. A sign out the front says *Rooms from $50*, so the price, at least, is right. 'Why that one?'

Haruko points at the garden. 'Best trees are pine and bamboo.'

'Why?'

'Pine because it lives a long time, it is strong, and bamboo because it is straight and honest.'

This seems as good a criterion for choosing motels as any. The motel she has pointed at has a single pine tree on the grass in front of it. A dense screen of bamboo forest separates its lawn from the petrol station next door.

We approach the motel – a faded pink structure with rusting metal verandah railings. There are no cars outside. It seems to be deserted. I knock. A sound comes from inside. The handle on the heavy brown door turns and it opens. My eyes are so dazzled from the sun that at first I see only a shadowy outline.

'Yes?' The voice is male, not Australian, some form of European.

'Do you have a room?'

As my eyes clear, I make him out. He is tall, with black hair that waves off his forehead. He is wearing a white shirt with rolled-up sleeves and seems too polished, too cosmopolitan, to appear here in suburban Ballina.

Inside the reception area it is cool and shady. Our host is distant, but polite. I book us into separate rooms again; we both need our space.

Haruko jiggles her giant plastic key ring in her hand as we pause outside our pink-painted doors. The afternoon sun casts long shadows across the car park. We could squeeze in the Big Prawn this afternoon, but it has been a tiring day and it would be nice to see the beach.

'Now we go for walk with dolls?' says Haruko.

I nod, although I am not sure what this might entail. We are going to throw them in the water, that much I know. The rest is a mystery.

Haruko smiles and pushes her glasses up her nose. 'First, I will get changed.'

Twenty minutes later, Haruko knocks on my door and I open it to see a vision in pink. The kimono must have been in her briefcase, although it is hard to imagine how. She has gathered her hair up behind her head in a tidy bun. Haruko bows deeply and smiles when she comes up. 'Now, I am proper Japanese girl.' She puts out her arms and twirls so I can admire her. Her kimono has an orange pattern through it, like a wash. 'Autumn is coming,' says Haruko, gesturing at the orange lines. 'Although, in Japan, will soon be cherry blossom time.'

She is right. It does feel like the season is changing. I don't know if it is just because we are back on the coast, but for the first time in weeks, the humidity has gone and the air feels fresh. 'Should I wear something different?' I am still in my all-white pilgrimage outfit. Then I remember that this question is superfluous. Since I lost my suitcase I only have one change of clothes that I picked up at a second-hand shop in Brisbane and they are nothing to get excited about.

Haruko shakes her head. 'You are perfect. Have you got doll?'

I pick up my doll from the table near the door. Its cloth face is impassive, serene.

Haruko's dolls dangle from her hand.

'Why do you need two?' I ask.

'You will see. Where do we go to throw dolls?'

I consult the tourist map in the plastic folder that has been left on the table. 'This looks like a good place.' I point. 'At the river mouth.'

Haruko studies the map. Next to the river mouth is a beach with a picture of a surfer drawn on it. 'I will bring surfboard too.' She smiles suddenly. 'First dolls, then surf.' She tucks her dolls inside the top of her kimono and picks up her board.

So now, finally, I will get to see Haruko surf. I am looking forward to it. I smuggle Inari out of the room – dogs are not allowed – then set her down on the footpath.

Haruko, Inari and I head towards the river and find a path stretching out along the top of a large break wall which guides the river to the sea. The path is busy with dog walkers, power walkers, cyclists and joggers, some with surfboards under their arms. I don't suppose they've ever seen a girl in a pink kimono carrying a surfboard before, but they try not to stare.

At the end of the path, the rock wall juts out into the ocean. On one side is the clear blue and lazy river, on the other the churning sea. The two water bodies meet in a flurry of waves and chop. The offshore breeze picks up the tops of the waves and whisks them into the air. I breathe in the salt. The colours seem brighter today. Everything is shiny and new in the nice weather.

We are a few metres short of the end of the wall when Haruko stops. 'Here, I think.' She puts down her surfboard and looks over the edge. 'Come on, Misaki.' Haruko picks up the edge of her kimono. Beneath it she is wearing black basketball shoes. She clambers down over the large boulders and Inari and I follow.

Soon we are perched on half-submerged rocks at the edge of the river. Haruko glances at me, then without any ceremony, flings one of her dolls into the water. It floats, rising and falling on the chop, moving slowly towards the sea.

'Just like that?'

She nods.

'Do I have to think of anything special?'

'Think of your bad luck floating away with it.'

I think of Ben, my mojo, my marriage, my cardboard shop . . . With a swing of my arm, I toss the doll. The doll rotates above the water, its blue kimono flaring, then lands with a faint splash. Inari jumps to her feet and looks about to jump in after it. 'No, Inari.' She sits down, her tail wagging. The doll bobs up and down as the river sweeps it towards the sea and soon it has vanished.

Haruko smiles. 'Feel good?'

'Yes.' Somehow I do feel lighter.

Haruko is still holding her other doll. This one wears a red kimono.

'So, what's that one for?'

Haruko gazes down at the doll as she speaks, turning it slowly in her hands. 'In Japan, we have shrines for children who die. Or babies who aren't born. They are called mizuko.'

'Mizuko?'

'It means water children.'

The breath catches in my throat. I don't speak. I don't think I could.

Her eyes dart towards me and then back to the doll. 'Sometimes the shrine has a statue of the Jizo Bodhisattva who cares for children. We don't have Jizo Bodhisattva here, but . . .' Haruko looks at me. 'Do you want it?' She holds out the doll.

'For me? But . . .' How did Haruko know? I don't really need to ask that question. Haruko has eight million kami whispering in her ear. And besides, I am a forty-one-year-old woman with no child.

I take the doll. The surf roars louder in my ears as I think about my water child.

Soon after I met Adam, I got pregnant. I was too young, I thought. I hadn't finished my degree. 'There will be a better time,' Adam said. Only, as it turned out, when the time was right, when I stopped taking the Pill and waited expectantly, it never happened.

While the abortion was almost painless and soon dismissed, as the infertile years went on I began to remember it more. That lost child grew in my imagination. I dreamt of a ten-year-old, a twelve-year-old, her thirteenth birthday – she was always a girl.

As I turn the doll in my hands it dawns on me – that baby would be exactly Haruko's age now. But then I think I knew that from the moment I met her. I knew it in my heart if not my head.

'Just put it where you want,' says Haruko.

I place the doll in a crack between two rocks where she can see the river, a place where she won't blow away or get wet with rain. Like a little cave. And I think about the water child who would have been the same age as Haruko.

'Good spot,' says Haruko. 'Like a shrine.' She reaches inside her kimono, pulls out a red scarf and tucks it around the doll. 'Keep the spirit warm.' She touches her hands together and bows her head briefly.

Inari noses the doll, then sits down again.

'Thank you.' I bite the inside of my lip. I don't know how to pray – that's never mattered until now. *Goodbye.* I wait for the water child's voice inside my head, but it doesn't come. Somehow I know that I will never hear her again.

We clamber up the rocks to the top. Haruko looks out to sea. 'On Shikoku is place near the sea. Very wild. Very lonely. People set out by boat, searching for Pure Land of the South. Religious people.'

'Do they ever come back?'

She shakes her head. 'Better not to go, I think. Better to stay here on land.' She turns to me and smiles.

We are quiet together for some time, gazing out to sea. Somewhere out there a doll in a blue kimono is taking my bad luck with it.

'We go to beach?' Haruko breaks the silence. She has picked up her board.

I nod and we clamber down the other side of the rocks to the beach.

'Now, I surf.' Haruko peels off her kimono to reveal a pink one-piece swimsuit beneath.

I settle myself on the sand while Haruko paddles, splashes and glides in the small waves. I don't know much about surfing, but she seems to be a very dainty surfer. Her hair stays almost dry. She jumps to her feet, as graceful as a dancer, and I can't stop the words that spring to my mind – *water child.*

A few metres away from me, a mother watches her child dig holes in the sand. I think of the doll in the cave on the other side of the wall and I find my hands pressed together in what just might be a prayer.

Twenty-six

The next morning I wake just after eight o'clock. I have slept badly and I lie there for a while, staring at the wall, feeling grumpy and tired. Last night, I was consumed by a desperate urge to be with Adam. I needed to tell him about the dolls, about Haruko, about the water child.

But I couldn't talk to him about something so tender, so raw, on the phone. Not while we are on such distant terms. And not talking to him felt like suffocating.

I had never told Adam about my water child. It would have seemed like a reproach. While I didn't talk about her I could pretend she wasn't important. And mainly that worked. But it now seems to me that the water child has stood between us for our whole marriage.

Adam encouraged me – gently, tentatively – to get the abortion. I let him think it was what I wanted. *There will be a better time* . . . He never would have said that if he had understood how I really felt. He would have stood by me. We would have made it work. But I did the sensible thing. I put it behind me. I never told him, never acknowledged – even to myself – how much I wanted that child.

Was the water child the unseen crack in our marriage that became a hole – an unnoticed gap that Ben rushed to fill? Perhaps.

Four empty mini-bar bottles – two of gin and two of scotch – on my bedside table remind me that I have now broken the no alcohol rule. I hadn't drunk like that for some time, but last night it seemed a necessity. *Meat, sex, alcohol, quarrelling* . . . I am a bad, bad pilgrim. Luckily I am in no danger of breaking the rules about having too much money or baggage.

Underneath the bottles are my divorce papers – in triplicate. I lift the bottles and pull the papers towards me. My eyes skim over the typed wording then come to rest on the names at the end. *Adam Douglas. Arkie Douglas.* I touch Adam's signature with my finger. Even if we divorce I will still have his name. It seems unreal, that you can end a marriage just like that. Of course in some countries it is even easier.

I divorce you.

I divorce you.

I divorce you.

Three texts – that's all it takes in Malaysia, I hear. For a man, that is, of course. For women, I imagine it is more difficult.

I stretch out again in the bed, my hands beneath my head. I no longer feel certain that things will work out between us. As the memory of Adam's skin against mine weakens, so too does my confidence. Perhaps it really *was* just sex. It felt like love, but how would I know?

As if prompted by my thoughts, my phone rings. I reach for it.

'Arkie?'

'Yes.' It is him.

'Where are you?'

'Why do you want to know?'

He sighs.

'Are you tracing this call?' I am only half-joking.

There is a long silence between us. It goes on and on. I wonder who will be the first to say something – the first to hang up. *Not me.* All the things I want to say are stuck in my throat, choking me. If only I could open my mouth, let them out, but I can't.

There is a knock on the door. 'Breakfast.'

'That's my breakfast.' Holding on to the phone, I walk over to the door and collect the tray that has been left outside.

'What have you got?' says Adam.

Despite myself, I smile at the question; it is like I am just away from home on a business trip. 'Eggs, toast, bacon, mushrooms, juice, croissants, hash browns and Coco Pops.' It feels healing to talk to him, even about trivialities.

He laughs. 'I don't believe it.' Adam knows I never eat like that.

'Okay, just toast.' Our easy banter makes me feel like we are friends again.

'We can't go on like this, Arkie. We really can't.' His voice is soft.

I plummet back to ground. 'No. I know that.' Tears prick at my eyes. I swallow, force down the words I want to say. For a moment there I almost thought I had a chance. I pick up the divorce papers and rustle them next to the phone. 'Hear that? That's the sound of our marriage ending.' I press *end* and sink to the bed.

Gulping sobs tear their way out of my chest. I press my face into the pillow and shriek my misery into the foam, the grief surprising me all over again with its force. Inari presses her nose to my face. Licks my cheek.

Adam doesn't ring back. Once he would have, but now I am alone.

Eventually the storm subsides. I lie on the bed, limp and crumpled – a piece of flotsam washed up on the beach. It is over. We are over. My water child has gone, and now Adam has gone too. There is just me. It's a strange feeling.

Dragging myself upright, I take the papers and tuck them back in my bag. Perhaps I will post them to Adam. That is what I should do. There is no point in trying to hang on any longer. They say a clean cut heals quicker. But I imagine that's only if it doesn't sever an artery.

I boil the jug and make myself tea in my Tanuki teapot. The ritual calms me. Going outside, I sit on the little chair next to the obligatory Buddha statue and nibble on my now cold and rubbery toast. Inari enjoys the bacon and eggs.

The plastic folder of tourist information lies on the table between my room and the next. Looking for distraction, I flick through it, pausing when I come to a picture of the Big Prawn. Some pages from the local paper have been inserted into the plastic sleeves.

Big Prawn Escapes the Net, says the headline.

The piece is a couple of years old. It seems that the Big Prawn was scheduled for demolition but the new owners of the site, a hardware chain, decided to keep it as part of their development. There are more old articles on this long-running story.

Prawn sinks to lowest depths.
Prawn gets raw deal.
Councillor floats new Prawn plan.

What a gift to headline writers the prawn has been.

The saga of the prawn's fate had apparently spread far and wide, even getting a mention on *The Late Show with David Letterman* in America – fame indeed. One of Australia's best-loved Big Things, says the article, it was built in 1989.

The year I turned seventeen,
Hip hop,
Acid-washed jeans,
Brie with sun-dried tomato topping,
'Look Away' by Chicago, and
The fall of the Berlin Wall.

It's easy to win this game when you're playing by yourself.

Haruko appears through the entrance of the motel. She has been out walking. Today, she is wearing a black pleated mini skirt which juts out from her hips. At the bottom of her pale legs she has black ankle boots and purple socks that stretch up to her knees.

Again, I wonder how she does it. How do all these clothes appear out of her tiny briefcase?

On her head is something made out of a little bit of black net.

I catch a faint whiff of seaweed as she comes towards me.

'I have been on the beach.' Haruko pats her head.

Only Haruko could pick up some fishnet on the beach, add it to her outfit and end up looking like something from Paris Fashion Week.

Haruko opens her briefcase and pulls out a black object about the size of a pinecone. 'This would be good as dress.'

The object is rubbery and shaped like a spiral. I can't imagine how you could possibly wear it as a dress.

Haruko holds the object in front of her and gestures with her spare hand. Suddenly I visualise a model with a spiral-shaped hat and twirling skirt.

Haruko smiles as she sees me get it. 'Beach rubbish is the next Big Thing.'

'Could be.'

Haruko sits down in the spare chair and examines me closely.

I suspect my eyes are still red from all that crying.

'Pilgrimage can lead to upwelling of feeling,' she says. 'Pilgrim has time to reflect on past mistakes.'

I nod. Haruko is a mind-reader.

'Pain is . . . healing,' she says. 'You go through. To other side.'

'That's a good way of looking at it.' I gesture at the teapot. 'Would you like a cup of tea?' I refill my cup and place it in front of her.

She hesitates. 'Tanuki teapot?' She inspects it. 'You have cleaned it up.' She sips, then drinks half the cup in a gulp. As she places it on the table, she looks me up and down. A crease forms between her eyebrows.

I suddenly see myself through her eyes. I have had to wash my white pilgrim's outfit; it is still drying on the clothesline. In the meantime I am wearing my Op Shop outfit – brown baggy shorts and a loose brown T-shirt which says *Aotearoa* in colourful writing. On my feet are black rubber thongs that I bought at the supermarket yesterday. I am even wearing a blue baseball cap with the name of a bank on it. What is wrong with me? Even when I was about to throw myself under a train, I dressed better than this.

Haruko stands up and steps towards me. 'Do you mind?' She doesn't wait for my answer before pulling off my baseball cap. She opens her briefcase and extracts bobby pins with the urgent attention of someone about to defuse a bomb that will explode in three seconds. In a moment my hair is arranged extravagantly on top of my head with Haruko's beach flotsam the crowning glory. Haruko swivels me towards the motel room window.

I can't see myself very well. My reflection is a semi-transparent outline. But what I do see makes me smile. I look . . .

'Like mermaid,' says Haruko.

This is almost right. In fact from the shoulders up I am ready for the VIP tent at the Melbourne Cup. My flotsam fascinator would be the talk of the town; I would be queen of the hat parade. 'I think my clothes are dry.' I gesture towards the washing line. 'I'll just get changed.'

Haruko shakes her head. 'Not finished yet. Today, no white clothes. Today . . .' She smiles. 'Renewal.'

Renewal. 'Do you think I am ready for that?'

'Oh yes, Misaki. Today you are ready.'

'Now . . .' Haruko pulls something thin and silky from her briefcase. She opens the door to my motel room. 'You get changed.' She pushes me gently in the small of my back and I almost jog over the threshold.

She shuts the door behind us and hands me what appears to be a black negligee. I hesitate and she gives me a stern nod.

Once I am dressed in the negligee, she opens her briefcase again. It is a magical compartment in there. No matter what she takes out, there is always more. Haruko pulls out another piece of fishing net. She drapes it around me, tucks and pulls, twisting me this way and that, and next minute I am an elegant fish-netted creature pulled up from the sea. She places a sea urchin shell in position as a brooch, fastens it in some mysterious manner and nods with satisfaction. 'Now we ready for Big Prawn.'

'Because I look like something caught in a trawling net?' I say.

Haruko shakes her head. 'You are sea goddess.' Opening the door, she picks up her half-drunk tea from the table and swallows it down. *'Tan, tan, Tanuki's testicles,'* she sings.

I catch a glimpse of myself in the mirror as I lift my day-pack. For a moment, I wonder if I am the kind of person I would avoid in the street. Inari presses her nose into my hand. No, I decide, I look otherworldly – like someone with power. I look like . . .

Masked Mermaid in Black. A small print of Dali's painting used to hang in our hallway. The 'mermaid' could have doubled as a dominatrix – she wore spiky black rubber from her head to her toes. I spin on my heel and straighten my shoulders as I leave the room, shutting the door with a bang.

The motel owner comes out as we leave. He is sharply dressed in a long-sleeved white shirt and black pants. He hardly noticed me yesterday, but now he stops dead, as if struck by a vision. 'Bella,' he says and gives a small bow.

Bella. I'm not sure if this is Italian or Spanish. As I am currently under the influence of Dali, I decide on the latter. I smile, as if I am used to being admired by Spanish motel owners. 'Gracias.'

This seems to be the correct reply as he nods. 'Where are you going today?' He glances at Inari, who I have forgotten to hide in my bag, but he doesn't comment.

'To the Big Prawn.'

'And the Big Banana,' adds Haruko. 'We are on pilgrimage to Big Things.'

'Big things?' The man raises one eyebrow. 'In Spain, we have a very good pilgrimage – the Camino. You should do that one.'

'Yes, I'd like to,' I say. 'Sometime.'

'Where have you been so far?'

I fill him in on our progress.

'Ah,' he says. 'But you have not been to the Big Buddha.'

Haruko and I glance at each other. Her eyes are wide.

'Wait,' says the man, 'I will get you a brochure.' He darts inside and returns in a moment with a brochure, which he thrusts into my hands. *Crystal Castle* it says on the front and there is a picture of the Big Buddha.

I show Haruko the picture.

She screws up her nose. 'They are bigger in Japan.'

I put the brochure into my daypack. 'Thank you. We will see if we can make it.'

The man waves as we walk away. 'Come back some time,' he calls. 'You can bring your dog.'

'He likes you, I think.' Haruko eyes me up and down. 'All men like mermaids.' She smiles. 'But they are very dangerous.'

'I've never been dangerous before.'

'So it is time,' says Haruko.

Twenty-seven

Well, here we are, at the place that started me on this pilgrimage. I remember my dream – the beach, the pink temple, the way the prawn winked at me, my sense that I was completing part of a journey. And now I am at the *Lobster Telephone* dressed as another Dali vision, the *Mermaid in Black*. Surely that has to mean something.

The prawn is mounted on high metal legs at the entrance to the hardware store car park. It is freshly painted in a colour that is closer to orange than pink and, unlike some other big things I could name, is completely unmissable. It being only eight am, the store is closed and the vast car park empty. A salty breeze blows in from the sea, bringing with it the smell of seaweed. Or is that my fishnet hat? I touch my head. I had almost forgotten it was there. I feel different dressed like this – bold, quirky, *dangerous*. I feel like I am coming back to myself.

As we stand on the footpath I mentally compare the remarkable prawn in front of me with the pictures in the newspaper articles I'd read earlier. In the old pictures, the Big Prawn had been perched on top of – and seemed to be mating with – a building that used to house a souvenir shop. This juxtaposition seemed appropriate as, after all, Big Things and souvenirs are a match made in heaven. I wonder if they still sell prawn souvenirs in the hardware store.

'Do you buy souvenirs in Japan?' I say. 'When you go somewhere special.'

'Of course. Always. Japanese love souvenirs. We like to bring home something new from a region or sweets to share.'

'Strange things, aren't they? So useless.'

Haruko nods. 'They are nothing, except memory of place.'

It's an interesting idea, the object as a storeroom for a memory. My hand drops into my bag and I finger my Seven Lucky Gods – souvenir of my re-entry back into life.

Haruko is studying the prawn. 'In Shikoku, one temple hangs on cliff-side,' she says. 'Very sacred.'

I turn from the towering prawn to gaze at her. 'You think this is like that?'

She purses her lips and cocks her head to one side. 'No. Not much like.'

I would have to agree.

'But it is very . . .' Haruko pauses, 'confident.'

She has hit the nail right on the head. The prawn radiates an optimistic spirit that makes me smile. 'There is something very nicely tongue in cheek about a town which brands itself with a giant crustacean, don't you think, Haruko?'

Haruko pokes her tongue in her cheek and gives me a puzzled frown.

'It means . . . that it is not to be taken too seriously.'

She smiles. 'I like it.'

Although I have seen the prawn before from a taxi, standing on the ground next to it is a completely different proposition. It is quite intimidating. I can't imagine it being knocked down – it would leave an enormous prawn-shaped hole in the sky.

I believe prawns are carnivores. This being the case, I am grateful they are small. A twenty-five-metre prawn would be enough to make me flee the water forever.

I scan the vicinity for any sight of Fabian in his grey BMW then wonder why I still care. I already know that Adam is not coming back to me. But – I think of the divorce papers in my daypack – I want to surrender on my own terms. I will give the papers to Adam myself. I will look him in the eyes and admit that our marriage is over. It is a matter of pride. I can't let Fabian get the better of me.

Standing here next to the Big Prawn makes me feel exposed. Fabian can't be far away. Surely he has deduced that we were heading prawn-wards? How could we resist such a delightfully big, Big Thing? But there is no sign of him as yet. I turn back to the prawn.

Apart from being very large, it is also rather lifelike. Whisker-like protrusions trail from the bottom of its face, and a spiky horn extends from its forehead. Its curving tail almost touches its nose. This tail is a new addition; it wasn't there when the prawn sat on top of the souvenir shop. 'You used to be able to climb up and see out through the eyes,' I say. This is what the taxi driver told me on my tour.

'I wish we could do that,' says Haruko.

'I wonder what the world looks like through a prawn's eyes.'

'Scary, I think,' says Haruko. 'If you are a small prawn.'

I take a photo of Haruko and Inari, with the prawn in the background. Haruko has her surfboard under one arm and her briefcase in the other hand. Her jaunty fishnet hat perches on her silky black hair. Inari sits at her feet, absolutely immobile, her nose pointed directly at the camera. They look like they are in a very quirky fashion shoot.

I click the shutter, then inspect the image on the camera screen. Goose bumps rise on my arms. I pull Haruko's pilgrimage proposal out of my bag and flick through it. 'Look, Haruko.' I show her the picture. 'Inari is exactly like the fox statues in that temple in Kyoto.'

Haruko nods. 'She is guarding the temple.'

Despite my worry over Haruko and the Big Prawn, now that we are here she seems cheerful, even eager. She strides towards the base of the prawn without hesitating – a travel companion after my own heart. Inari, of course, is already there. After a quick glance around the car park, I follow. I am still a little anxious about Fabian.

A fat pigeon with a green breast is pecking at the dirty concrete. It flies off with a whirr of wings as we approach.

Haruko watches it go. 'You have your Lucky Gods?'

I take them out of my handbag.

Haruko opens the drawstring bag and pulls out one god. 'Bishamonten. Pigeons always land on his shrines.'

Bishamonten is the only god with a black beard. He holds a sword in one hand and a miniature pagoda in the other.

'Bishamonten is terror for evil people, god of treasure and heal sick. He guards place where Buddha preach,' says Haruko.

Haruko and I stretch our necks to gaze up at the prawn. The traffic roars behind us but we are all alone here, beside a huge, empty car park. 'It's hard to imagine Buddha preaching anywhere near here,' I say.

Haruko shrugs. 'You don't know.' She walks closer to the prawn then stops suddenly. 'Yakuza.'

'Pardon?'

Haruko points.

Inari yaps.

We are not all alone, after all. Walking around the side of the hardware store is a man who looks like a young Japanese Elvis. His hair curls in a wave over his forehead and he is wearing a tight black body shirt with trousers that hug his hips and end in pointy-toed boots. He walks with the slight swagger of a gangster.

Haruko puts down her surfboard and briefcase and folds her arms. 'It is prawn.'

'Prawn?'

'His nickname, Ebi, means prawn. He is Yakuza.'

I think of Haruko's reaction to the Big Prawn. Is this who she was thinking of – the fearsome prawn? She seems remarkably calm. I thought she was fleeing the Yakuza. And they do have a terrible reputation. Now, however, she seems only mildly irritated.

Inari stands in front of us, the hair raised on her neck. She is only the size of a watermelon, but she has a valiant heart.

The man is wearing round Lennon-type sunglasses. As he comes closer, I notice his sleeves are rolled up to reveal well-toned biceps and the edge of a tattoo. It looks like –

'Prawn,' says Haruko.

I glance at her.

She nods and touches her shoulder. 'He has prawn tattoo.'

So, Haruko has seen this man with his shirt off . . . Her prawn reaction now takes on a different context.

The man stops short of Inari, who makes a noise like a toy aeroplane taking off. 'Haruko.' Inari yaps and he steps backwards quickly. He doesn't seem a very formidable Yakuza.

Haruko speaks rapidly in Japanese. She gestures with her hands, making a shooing gesture.

I move closer to her, ready to try to fight him off if necessary. He doesn't appear to be carrying any weapons, but even so . . .

The man replies.

Even with no knowledge of Japanese, I can tell he is not aggressive. He puts his hands out, like he is pleading with her.

Haruko crosses her arms more tightly.

Suddenly the man drops to one knee.

Inari jumps up on him, placing her paws on his shoulder. She licks his face and he doesn't try to stop her.

Haruko turns her back on him.

The man's face falls a little, but he doesn't move. He talks softly to Inari in Japanese and strokes her. She rolls over to have her stomach scratched – not such a valiant guard dog, after all.

Haruko tosses her hair in a disdainful way, still with her back turned.

'Haruko, he seems quite nice,' I murmur.

Haruko snorts. 'Oh yes, he quite nice. Ask him why Yakuza chasing me then.'

I turn back to the man. He is still kneeling on the ground, his hair immaculate and his Lennon glasses in place. Inari squirms with delight as he scratches her. He gives me a cheeky smile. 'Yakuza are not chasing,' he says, 'only me.'

Twenty-eight

The Big Prawn watches over our frozen tableau. All is silent except for the roar of the traffic. We make a strange group clustered there in its shade, as if gathered for an eccentric pagan ritual.

Ebi kneels – a supplicant seeking forgiveness.

Haruko's hair shifts in the breeze like a sheet of silk.

Inari – who seems to be on Ebi's team now – sits beside him, her button-black eyes on Haruko.

At last Haruko swings around. Hands on her hips, she glares at Ebi. A torrent of rapid Japanese pours from her lips.

Inari's ears prick hopefully.

Haruko keeps talking and Inari's ears flop. She whines and licks Ebi's hand. He strokes her head.

'So?' says Haruko.

'My friends helping me find you,' says Ebi. 'That is all.'

She speaks again in Japanese.

He replies in English. 'I pay your bill. It is finished.'

Haruko's attitude softens a little. 'Get up.' She lifts her chin. 'So why you here?'

Ebi stands up and brushes the dust from the knees of his otherwise spotless trousers. 'You didn't finish class.'

Haruko frowns. 'So?'

'I miss you. When will you come back?'

Haruko's hands are still on her hips. 'You come all the way here to ask me that?'

Ebi shrugs. 'It is not so far. Only nine hours Tokyo to Gold Coast.'

'So. You are here. Now what?'

Ebi tilts his head. 'I take you for lunch?'

Haruko snorts. 'I am busy.'

I feel sorry for Ebi. 'He's come all this way, Haruko.'

Inari yaps in apparent support.

'Not so far,' she says. 'Only nine hours. And I did not ask him to.'

Inari trots over to Haruko and, jumping up, licks her hand. 'Oh, you take his side.' Haruko pats her head.

'There was man here before.' Ebi makes a gesture over his stomach. 'Fat man. Looking for woman in white with Japanese girl. I tell him you are already gone.'

Haruko and I exchange a glance.

'Thank you, Ebi. That was very clever of you,' I say. 'How did you know we didn't want to see him?'

Ebi shrugs. 'Just usual method.'

'Usual for Yakuza, he means,' says Haruko. 'Don't give out any information.'

'I have phone number,' Ebi says. 'If you want to talk to him? I said I give it to you if you come back.' Ebi holds out his phone with Fabian's number on the screen.

I shake my head. 'No thanks.'

'He say he is going to Big Buddha,' says Ebi.

Haruko and I exchange another glance. Clearly we will have to strike that one off our list for now.

'It is not so big anyway,' Haruko says dismissively.

'Can I drive you to somewhere?' Ebi looks at me, trying to enlist me to his cause. 'Drive you both?' He turns to Inari. 'And dog?'

Haruko tosses her hair. 'You have car?'

Ebi points at a shiny black sports car parked on the edge of the road, beyond the car park.

Haruko glances at me.

I give a small nod.

'You can take us to Big Banana.' She says this as if granting a huge favour. 'We are on pilgrimage.'

Ebi smiles, like he has won the lottery. He steps forward and it seems that he might be about to kiss Haruko, but she pushes him on the chest with her hands.

'Just driving,' she says, but then she smiles. She strides off towards the car, her heels clacking on the footpath, and I think her hips might be swaying a little more than usual.

Ebi straightens his glasses. He gazes after Haruko as if she is the Holy Grail, and I can't help liking him for that. He is trying to keep his cool, but an enormous smile that won't stay off his face is totally ruining his bad boy attitude.

'Happy?' I say.

'Very much happy,' he says.

So now we are four, Haruko, Inari, Ebi and me. My pilgrimage is becoming quite crowded. Haruko jumps into the back seat with her surfboard, leaving me to share the front with Ebi. Inari sits on my lap.

Once we are in, Ebi presses a button and the top of the car lifts off and retracts behind us. 'Nice day,' he says. He glances in the mirror to get Haruko's reaction, but she is resolutely unimpressed. He looks deflated.

'Nice car,' I say to cheer him up.

He smiles politely.

Obviously he would prefer it if I wasn't here, but he is making the best of a bad job. I feel like a mother-in-law tagging along on a date.

'Arkie. Arkie.' Someone is calling my name. I crane my head around and see a big man running down the footpath towards us. For a moment I think it is Fabian, but no, Fabian doesn't wear shorts.

The man runs, panting, to the car, his pink legs eating up the distance between us. I recognise those legs.

'Big Redback man,' says Haruko.

Chris stops at the door. 'Thought I'd,' he catches his breath, 'missed you.'

'What are you doing here?' I say.

'Got the day off. Weekend off. Thought I'd come to Ballina. Do some fishing.' He pants again. 'Read your blog. Thought you'd be here. Wanted to say hello.'

'That's nice. Good to see you again.'

'You too.' Chris takes in my sea-inspired ensemble. He looks impressed. 'I was wondering,' he says, 'if I could see your Lucky Gods.'

'Of course.' I pull them out of my bag and hand them to him.

Chris stands there, turning them over in his huge hands, as if imprinting them on his mind. He has a small backpack slung across one shoulder.

Ebi taps his fingers on the wheel. Haruko sighs loudly.

I don't want to be rude, but we have a big day ahead of us. 'Um, we're going to the Big Banana.'

Chris's head comes up. 'I've never been to the Big Banana.'

'Do you want to come?' The words are out before I can pull them back.

Ebi gives me a blank stare and I can feel Haruko's disapproval radiating from the back seat.

I can see their point. Chris is almost the size of the whole car. 'But perhaps you have other plans?' I add.

Chris gives a broad smile and I think he is going to join us, but then he looks at the car, taking in the cramped back seat. 'I'd love to. But I want to go fishing. Thanks.'

He hands me back the gods. 'I've ordered some in. For the garden shop, but it's good to see your ones. So I can compare. Nice to see you again. I'll let you get on.'

Ebi and Haruko smile politely.

'Great car,' Chris says.

Ebi nods. 'Thank you. I have better one in Japan.'

I look in the rear-view mirror as we drive off. Chris is standing on the side of the road waving.

'He would not fit,' says Haruko.

I glance in the back seat. She is right. With Haruko and her surfboard, things are already quite crowded back there. And he does have incredibly large legs.

'Was that a bit strange, do you think – how he came all the way here, just to meet me?' I say to Haruko. 'And how did he know we'd be at the Big Prawn right now?'

She waves her hand breezily. 'That happen to pilgrim all the time. You are guru now, Misaki. People sense that. They want to learn what you have to teach.'

'I don't feel like a guru.'

'Sometimes guru is last to know,' she says. 'Takamure is always telling people, go away, go away, I am not a guru. But they know.'

We zoom down the highway in silence, the wind in our hair. I hold on to my fishnet hat. Amazingly, Ebi's carefully arranged pompadour hairdo is undisturbed. Inari pokes her nose into the breeze, her fur flying back around her.

'Like fox,' Ebi says, observing her. 'White fox.'

'We call her Inari,' I say.

He smiles. 'Very good name. Fox spirit very lucky.'

Haruko pulls out her computer in the back and types away. Her phone rings. 'Hello?' She is silent for some time, apart from the occasional 'mmm'. Eventually she says, 'Okay. Big Banana,' hangs up and immediately places the buds for her music in her ears.

'Who was that?' I peer around at her.

Haruko pretends not to hear me. She nods her head in time with some unheard music and bends to her typing.

'Very annoying girl sometimes,' says Ebi.

I smile at him. 'Have you known her long?'

'Twenty years,' he says.

I stare at him, unsure if I have understood correctly. 'Twenty?'

He nods. 'I live next door. I know her since baby.' He glances at her in the mirror. 'She really something else.'

'Yes, she is, isn't she?' I sense a chance to learn more about Haruko. I lower my voice. 'She told me she was a prostitute. Is that right?'

Ebi shakes his head decisively. 'No. Definitely not prostitute.' He sounds shocked.

'Oh.' I feel relieved.

'She take presents, maybe money from men, but not prostitute.'

'Oh.' I feel not quite so relieved. Possibly there is a cultural difference going on here with definitions.

'Lot of girls do that,' says Ebi. 'Money for clothes, jewellery, drinks . . . Prostitute is different.'

I nod. I suppose there is a subtle difference.

'Hostess,' says Ebi. 'Little bit like geisha. Just talk, laugh, pour drinks.'

'Oh, hostess.' That doesn't sound too bad.

'I don't like though,' says Ebi, his voice low. 'I ask her to stop. We have fight. She disappear.'

'So you've come to take her home?'

He nods. 'I hope. I want to marry her. She the only one I want.'

The sun vanishes behind a cloud and goose bumps rise on my arms. I suppose I knew this would happen sometime, that Haruko would go home. But I was hoping it wouldn't be quite so soon. 'She has a gift, you know. She should use it.'

Ebi nods. 'She always been special. I see now though,' he glances at me. 'She is happy. She more . . . confident. I only want her happy. She can do what she want.'

'So you are a Yakuza?' I feel like I am conducting an interview with a prospective son-in-law.

'Yes.' Ebi appears uncomfortable, as if this might hurt his prospects. 'But maybe I retire.'

In the back seat I sense a stirring. Haruko is listening.

'Haruko doesn't like,' says Ebi. 'But it is . . . complicated.' He holds out his left hand and I see that the tip of his little finger is missing. 'I give this to Yakuza boss,' he says.

'Why?'

'Apology. For . . . touching Haruko.'

A surge of angry Japanese comes from the back seat.

Ebi blushes. 'She say I should have told her father we are in love, not give him finger.'

'Haruko's father is the Yakuza boss?'

Ebi stares at me in surprise. 'Everyone know that.'

'Yakuza treat women like object,' says Haruko. 'Buy and sell bad girls. Nice girls stay home and cook and clean. I don't want to be nice Yakuza home-style girl. Don't want to be bought or sold. I sell myself instead. Cut out middle man.'

I can see her perverse logic – the satisfaction involved in beating her father at his own game.

Ebi looks at her in the mirror. 'I will leave if you marry me.'

I stare out the window, pretend I'm not here.

Haruko doesn't say anything, but the expression on Ebi's face when I turn back tells me he lives in hope.

Twenty-nine

After two hours on the road, we are on the outskirts of Coffs Harbour. My phone goes *ting*. I have a comment on my blog from the Big Scotsman.

> Awrite!
> You are entering the fortress of the oppressor. Stay alert. Don't let them sway you with their sweet-talking banana ways. Make the eejits admit the error of their conduct!
> The Big Scotsman
> THE ORIGINAL AND STILL THE BEST

I smile. The most peculiar people come out of the woodwork when you blog. I am starting to feel quite fond of the crazy Scotsman, but I don't reply. I don't want to encourage him.

I also have a comment from Bertie in Tewantin. She seems to be in a contemplative mood.

Dear Arkie,
Now that I've started thinking about travel, the idea won't leave me alone. I went inside the Big Shell yesterday and thought about the strangest things. Like scones. I wouldn't mind seeing a place where they don't make scones. What do ladies bring to cake stalls in those countries? Do you know?

When I closed my eyes I could picture them in America. They were leaping out of a Cadillac in sunglasses and high heels with a plate of Pecan Pie. I imagined them in Austria – skiing through the pine trees holding a steaming Apple Strudel. But what do the mothers do in Japan when the school needs to raise money? Hold a sushi stall?

I never had a mid-life crisis, but I hear they're very popular these days. My friends' daughters are all starting university again in their forties or leaving their husbands to follow an Indian guru. Is it too late to have my mid-life crisis now, do you think?

Yours,
Bertie Webster

I pose the sushi question to Ebi, then reply.

Dear Bertie,
In my opinion it is never too late to have a mid-life crisis, particularly one involving exotic travel, gurus or a pilgrimage.

It sounds like the travel bug has started to bite you. I have it on good authority that in Japanese schools they usually stage a music recital to raise funds.

Yours,

Arkie.

Ebi turns at a sign advertising the Big Banana and we roar into a vast and nearly empty car park. He pulls up next to an arrow which reads *Tobogganing*. It points towards a long, narrow building which follows the slope of the hill. Ebi looks over his shoulder at Haruko and cocks his head.

'Okay,' she says.

Ebi's face breaks into a broad grin. 'Me and Haruko. We always toboggan when we are children. In mountains outside Tokyo. Will you come, Arkie?'

I shake my head. I wouldn't be so cruel. 'I'm going to check out the banana.'

Ebi does a good job of hiding his relief.

Ebi and Haruko head towards the toboggan slope. Haruko is keeping her distance, but they are talking.

Inari hesitates, then follows me. The Big Banana is surprisingly hard to find. I wander across the empty car park and under an archway saying *A Whole Bunch of Fun*. A row of signs advertise a combination of offerings including *Banana Theatre*, *Plantation Tour*, *Ice Rink*, *Water Slide* and *Toboggan*. And *Fresh Banana's*. The sign writer has been struck by the random apostrophe disease so common to their trade. An arrow points to a boarded-up ticket window. I can see no evidence of bananas and no apparent way in.

Eventually a family – a mother and father and two pre-teenage kids – emerges from behind some bushes. 'Excuse me, do you know where the banana is?' I say.

They look me over, and I remember what I am wearing. I adjust my sea-urchin brooch and straighten my shoulders. Attitude is everything.

But they don't seem alarmed by my appearance – more cautiously impressed. 'In there.' They gesture behind them and I notice a narrow pathway among the foliage. 'You can't go through it though. It's closed for renovation,' says the father.

'We were a bit disappointed,' says the mother.

'Oh, I'm used to it.' I sound like a jaded world traveller. By this stage I would be almost shocked to find a Big Thing in full working order.

I walk through the bushes, expecting at any moment to be amazed by a towering banana. But the Big Banana, when I do spot it, is no Big Prawn. It is reclining shyly, rather than thrusting skyward. I had imagined a golden pagoda, but this is more of a yellow log.

A walkway that obviously leads inside is blocked by a sign saying *Closed for repairs*. What a tease these Big Things are.

My face must show my disenchantment as a woman leaning on the verandah railing above me says, 'Well, it's bigger than a real banana.'

This seems a very Pollyanna-ish view. Since when is bigger than a real banana big enough? She is clearly a low achiever; the Pyramids and the Taj Mahal would never have been built with an attitude like that. I can't imagine Ramses the Great saying, 'She'll be right; it's bigger than a shed.'

'I think it's shrunk,' the woman adds. 'I came here when I was ten and it was definitely bigger.' She smiles and waves before wandering off in the direction of the shop.

At the front of the banana is a plaque. I move closer, so I can read it.

This plaque commemorates 40 years of
THE BIG BANANA
Opened in December 1964, to advance the Banana Industry and Tourism in Coffs Harbour, the Big Banana generated a spirit of warmth, goodwill and entrepreneurial endeavour, which resulted in many similar developments across our continent.
'Big Things' are now a form of artistic expression unique to Australia.

The sign goes on to name a number of dignitaries involved in its unveiling.

This plaque raises more questions than it answers. Hadn't Max at the Big Pineapple said that Big Things originated in America? Though perhaps they do it differently there . . . In which case they would still be unique to Australia in a sense.

And what about the Big Scotsman? I remember his sign-off – *the original and still the best.* The Big Scotsman may be deranged, but perhaps he also has a point. Where does the Scotsman fit in, in the history of Big Things? I look at the date again. *1964* . . . That was a long time ago.

Eight years before I was born,
'I Want to Hold Your Hand',
Pork with prunes, and
Mini skirts.

Yep, while some were fainting at Beatles concerts, others were building Big Bananas. What a diverse world it is. A long breath escapes me. Despite my world-weary air I was expecting more. Perhaps the meaning of the Big Banana, if it has one, is to be found in the souvenir shop. I walk up the stairs onto the verandah.

Outside the shop a brightly painted monkey mounts a large model of a banana. I try to drag my mind out of the gutter, but it is difficult. Inari runs up and sniffs at the monkey. Disappointed, she follows her nose inside.

While the banana was underwhelming, the souvenir shop is the opposite – row upon row of banana shaped items stretch into the distance. Banana soft toys hang from the ceiling, banana soaps crowd the shelves . . . Who knew that there was a market for banana-shaped phones or pencils? Phallic symbols everywhere; it is like I have slid through a portal into a Kings Cross sex shop. At least there are no banana-themed Buddhas.

How do they manage to keep such a wide selection of banana objects in stock? Surely there can't be much demand. Somewhere in a factory in China they must be churning out banana memorabilia by the dozen. It's a strange thought. A sign on the wall advertises that it is *The World's Largest Collection of Banana-Themed Souvenirs*. Also the *only*, I'd imagine.

The Pollyanna woman is now at the counter buying a yellow plastic sex toy. Or maybe it is a box designed to protect bananas. Hard to know. I imagine an innocent child pulling it out of their lunch box at school. At least it will give them something to talk about with their psychotherapist in later life. As Freud said, sometimes a cigar is just a cigar, but usually . . .

The phone rings and the shop girl picks it up. Her eyes scan the room. 'No, there's no woman in white with a Japanese girl here. Okay, yes.' She writes down a phone number. 'I'll let you know. Why don't you try the Big Windmill?' She hangs up.

I look away casually. It is Fabian, no doubt. It's lucky I changed my outfit for today. On the counter is a book titled *Big Aussie Icons – 50 of Australia's craziest roadside attractions*. I flick through it. 'The original and, as many would argue, still the best', starts the introduction to the section on the Big Banana. I go to the index and look for the Big Scotsman. It is there, and built one year earlier in 1963. What is going on here? How can the book say that the Big Banana is the original if the Big Scotsman came first? Is this some kind of Orwellian double-speak? It's very confusing.

The Pollyanna woman has walked off clutching her phallic-shaped parcel. The shop girl is now filing her yellow-painted nails with a banana-shaped nail file. She is wearing a tight yellow dress and, being tall and curvaceous, has a rather banana-like appearance herself. I cough to attract her attention and point at the book. 'Why does it say in here that the Big Banana was the original Big Thing, when the Big Scotsman was built one year earlier?'

The girl stops her manicure. 'Never heard of it.'

'But the Big Scotsman was built in 1963 and the Big Banana in 1964.'

She has been well trained. 'I don't think so. The Big Banana is the original and the best.' She smiles the automatic smile of check-out chicks everywhere.

'But how can it be?' I hold out the picture of the Big Scotsman. 'This was built first.'

She looks around the shop, possibly searching for reinforcements. Her eyes come back and rest on my fishnet hat, trail down over my outfit. Her haughty look falters. She may be the banana queen, but she is no match for my mermaid. She glances at the Scotsman. 'It's not very big. And it's not an agricultural product. Big Things are supposed to be agricultural products.' She smiles as if claiming victory.

'It's in the Big Things book, so it must be a Big Thing, mustn't it?' I place my hands on the counter, raise myself to my full height. I'm not sure why I care so much, but somehow it seems important. I owe it to the Big Scotsman. 'I'm not trying to be difficult; I just want to get to the bottom of this. I accept that the Big Banana is the first big agricultural product, but it may not be the first Big Thing. If you agree that a Big Thing is at least twice the size of the object it –'

'You'll have to speak to the manager. He knows the guidelines.' Her hand reaches below the counter. Is she pressing an alarm? Will a man in yellow emerge from the shadows and take my arm? Will I end up in a dungeon along with other supporters of the Big Scotsman who have wandered in over the years? I am starting to feel like Braveheart leading the charge against the English oppressors. 'Onwards, men!' I cry as I lead the mob across the windy moors. A cold wind blows in under my imaginary kilt. I seem to recall things didn't end too well for him.

'We don't talk about the Scotsman here,' says a voice behind me.

My heart jumps. I turn, expecting the banana mafia. But, no, it is even more surprising than that. If I made a list of all the people I least expected to see, he would be right at the top.

It is Ben.

Thirty

I stare at Ben, taking in his face – the face that once meant so much to me. He is wearing shorts and thongs and eating a frozen chocolate-coated banana on a stick. I have never seen Ben in public less than immaculately groomed. And why is he eating something so incredibly gross? He seems like a downmarket version of himself.

'What?' He holds up his banana. 'You got a problem with my banana?' He smiles, as if attempting to make this encounter less weird.

I shake my head. 'I'm just . . . surprised.' I could never have imagined meeting like this. Here, among the bananas. Possibly it is appropriate. Apart from on television, I haven't seen Ben since he dumped me. I test my reaction, waiting for the surge of blood, the heart palpitations. But it is like those feelings belonged to someone else. He looks like an ordinary man, early forties, better looking than average, but with a hint of softness around the middle. Too many chocolate-coated bananas? His aura seems a little flat. If he did steal my mojo he must have misplaced it.

Something has changed. Perhaps it is me.

He steps a little closer, a half-smile still on his face.

I think he is going to hug me and I'm not sure how I feel about that. I don't think we are on hugging terms. And I don't want to come any closer to that banana.

Ben sees my reluctance. His hands, which were half-raised, drop to his sides. 'Can we talk?' He takes a bite of his banana. A smear of chocolate stains the side of his face and he wipes it away with his hand.

'Yes.' I suppose it is time to build a bridge over that pit of unspoken words between us.

'Outside?'

I nod.

Ben walks outside. I follow. He sits down on the pedestal at the base of the Big Banana and pats the concrete beside him.

I sit, warily. The banana casts a curving shadow over the two of us. Inari lies down on the grass and promptly falls asleep.

'Funny dog,' says Ben. 'Is it yours?'

'Long story. Short answer, yes.'

Ben glances at me out of the corner of his eye. He is waiting for me to begin, but that isn't how it is going to work. Not this time.

'You look well, Arkie.' His eyes flicker up and down my mermaid outfit. 'New clothes?'

I nod. 'New to me, anyway.'

He studies my outfit for a bit longer. 'Not many people could carry that off.' It is almost a backhanded compliment, but he sounds admiring. 'Isn't this the strangest place?' he says.

This is my cue for a witty comment. 'Yes,' I say. There is much that I could add, but I choose not to. I wonder why he is here. What he wants. I'm pretty sure he isn't here for a chat about the Big Banana.

Ben takes another bite of his banana and chews rapidly. He seems a little uptight. His hair is ruffled and a two-day growth stubbles his chin. 'Have you tried these?' He gestures towards me with his banana. I shrink backwards. 'They're surprisingly good.'

I shake my head. I have nothing to add on the subject of chocolate-coated fruit. Once I would have, but I am not in the mood for banter. I don't want to play that game anymore.

I see him note my recalcitrance. Ben's interest was always conditional on my being entertaining. I tried so hard to be upbeat, intelligent, sparkling. When I wasn't at my best he would remember an urgent appointment he hadn't mentioned previously. After he left I would curse myself for being so dull. It never occurred to me to recognise this as a failure on his part.

I observe him out of the corner of my eye as he eats his banana. Even now, when I am not sure I like him, he rattles my mind. I still feel a frustrated desire for connection, I don't know why. It is like our cogs don't quite mesh and I can't help wanting to tinker until they do. 'Haruko teed you up to come here, huh?' I say, remembering her conversation in the car.

'I asked her to. I thought we should . . .'

'Have closure?'

Ben nods. He finishes his banana, but still holds the stick. 'I could eat another one of those.'

'I'm not going to spoil your election campaign if that's what you're worried about. I'm not Monica Lewinsky.'

'That's not why I wanted to see you.'

I snort, but he continues.

'You said something to me once. On the phone.' He twists the banana stick in his hands.

I know immediately what he means. 'About my mojo?'

Now he is tearing pieces off the stick with his fingernails, shredding it. He speaks rapidly, as if trying to get the words out of his mouth before they choke him. 'I thought you were out of your mind. Maybe you were right, though.'

I tilt my head.

'You had so much . . .' he searches for a word, 'intuition and . . .' He frowns, loses the struggle. 'It seems a bit strange to say this, but . . . It was like it transferred itself. Is that too weird?' He turns to me, his banana stick in pieces in his lap.

'Not to me.'

Ben spreads his hands. He looks me in the eye. 'You already know what's happened, don't you?'

I hold his gaze, testing myself again, waiting for the pull in my stomach, the weakness in my legs, but it doesn't happen. 'It's gone?'

He nods. 'That indefinable something has packed up and left.' He brushes the remnants of his stick off his lap. 'I've never felt like this before. I just feel totally . . . deflated.'

'I know exactly what that is like.'

'I'm in the middle of an election campaign and I just don't have any . . .'

'Charisma?'

'Oh, God.' He puts his face in his hands. 'I haven't, have I?' He drops his hands. 'What can I do, Arkie?'

'So, when did you start deflating?' I raise my eyebrow to make it seem like I could be joking but I don't feel ironic at all inside.

Ben shrugs. 'It's been a gradual thing, but then . . .'

'Two days ago?'

He looks at me sharply and he doesn't say anything.

I know I am right. *The night I spent with Adam.* I rein myself in. I may be getting too far into woo woo territory.

'Has it found its way back to you?' he says. He sounds embarrassed.

A warm breeze blows towards us where we sit beneath the banana. The Pacific Highway traffic roars in the distance. I hear Haruko giggle. She must have finished tobogganing.

I nod slowly. 'Yes, I think it's coming back. I seem to be reinflating.'

We eye each other uneasily. I think we both know this is a strange conversation to have.

Ben runs his hands through his hair. It sticks up on end like a mad professor. 'Can you help me?'

I think of how he cut me off when I needed help, refused to talk to me, hurt me in a million ways, yet I can't bring myself to do the same. 'You're going to have to find it for yourself, Ben. I haven't got your mojo.' He seems so pitiful that I add, 'You could try doing a pilgrimage.'

A spark of hope appears in his eyes. 'A pilgrimage? Where to?'

Inari is awake now. Her black eyes move between us, as if she is following the conversation. I have a sudden image of Ben and I sitting beneath the banana, me in my mermaid outfit and he a dishevelled mess. I am glad now that Haruko took charge of my appearance today. Was she adorning me for my meeting with Ben? I touch my net hat and straighten my shoulders. 'You should undertake a pilgrimage to eighty-eight Big Things,' I pronounce. Perhaps I really am becoming a guru.

'Eighty-eight? But I have my election campaign . . .'

I regard him with compassion. 'Ben, there won't be an election campaign if you don't have any mojo.'

He nods. 'Yes. Of course. Do you think it will work?'

'It will. If you do it in the right spirit.'

He slumps forward onto his elbows. 'We had fun, didn't we? You and me.' He sounds like he is seeking reassurance.

'Some of it was fun. Some of it wasn't.'

He gazes at me from under his hair. 'You never really loved me, did you?'

As he says this, it hits me – he is right. Ben was a drug that has now worn off. Not love then, madness – the mind playing tricks. 'No. I guess I never did.'

'I really could have fallen hard for you, Arkie.' Ben smiles ruefully. 'But . . . it's not what I do. I don't think we were very good for each other.'

'Or for your election campaign?'

Ben's eyes meet mine. He hesitates, then replies. 'Possibly not. No. It wouldn't have helped.'

'How is Elaine?'

'She's well. We co-exist quite happily.'

Co-exist. All at once I feel sorry for him, settling for that. But perhaps it seems worth it. Maybe passion is over-rated.

Ben gazes out towards the horizon. 'Do you regret it?'

'Oh.' I think of everything that has happened – meeting Haruko, the pilgrimage, falling in love with Adam all over again. None of that would have happened if not for Ben coming into my life. And it's hard to regret any of it. 'Perhaps it was necessary,' I say. But then I remember how Adam left me. How I didn't get out of bed to say goodbye. How I have probably lost him forever. 'But I regret hurting Adam.'

'I hope things work out for you,' he says. 'I never meant . . .'

'I know you never meant.' It is pointless going down this track; recriminations will serve no purpose. 'I hope things work out for you too. Good luck with the mojo. You should find it eventually. Do the pilgrimage. Open yourself up to it.'

We smile, warily, like two wounded enemy soldiers. We have hurt each other enough. Inari licks my hand.

Part Three

'There is no place like home.'

The Wonderful Wizard of Oz, ***L. Frank Baum***

Thirty-one

Haruko and Ebi emerge through the bushes beneath us. They are holding hands and Haruko's cheeks are flushed pink. They stop when they see us. Haruko points with her spare hand. She seems to be holding a banana-shaped water pistol. 'There it is.' She waves the banana pistol at me. 'We have been looking for banana everywhere.'

Inari jumps up with a yap and runs towards them, tail wagging.

Ben touches my shoulder. 'I'm going to head off.' He raises his hand to Haruko.

Haruko gives an impenetrable smile, like a Zen monk. Their eyes meet for a moment, then Ben stands and leaves.

I check my arms just in case, but I already know there is nothing to see. No rush of blood has left its imprint on me. Whatever power he had over me is gone. I stand too, and stretch. 'Did you see any Buddhas, Haruko?'

She shakes her head. 'None.'

The Big Banana is a Buddha-free land. 'Our eleventh temple, Haruko,' I say. 'Is there anything like this in Japan?'

Haruko hands her banana pistol to Ebi, who puts it in his pocket – suggestively, I think. Haruko's mouth quivers, she smooths her hair behind her ears. She gives a fleeting glance towards the Big Banana. 'There is place called Taga-jinja sex shrine on Shikoku. It is fertility shrine. It has many, many . . .' she gestures at the banana, 'banana-shaped stones.' She giggles.

Ebi says something in Japanese and Haruko giggles. 'You can get fortune. It tells you how . . . good you are, you and partner,' she says.

'Compatible?'

'Yes. Compatible. There is statue that comes with it.'

'Bit like that.' Ebi points at the lewd monkey outside the souvenir shop.

This conjures up a strange image. 'I can imagine,' I murmur.

The souvenir shop is shutting. The shop girl drags the monkey inside and slides the door shut – banana accessory sales are closed for today.

As the sun sinks towards the trees the banana shadow creeps across the grass. A bat suddenly emerges from the forest behind, startling me as its wings rush overhead.

Frightened, Inari runs between my legs.

The bat glides over our heads, then flaps towards the coast.

Haruko follows its progress. 'Fukurokuju,' she looks back at me, 'is usually accompanied by bat.'

I slide my hand in my bag and pull out my Lucky Gods. Ebisu, Daikokuten, Bishamonten, Benzaiten, Hotei, Jurojin, and the last one, Fukurokuju . . . My Fukurokuju has a high forehead. He is bald, with long whiskers and wears a lime-green robe.

'God of wisdom,' says Haruko.

Wisdom. That would be nice. I've been to all these places, seen all these Big Things . . . Am I any wiser than when I first set out? I don't know, but now something is happening. A tingle fills my fingers. It works its way up my arms, my shoulders, my chest. As it reaches my head a scent fills my nostrils, a vision crowds my mind. I have vanquished Ben and now . . . 'I think we should go to Sydney next,' I say. 'I have something I need to do.' I think of Adam. 'Two things I need to do.'

'Are there Big Things there?' says Haruko.

'I don't think so. But, Haruko, back in Brisbane you said that pilgrimages were about transition.'

Haruko nods. 'They are sacred journey. You are cleaned of your sins.'

'And also transform yourself.'

'Yes. You come back changed.' Haruko smiles and looks me up and down. 'Like you. You are changed. So . . . are we still on pilgrimage?'

'I don't know. Maybe this is the end. For now.'

Haruko tilts her head to one side. 'You have been only to eleven Big Things, not eighty-eight.'

'Does that matter?'

'Eleven is lucky number too.' Haruko smiles. 'Mini-pilgrimage. Like me on Shikoku. I only do eleven. You have rest of life to finish.'

Haruko, Ebi, Inari and I turn south down the highway.

We stop for the night in a nameless town with a motel called Highway Comfort.

There is confusion at the check-in.

'One room?' says the fiftyish woman with a waist like a barrel.

'Two?' says Ebi.

'Three.' Haruko is firm.

Ebi pouts.

I smuggle Inari into my room. Soon after, Haruko and Ebi knock on my door. 'We are going to KFC,' says Haruko.

I raise my eyebrows.

Haruko seems slightly embarrassed. 'Do you mind? Pilgrimage is over for now, yes?'

How could I mind? I have broken almost every rule in the book and I probably would have broken the others too, given the opportunity. 'Of course I don't mind. Have fun. I'm worn out. I'll get room service.' I think they need some time together. I order a meal for myself and Inari – vegetarian for me. I am paying penance and I don't think my pilgrimage is finished just yet. When I turn on the TV, Ben is on the news, talking about the importance of Big Things to tourism.

'I'm planning to visit as many Big Things as I can throughout my election campaign,' he says. 'I think the importance of Big Things to the economy and identity of Australia has been under –'

The newsreader cuts him off. 'I'm sorry, we might have to leave it there.'

Ben's mouth hangs open as the camera pans away. They never would have done that in the past.

But it suits him, I think, this new low-key persona. Now he seems less like a cult leader and more like someone you could trust.

I think about Ben and my idea that we had met in a past life. It is flaky, but somehow it fits. People always think they were royalty in a past life, don't they? More likely we were peasants in adjoining shacks. How the mud pies would have flown across our thatched straw fence.

Maybe I will bump into him, life after life. Perhaps we are meant to be nothing more than the grit in each other's oyster, existing solely to create change when it is needed.

I make myself a cup of tea in my Tanuki teapot, turn on my iPad and scroll through the photos from my pilgrimage. Am I really ready to finish? Ending the pilgrimage means returning to the real world. Accepting that the life I have is the life I have created.

I didn't get anywhere near eighty-eight temples, but as Haruko says I have the rest of my life. And there is always Shikoku.

But now I must think about tomorrow, the future. As I take a sip of tea, I remember a picture that used to hang on our balcony – *The Future Revealed*. In the painting, mist drifts, dreamlike, across the face of a woman. I never really understood what it meant. There was no point in asking Adam. 'If you have to ask the meaning of a surrealist work then you have missed the point,' he'd always say.

It was like that stupid joke he used to pick me up – how many surrealists does it take to change a lightbulb? You either get it or you don't. *The Future Revealed* . . . I think maybe I do understand it now.

The pictures are arrayed in thumbnails on my screen. I rearrange them into the chronological order of their creation, then find a pen and open my notebook.

1. *The Big Banana – 1964.*
   'I Want to Hold Your Hand' by The Beatles,
   Pork with prunes, and
   Mini skirts.
2. *The Big Shell – 1967 (a guess)*
   'To Sir with Love' by Lulu,
   Flower power, and
   Frisbees.

3. *The Big Pineapple – 1971*

Hot pants,

Pineapple cheese ball,

'Joy to the World' by Three Dog Night, and

Disco.

I go on. 4. *The Big Mower –1975*, 5. *The Big Cow – 1976*, 6. *The Big Pelican – 1977.*

I take another sip of tea and, as I click and drag the next photo, I notice an image I haven't seen before. I have no idea where it came from. It is of me; Haruko must have taken it. I touch my finger to it so it fills the frame. It takes me a moment to recognise the setting. No, Haruko didn't take it.

I am in Adam's bed in the Brisbane unit. Asleep. It is morning – he must have taken it just before I woke. My hand is open on the pillow, my cheeks are pink and my tangled hair is the colour of autumn. I look about twenty years old.

I touch the screen. 'Why did Adam take that photo, Inari?'

Inari pricks her ears and wags her tail across the carpet.

I think of the picture I found in his sketchbook in Brisbane. *Two Faces.* It was harsh, but he was right. I was lying to him and to myself. I open an email and type in his address, attach the photo. *I think this is yours. Only one face now, Adam*, I write. I press *send* before I can change my mind.

Then I move the photo to another folder. I can't bear to look at it, to imagine him taking that photo and all the time thinking of me like that. I go on with my sorting.

7. *The Big Macadamia – 1978*

Platform shoes,
Curly perms for men,
Strawberry Shortcake Doll,
Watership Down, *and*
Dallas *on TV*

8. *The Big Avocado – 1983, 9. The Big Prawn – 1989, 10. The Big Redback – 1996 and 11. The Big Pie – 1999.*

There is a trend here. I'm not yet sure what it is, but I am – I think – getting closer. Trends are like rare and timid wildlife, you must sneak up on them. Approach them from downwind, stealthily.

I take Inari outside for a walk before going to bed. It is cool and the sky is filled with a million stars. Not far away, the traffic roars down the highway, but in this back street, only the odd car goes by. I hardly notice my surrounds, my head is a swirling galaxy of trends.

The next Big Thing. The next Big Thing. The trends whirl around and around in my mind. *Pokémon, Macarena, hip hop, hot pants* . . . Fads and events. Fads feed the events, events feed the fads. It is the circle of life. *And what about the Buddhas?* What does it all mean? That is the question. There is only one thing to do. Sleep on it – let the subconscious do its thing. *Dream . . .*

Back inside, I lie down and close my eyes but sleep is a long time coming. Ten o'clock. *Pork with prunes, hot pants, mood rings, Buddhas, Adam.* Eleven o'clock. *Tank tops, platforms, Rubik's Cube, hip hop, Buddhas, Adam.* Twelve o'clock. *Bomber jackets, piercings, Pokémon, Buddhas, Adam.* One o'clock, two o'clock, three o'clock. *Adam, Adam, Adam.*

Thirty-two

I am dreaming I am inside my cardboard Revitashelter when a knock on the door wakes me. I have ordered breakfast for seven o'clock. Not long ago, this dream would have been a nightmare but just now it was, in fact, a happy dream. I bring in my breakfast tray and as I boil the kettle I remember how, just before I woke, I burst out of my Revitashelter like a Playboy Bunny out of a cake.

'Tan, tan, Tanuki's testicles,' I sing, pouring water into the teapot.

Inari wags her tail in a mad arc and prances about as if sharing the joke.

I move on to the toast and the single-serve box of Sultana Bran and contemplate what today will bring. A vision is still brewing in my subconscious. The air smells like the future. My mojo is returning. I am almost sure of it.

Haruko knocks on my door at seven-thirty. She is dressed in black from head to toe. It is not a monotone though; she graduates from ebony on her shoes to an off-the-shoulder blouse with the merest hint of grey. 'Black is the new black,' she says.

'How do you do that?'

Haruko cocks her head, her silky hair swinging out.

'You have this tiny bag and yet . . .' I gesture at her outfit, 'this comes out.'

Haruko smiles, exposing the gap between her teeth. 'There are more possibility in universe than most people realise. And Japanese are very good packers.'

I smile. 'Keep your secrets then.'

Haruko slides her hair behind her ears and studies my face. 'You've got it back now, haven't you? You took from him. I knew you would if you saw him.'

I'm not ready to answer that question until I am sure. I take a deep breath and look around. My motel room is in dire need of renovation. The orange carpet and fluffy-dog print hints at the seventies. I already know that there's no Buddha; this motel hasn't kept up with the times. My iPad is propped up on my bedside table, still scrolling through photos from my journey.

Everything is coming together. *Millions of gods are talking to you; you just have to listen.* Yes the universe is whispering to me. A surge of elation rushes up my body from my toes to my head. Fizzing bubbles of joy invite me to dance, to sing. It is like falling in love, but without the anxiety of wondering if they love you back. Yes. Everything I need, I already have.

Haruko smiles. She doesn't need me to answer. She looks me up and down. I have gone back to my white pilgrim's outfit today. My mermaid dress lies on the counter – a small pile of silk and net, a discarded shell. It is hard to imagine that crumpled mound once clothed me, made me feel like a sea goddess. The power has evaporated now.

Haruko shakes her head. She opens her briefcase and pulls out a pink petticoat, the smallest handful of silk. 'Today, you wear pink.'

'Haruko, I never wear pink.' I gesture at my red hair. 'Do you have any other colours?'

'I have other colour, but today you wear pink.' She raises her chin in an imperious way.

Haruko is so insistent and what does it matter, after all, if my dress clashes with my hair? I take off my pilgrim's clothes and slide on the petticoat.

Haruko smiles. She reaches into her briefcase and pulls out a pink hair clasp, gathers my hair onto the top of my head and secures it. Then, taking the tops of my shoulders, she turns me towards the mirror.

I have never, ever in my life worn pink, but now I see that Haruko is right. My face seems brighter, my hair more vivid. I look younger, fresher.

'Like Benzaiten,' she says.

The goddess of flow. Amiable, fertile and a competent wife. I nod. 'Yes, pink is right for today. Thank you, Haruko.'

'And one more thing.' Haruko rummages in her briefcase again and pulls out a red ball. She pulls it apart and I see it is a pair of ballet slippers. She hands them to me.

'Ruby-red slippers?'

Haruko nods. 'Like Dorothy. Because today, maybe, you find your way home.'

I have to blink rapidly to stop the tears though I hardly know why. I slide the slippers on my feet and while the red slippers/pink petticoat/red hair combination should be a disaster, in fact it is absolutely perfect.

There is a knock on the door and Ebi appears. His hair is again swept back, carefully arranged. I wonder what it's like when he gets out of bed in the morning, how long it takes him to get it in place.

Haruko turns and her face softens. He rests his chin on her shoulder and she doesn't shrug him off. They look good together.

'Sydney?' he says.

The sun is shining, so Ebi puts the car hood down again.

'Do you want the front?' I ask Haruko.

She nods and slides herself onto the leather seat.

Ebi's shoulders straighten. He adjusts his sunglasses. Today he is wearing silver aviators and black jeans with chains hanging off them. His tight white T-shirt reads *Hope Should Have in Anytimes*. He has rolled up the sleeves and his prawn tattoo flexes on his muscled shoulder as if it is swimming.

Inari and I hop in the back. 'Why the prawn?' I say. I am imagining something sinister – don't prawns eat dead things on the bottom of the ocean? Is there a mafia connection?

Ebi looks over his shoulder. He smiles in a sheepish way. 'Because I like prawn sushi too much.'

Haruko giggles and says something in rapid Japanese.

'When we are in high school, I make myself sick at party eating too much prawn. That is how I get nickname. Then, when I join Yakuza, I get tattoo.'

Ebi turns the radio up loud as we cruise down the highway; Bruce Springsteen is singing 'Born to Be Wild'. We all sing along as the wind blows Haruko's and my hair around. Ebi's hair doesn't move. He is obviously on excellent terms with his styling products.

Ebi glances in his rear-view mirror every now and then. 'That car is behind us for two hours,' he says as we reach the outskirts of Sydney.

I crane around in my seat and see a bearded man at the wheel of the car behind us. He slumps lower in his seat as he sees me. Fabian. 'Try to lose him.'

Ebi accelerates as the lights go red and takes a turn down a side street. I twist around and see Fabian stopped at the lights, his fleshy hands gripping the wheel. *Ha.* Lawyers don't break road rules and, besides, the cross-traffic is starting to flow. I can't resist waving at him gaily. His face is impassive behind his sunglasses. The last I see of him, he appears to be talking on his hands-free phone.

'Where we going?' says Haruko.

'You will see. Mystery tour. Turn right here,' I say to Ebi.

Soon we are in Paddington. It is Sunday, but the streets are busy with men in trendy casual wear and well-groomed yummy mummies pushing prams. Eventually we find a park.

'This way.' I head towards the shopping strip and down a side street.

Along the way we pass a number of boutiques catering for those with expensive tastes, an antique shop, a trendy cafe, a flower shop and – the only dark window in a brightly lit row – Arkie's Ark. I run my tongue over my lips as I see it, suddenly nervous. The shop brings back memories. Last time I was here I was demented, crazy with love and loss.

But I am not that woman anymore. I take a deep breath and smile at Haruko and Ebi. 'Ready?' Opening my day-pack, I pull the key out of the zip pocket and unlock the glass sliding doors. Inside the glass is another set of doors. Once so beautiful, my cardboard doors are now crumpled and stained with damp.

My heart beats a little faster as I see them. I feel like a hero returned from a journey with a magic charm. But will it work in the real world? I extend one finger, press it to the door. No nausea, no revulsion strikes me. My heart rate slows. I press my whole hand against it. Cautiously, I lean closer, breathe in its papery smell, touch it with my nose.

Yes, the magic works, the journey was a success – the dry, papery texture holds no fears for me. My cardboard phobia is gone. I pull the doors open, tentatively, like an explorer entering a tomb that has been sealed for thousands of years. I am stepping not only into the darkness of a disused shop, but back into my past. I feel for the switch and the lights come on.

Inari rushes in and immediately commences an olfactory tour.

Ebi and Haruko are quiet behind me. I turn. 'So . . . what do you think?'

Haruko spins on her heels, taking it all in, the cardboard shelving, cardboard hats, cardboard toys and the pièce de résistance, the cardboard coffin. She cocks her head on one side. 'It could work, but . . .'

'It doesn't,' I say.

'Wrong energy,' says Haruko.

I nod. 'I got it wrong. I thought people wanted a reinvented simplicity, but what they want is actually a return to the past.'

Haruko nods. 'Long-term trends reflect deepest needs and desires.'

'The need for connection,' I say.

'Need for innocent pleasure,' says Haruko.

I have trained her well. I pull out my iPad and hold it up, flicking through my photos of Big Things.

Haruko nods as each picture comes up. I can see her remembering.

'Imagine a time when people were happy to be amazed by the view from the top of a pineapple's crown.'

'When ride on train through banana plantation was the most excitement,' says Haruko.

'When kitsch was big.'

'And wearing kaftans.'

'Eating angels on horseback.'

'And fondue parties.'

'People who were there will want to be there again. People who weren't there . . .'

'Wish they were.'

I get a warm feeling in my stomach. It's the real deal. I am firing on all cylinders. 'This shop will be a celebration of the sixties and seventies.'

'Of simple way,' says Haruko.

'And the Australian rural life.'

'And Big Thing,' says Haruko.

'But not only that,' I say. 'This shop will take nostalgia to a new level. It will celebrate the good old Aussie love of surrealism as it expresses itself in the pursuit of Big Things. And it won't only be a shop, but the new head-quarters for my trend-spotting business. I will call it . . .' Haruko and Ebi wait expectantly, 'The Next Big Thing.'

Haruko smiles. She turns to Ebi. 'What you think?'

'Very cool,' he says. 'Very retro. Japanese love this sort of thing.'

'I'd buy it.' A man speaks from the door.

We all turn.

It is Adam.

Thirty-three

Adam is casually dressed in an orange-checked shirt and loose navy pants. A car key dangles from one hand. 'Fabian told me you were in town. I figured you might come here.' He looks relaxed, as if this is an informal visit.

I still have the divorce papers in my daypack. My hand goes instinctively to the bag, as if he might snatch it off me. I'll give them to him. Soon. Just not yet.

His gaze moves towards Haruko and Ebi. 'Adam, this is Haruko and Ebi.' I turn to them. 'Adam is my . . . husband.' I cannot bring myself to call him anything else.

Something passes over his face, but he does not contradict me.

'And Inari,' I add, as she trots over to sniff him.

'Ebi.' Haruko takes his arm. 'Let us go and get coffee.'

'So,' says Adam after they have gone. 'The divorce papers?'

I unzip my bag, pull out two copies and hand them to him. 'I was going to give them to you. You didn't need to come after me.'

He takes them from me, folds them carefully and slides them into the pocket of his pants.

'Just like that?' I say.

Adam's shoulders lift slightly. He scans the shop, then walks over to a high cardboard bar stool and perches on it.

At least he is not leaving straight away.

'I haven't been here before,' he says. 'It's, um, interesting.' He jiggles his car keys in his hand.

So we are going to make small talk. 'Do you like the coffin?' I say.

'Why did you do it?' He looks directly at me. And I can tell that this is no longer an informal visit. The keys are clenched in his hand.

My stomach jolts. And now I wish that we *were* making small talk. The question could mean many things, but I know we are not talking about cardboard. I meet his eyes. *Why did I steal the papers? Why did I go to bed with him?* No, I know what he means. *Why did I cheat?* There are so many things I could say, but I'm only going to get one chance. I close my eyes for a moment, then open them again. 'I was searching for something.'

'Did you find it?'

'I thought I had, but it wasn't real. It was a trick of the mind. I did find something else though.'

Adam waits.

'I found out that . . .' Something wet touches my fingers – Inari's nose. 'I found out that I love you. Still. After all these years.'

Adam studies me as if he is trying to read my mind, to see the truth there. His face doesn't give much away.

A shimmer lights up my body. For some reason I think of a painting that used to hang in our bedroom. A woman's hand poked through a gap in the wall, her fingers crossed. I never knew if they were crossed for hope, or to counteract the effect of a lie. Behind my back I cross my fingers. *For hope.* He is thinking about it. He wants to know if he can trust me. If he lets me back into his life, will I stomp all over his heart again? Once someone has cheated once, does that make them a cheater for life?

I speak quickly. 'Sometimes you have to go all over the world to find out that home is where you're meant to be. That's you, Adam. You're my home.' I don't know what else I can say.

'I haven't seen you in pink before.' And suddenly he smiles. I am looking at my old friend again. 'It suits you.'

I walk over to his chair, reach out and hold his hand. He doesn't resist, but neither does he squeeze my hand. 'I'm so sorry for hurting you,' I say.

'There you are.' A voice breaks the silence.

We turn towards the door.

Fabian Fernley is striding through the cardboard doors, additional copies of the divorce papers in his hands.

Sweat blooms under his armpits. His face is red and moist. 'Hold on to her,' he says.

Adam's hand squeezes mine, firmly. I couldn't pull away if I wanted to. His other hand pats his pocket. 'It's all right. I've got the papers here.'

But Fabian has too much momentum to stop now. He is like a tank on a victory lap of a conquered city. Charging up to me, he thrusts his papers into my spare hand. A broad smile bursts across his hairy face. He stands there puffing, catching his breath. 'Served. Finally.'

The divorce papers are in one hand. Adam holds my other hand. I study his face. He is biting his lip but I don't know if that's a good sign or a bad one. 'Adam?' I say.

Adam takes the papers from my hand and gives them back to Fabian. He pulls his copies from his pocket and also hands them over. 'Sorry, Fabian. Shred them.' He bursts out laughing and his eyes meet mine. 'How did we ever come to this, Arkie?'

I am too wrung out for euphoria. What I feel instead is a flood of relief, as if a blockage of misery inside me has washed away. I hadn't even known that misery was sitting there in my chest, but now it has gone I am much lighter.

Fabian looks from Adam to me. Realisation dawns. 'Don't tell me . . .' He flings the papers onto the floor. 'For fuck's sake. I've been to the Big Redback, the Big Cow, the Big Pelican, the Big Shell, the Big fucking Mango . . .' He stops to draw breath, then speaks again through gritted teeth. 'I've been to the bloody Big Pie, the effing

Big Prawn, the crapulous Big Mower, the ridiculous Big Macadamia . . .'

He moves closer to Adam and me. I am mesmerised, unable to speak. He is now so close that I can see the individual spidery veins in each of his chubby cheeks. He seems not to notice that he is now standing on top of the divorce papers. His breath is hot on my face and smells of salt and vinegar chips.

'I've been to the preposterous Big Pineapple, the ludicrous Big Avocado and the farcical Big fucking Buddha and now you're telling me,' he plants a fat white finger on Adam's chest, 'you don't want a divorce?'

Adam shakes his head – the tiniest movement.

Fabian's eyes swivel to me then back to Adam. 'You're making a mistake. May as well get it over with while you can. Are you sure?'

Adam doesn't say anything for a few moments.

I hold my breath, but then his fingers twine themselves through mine. A warm glow engulfs me. My stomach does strange things. The feeling moves lower. Can this really be the man I was married to for twenty years? My body thinks differently.

Adam releases my hand, but only to put his arm around my back, to curl his hand around my waist. 'I'm sure,' he says.

'Jesus.' Fabian notices for the first time that he is standing on the divorce papers. He grinds them under his massive foot, leaving a dirty mark across the white parchment paper. 'I'll send you the bill,' he says.

'How was the Big Buddha?' I ask, but Fabian is already on his way out the door.

It is quiet in the shop after Fabian has gone.

Adam's hand is still around my waist and I am suddenly aware of how thin my petticoat is, how silky beneath his touch.

'Does that door lock?' he says.

I nod. Wordlessly.

Adam squeezes my waist.

His fingers are stronger than I remember them. My legs feel suddenly not quite up to the task of supporting me in the manner to which I'm accustomed.

'Don't go away,' he says. In two steps he is at the door. The noise of the traffic outside dims as he slides it shut, locks it and turns to me. He smiles – a smile full of possibilities, love tinged with sadness, memories both good and bad. Our entire history is held in that moment.

We have come such a long way since that morning when we met at his art show. Such a long way, and yet somehow no distance at all.

I smile back, although I am fighting tears at the same time. The world is reduced to the two of us – his eyes, my eyes. I feel like my heart could burst out of my chest, it is beating so hard.

Adam breaks first; his eyes roam around the room and come to rest on the cardboard coffin. Its lid is propped open, displaying the lush, padded interior. 'All it needs is a chocolate on the pillow.' He meets my eyes again.

A long, slow blush starts at my feet and moves up to my face as I think about the things we could do in that coffin.

Adam smiles. 'You have a very devious mind, Arkie Douglas.' Then he is beside me again. He strokes my face and runs his hands down my arms and it seems that my petticoat was designed just for this; it falls away under his touch. 'You're so beautiful, Arkie.'

And I know he is not comparing me to anyone at all.

Thirty-four

Two days later, I am at the airport.

The past forty-eight hours have been a whirl – buying tickets, shopping for souvenirs and sightseeing. Haruko couldn't leave without visiting the Opera House and Taronga Zoo and taking a ride on a Sydney ferry. As we careered from Mosman to Manly I swung between elation and despair. Adam was back, but now Haruko was leaving. It was all happening so quickly.

Haruko and I sit on plastic seats clutching paper cups of coffee. Adam and Ebi are in the airport newsagent nearby, browsing the books. I glance over at them.

Ebi looks like he could be a model advertising something totally with it and funky. *A new drink, perhaps? Mobile phones?* His baggy pants flop down over half-laced high-top boots. The hood of his long-sleeved hooded

T-shirt is pulled over his head as he browses a *Mad* comic.

Adam has an art book in his hands. His hair falls over his face as he turns the pages. Watching him makes me warm inside. We are a puzzle that has been put back together – two people who make more sense together than apart.

'Tell me about the last temple,' I say.

'Okubo-ji is called *Place of Fulfilment of Vow,*' says Haruko. 'People hang crutches and plaster, that sort of thing, on walls.'

'People who have been cured?'

Haruko nods in a matter-of-fact way. 'They don't need anymore.'

'After the last temple, what do people usually do?'

'Some say you should go back to first temple to complete circle. Others say leave circle open.'

'Arkie?'

I look up. It is Bertie from Tewantin. She is pulling a small wheelie suitcase and looking very dapper in a white pantsuit and white leather shoes.

'I thought it was you,' she says.

'Bertie!' I glance at her suitcase. 'What are you up to?'

Bertie perches next to me on a vacant seat. She appears younger than she did when I first met her. Her cheeks have a rosy flush and her eyes are bright. 'I've just got off the flight from Brisbane. I've got a round-the-world ticket.'

'Goodness.' This seems inadequate, but I am a little lost for words.

'You got me thinking, dear – you and your pilgrimage. I started to think about travel. The idea that there might be completely different ways of doing things just wouldn't leave me alone. If it wasn't supermarkets in Sweden or petrol stations in Peru, it was toilets in Tokyo or ice-cream in Indonesia. So . . .' she gestures at her suitcase, 'here I am.'

'Where are you off to first?'

Bertie hesitates. 'I'm starting in Japan.' The way she says the word, it sounds incredibly exotic – the kind of place from which you might never return. 'I'm doing a pilgrimage, a bus one. I'm too old for all that walking.'

'Congratulations. Good for you.'

'My dear, departed Trevor would say that I'm as mad as a meat-axe. Tewantin was always enough for him. We went to Byron Bay for a holiday once, but he didn't like the hippies. He didn't like change at all, did Trevor. Liked things to stay the same. He wouldn't have been too happy about dying.'

I am not sure if this is a joke or a philosophical statement, so I don't laugh. 'It's the ultimate change, isn't it?' I murmur.

'Exactly,' says Bertie. 'I say, you may as well give change a whirl while you're alive to enjoy it.'

'Bravo. So, how are you feeling?'

'Nervous. I've never been overseas before. And Tokyo. All those people. I've heard they push you onto trains. I wouldn't like that much.'

'Only pushing at rush hour.' Haruko smiles. 'You will be on my flight I think. I can help, if you need? At Tokyo. But you will find it easy. Once you are used to it. Japan is very organised.'

Bertie's face creases into a million wrinkles as she smiles. 'Will you, dear? That would be very kind of you.' She leans over and kisses my cheek, then gets to her feet. 'You walked into that information centre at just the right moment, you know. Got me going. Bye now, I'm going in.' She makes it sound like she is about to leap out of the trenches.

'I will look for you,' says Haruko.

'Email me,' I say.

Bertie smiles and zips open her daypack to reveal a small notebook computer. 'I'm starting a blog. You can be my first subscriber.'

I watch her stout back vanishing towards the departure gate. 'She's very brave, isn't she?'

'She find her courage.' Haruko taps her chest. 'Inside herself.'

I gaze towards the departure gate in silence for a few moments. Soon it will be Haruko who is *going in*. 'It's a strange feeling, ending things,' I say.

'Endings are also beginnings,' says Haruko. 'Some people never give up pilgrimage. They just keep going. They get addicted. Go around other way, maybe.'

I imagine myself travelling around and around Australia, becoming the crazy Big Things lady. 'I don't think I'm the addictive type. Not for pilgrimages anyway.'

Haruko smiles. 'No. You have your husband. And your business. That is your new pilgrimage. The Next Big Thing. I like it. You remember Takamure Itsue?'

'Of course – the one who was running away from her two lovers.'

'Yes. She gain confidence through pilgrimage to become writer. Later in life, when she need reassurance, she just has to remember pilgrimage. It gives her strength.'

'I'll remember our pilgrimage to the Big Things for the rest of my life. Maybe we can do the Shikoku pilgrimage together one day?'

Haruko meets my eyes. 'Maybe.' Her voice is neutral, but she hasn't rejected the idea.

I will take that as encouragement. 'So, is Ebi going to leave the Yakuza?'

Haruko nods.

'Is that difficult?'

'Yes. When you have been Yakuza it is hard to do other things. And sometimes dangerous,' she adds. 'They don't like very much.'

'And you? Will you keep doing the trend forecasting? Back in Japan?'

'Of course.' Haruko smiles. 'Japanese love trend. It will be easy. You don't need to worry about us, Misaki. We will find our way all right. Me and Ebi, we are more tough than very old crocodile.'

I bite my lip to stop myself from asking her to stay. I know there is no point. 'I'll miss you.'

Haruko reaches out and squeezes my hand. 'I will miss you too. But I have to go home now. There is no place like home.' She clicks her heels together with a smile.

'No, there isn't, is there? Thank you for helping me.'

'We help each other.'

I have Inari in my bag. She pokes her nose out now and licks Haruko's hand. Today Haruko's fingernails are all different. Gold stars decorate her thumb, her index finger is striped red and blue, purple dots her pinkie finger . . .

When she sees me looking she smiles. 'Fake nails.' She puts one hand up and adjusts her pink beret, strokes Inari's head with the other hand. 'Inari is very good for fertility.' Her words hang in the air, like floating dust lit up in the sun.

Ebi and Adam are back now.

Ebi holds out his hand to her. 'Time to go through.'

Haruko smiles at him and I can see how right they are, these childhood sweethearts. I can't begrudge her to him, but as I kiss Haruko goodbye I wonder if love might be the greatest folly of all.

Haruko picks up her briefcase. Her surfboard has been checked in. 'Maybe this is last temple for you, Misaki?' she says.

And suddenly I understand. I think of the people hanging up their crutches and wheelchairs on the wall and I know what I must leave behind – something that I don't need anymore . . .

'Goodbye, Haruko.'

'She's like *Venus on Sixth Avenue*,' says Adam as we watch her go.

A print of the goddess Venus on a city street used to hang in our laundry. Above the washing machine was the ideal location for a picture about finding the divine in the mundane.

I take his hand and smile through my tears. It is the perfect thing to say.

Epilogue

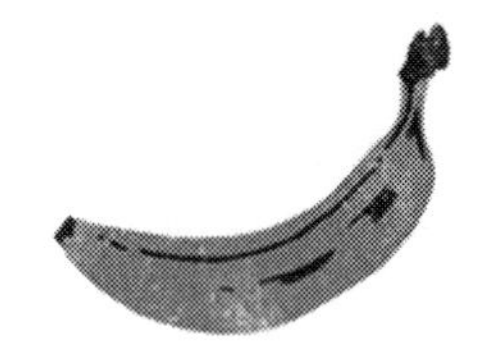

It is New Year's Eve. Adam and I stumble off the bus from Adelaide Airport. The street lights are on and our shadows dance in front of us as we walk. I can only imagine how hot it would have been just hours before.

Dogs are barking nearby. We have had to leave Inari behind, but she is well cared for. She loves our new house, especially the garden. She disappears into it for hours at a time, emerging mysteriously like a wild fox at mealtimes. She and Maisie get on well. Sometimes they get quite frisky together.

Adam and I are back in Blossom Road. Unknown to me, he had been there the whole year we were apart. The terrace we had rented just happened to come on the market at the same time we moved out of our apartment. Adam put down what money he had on a mortgage and started renovating.

We have gradually reacquired our surrealists. Some of them had never shifted from the local thrift shop in all those years. Others, we have had to hunt out.

The Joy of Living by Ernst hangs on our verandah. Its tangled and abundant foliage reflects our rampant garden. Adam and I have not yet learnt to trim and weed. Perhaps we never will. *Meditation* is over my desk in the study and *The First Pure Word* is next to our bed. The woman's crossed fingers remind me to treasure what I have regained.

I have hung *Venus on Sixth Avenue* back in the laundry and every time I look at it I think of Haruko. Like the goddess in the picture, she brought magic into my life. I have sent her many long emails and got short ones in reply. She told me that Ebi had left the Yakuza and that her father was not speaking to her. I still send her emails, but I haven't heard from her for some time.

I find her on Facebook every now and then and see her profile picture changing, so I know she is alive and well. That will have to be enough. Last week she was wearing a white dress and a jaunty bit of white net on her head. She looked like she could have been dressed for a wedding, but knowing Haruko she was just going shopping.

As we wait at a pedestrian crossing, my phone goes *ting*. I have an email. I scan it quickly.

'Who is it?' says Adam.

'You remember I told you about Chris at the Big Redback? He's going back to school to finish year twelve.' I read out part of the email.

. . . all this interest in Buddhas and Shinto Gods got me going. Maybe I'll go to university afterwards if it works out. Do Asian studies or something like that. Thanks for getting me started. Happy New Year.

Chris.

'Your pilgrimage has worked in mysterious ways,' says Adam.

I think of the people I met along the way and it's true that their lives have changed. Bertie was in Greenland last I heard, Chris is going back to school and Max and Cecilia have been reunited for six months now.

Max sent me a Christmas card she had made herself. It showed her and Cecilia on top of the Big Pineapple, the sun setting behind them. Max was wearing a clean pressed pair of khaki shorts and a startlingly white polo shirt and gave the appearance of having been put through a steam cleaner. Her cheeks were shiny, her hair glossy and she held aloft a glass of wine. Cecilia was small and dark-haired. She leant against Max, her cheeks flushed with wine, or sun. 'Going to South America in March,' Max had scrawled inside.

I think that sounds like an excellent idea. There is more to life than Big Things. After this one last trip, I plan to move on.

'Where are we going?' Adam says.

'I told you, it's a mystery tour.' I check my map then pull him along.

'You haven't got much stuff, Arkie.' Adam eyes my small backpack. His is about the same size.

'What do I need? Just thee and me.'

'You never used to pack like that.'

'No. That was before I realised I was a pantywaist.' I tell Adam about Grandma Gatewood and her solo jaunts along the Appalachian Trail.

'Inspirational,' he says. 'An army blanket, a raincoat and a shower curtain. Is that what you've got in there?'

I shake my head. 'A toothbrush, knickers and a T-shirt. We're staying in a motel this time. Oh yes, and my iPad and teapot.'

'Teapot?'

I nod. 'Just the essentials.'

I take Adam's hand and lead him along the footpath. Beside us, several lanes of cars whiz past, their lights flashing in our faces and then receding. 'Not far,' I say.

We link arms as we walk along. I feel like champagne is fizzing in my blood, although I haven't had a single drop to drink.

As we near our destination, Adam stops dead in his tracks. 'No way.' He starts to laugh. 'You brought me here from Sydney for this?' We walk closer and he peers up. 'Actually, it's pretty damn fine. I can't believe I haven't been here before.'

'You've never been here before?' I look at him closely.

'Never.' He shakes his head.

'Me neither. And it's fabulous, isn't it?'

'Totally fabulous.' He puts his arm around me and kisses my forehead. 'Quite stirring actually.'

'You wait. It's going to get better.'

The Big Scotsman is perched on the side of Scotty's Comfort Inn. He is not all that large, but meets Cecilia's requirements of a Big Thing, being about five metres tall. Lit up in the spotlight, he is really quite impressive.

My eyes start at the bottom and move upwards. He has long white socks topped with a strip of tartan. After a brief flash of knee, the kilt takes over, then the bagpipe and military green jacket. On his head, he is wearing a fluffy black hat with a red plume. His bagpipe is held to his lips which are topped by a black moustache and his eyes have a faintly startled expression.

'So, would you call that a Big Thing?' I say to Adam.

'Looks big to me,' he says.

'But is it big enough?'

Adam turns to me. 'You know, that's a very philosophical question, isn't it, Arkie? How big is big enough?'

'How much of anything is enough?' I say.

Adam's brown eyes rest on me. 'What do you think?'

'I think it's plenty big enough to be a Big Thing. I think the Scotsman was robbed.'

Adam avoids my eyes. 'So you think this is where it all started?' His tone is casual. 'The whole Big Things shebang.'

'Yep. Not at the Big Banana at all. Although the Big Banana was the first big highway agricultural product, so it did start that particular trend . . .'

'What do you plan to do about it?'

'Nothing.'

'Nothing?' he says.

'Nup.'

'Just keep it for those in the know, huh? Kind of like a cult thing.'

I nod.

'Yeah, that's probably the way to go. No point in taking on the Big Banana,' says Adam.

'You've got to pick your battles.'

'Never start a fight with a banana has always been my motto.'

'It's a good one. I wonder what Scotty's wearing underneath his kilt?' I say. We move closer and peer up, but no matter how we position ourselves the Scotsman's fibreglass kilt protects his modesty. Perhaps he is wearing tartan undies. 'We'll just have to assume that he's big enough,' I say.

'Has to be, if he's the original and still the best, doesn't he?' Adam raises one eyebrow.

Inside, I ask for the reservation for Douglas and get the key to the Superior Room. I have asked for a room with a view of the Scotsman. The woman behind the counter is about forty and fit-looking with curly black hair.

'Have you been here long?' I say.

'No, love, just a month or so.'

'Did you ever meet the original owners?'

'No, I'm not from round here.'

'What made them build a Scotsman, do you think?'

'Don't know really. Maybe they liked a drop. Of Scotch,' she adds.

'Do you think it was the first Big Thing in Australia?'

'Oh, couldn't say. Is that what you've heard?'

'Maybe. It's controversial.'

'Had terrible trouble working out how to build it, I hear,' she says. 'Took a few attempts. The bagpipe fell on one of the builders and broke his leg in one of the early models.'

'Nasty.'

'You're not wrong there.'

In our room, Adam and I plonk down our bags and drag our chairs over to the window, where we can see Scotty in all his glory.

I boil the kettle and pour tea for both of us out of my Tanuki teapot. It would be nice to serve it in little round porcelain bowls, but the motel's white mugs will have to do.

Adam raises his eyebrows as I place his mug in front of him. 'Tea?'

'You were hoping for something stronger? There's beer in the mini-bar.'

'No. It's all right; I'll have what you're having.'

I sip my tea then allow a sinister note to enter my voice. 'So. I suppose you're wondering why I brought you here.'

Adam looks at me out of the corner of his eye. 'To have a wild and crazy New Year's Eve?'

'It might seem like that so far, but no.' I switch on my iPad and put on a Scottish accent as I read. '*Thank goodness someone is finally looking into this issue. There has been a travesty of justice for too long.'* I raise my eyebrows as I lift my head.

Adam affects an innocent expression.

'You are entering the fortress of the oppressor. Stay alert. Don't let them sway you with their sweet-talking banana ways.' I drill him with my eyes again.

He is biting his lip, but a laugh escapes him. 'How did you guess?'

'Digital footprints, darling, or should I say . . . Scottie. I was looking for the opening times at Big W on your computer the other day and Google suggested Big Scotsman. Didn't do a very good job of covering up your tracks, did you?'

'Curses,' says Adam. 'Och, aye. Deception used to be easier in the olden days. I'm a blitherin eejit.'

I smile at him. 'Whatever made you do that?'

He shrugs. 'A misst ye sae muckle.'

I frown. 'Since when do you speak Scottish?'

'I don't. I just learnt a few phrases.'

'So what was that you just said?'

'I missed you so much.'

I take his hand. 'I thought you were a nutter.'

'Perhaps I am, lassie.'

We smile at each other. 'Well you're my nutter now.' I glance at my watch. 'Better get a wriggle on. Bingo starts at quarter past eleven.'

'Bingo?' Adam says. 'We're going to drink tea and play bingo on New Year's Eve?'

I nod.

'I hope we're not going to have to keep up this standard of decadence for the rest of our lives, Arkie. We're not twenty anymore, you know.'

'That's just the start. At quarter past twelve, I'll give you a present. I'm going to have to skip the soba noodles and the prayer. We started too late.'

'Be still my beating heart.' Adam smiles. 'This is going to be the best New Year's Eve ever.'

Adam and I play bingo sitting on the bed.

'Twenty-five.' He crosses the number off his card.

I flip up the next one. 'Ten.' One for me.

'Nineteen.'

'Forty-six.'

The pile of cards shrinks.

'Six,' says Adam.

'Bingo.' I wave my card. 'I win.'

I open my backpack and take out the facecloth with the cherry blossoms which Haruko gave me last year. It is still in its plastic wrapper. So much has happened since that night on the train station. So much that might never have happened at all. I tear open the wrapping and hold the cloth out to show Adam. 'It's lucky I won; I don't think I could bear to part with it.'

'It's beautiful,' says Adam.

It is fifteen minutes past midnight. 'So, it's time for your present now.'

'What have you got me?' Adam eyes my backpack. 'Nothing big, obviously.'

I unzip the backpack, pull out the drawstring bag which holds my Seven Lucky Gods and line them up on the coffee table. 'Take your pick.'

Adam gives me a playful look. 'Any one I want?'

I nod.

His hand lands immediately on Hotei, the chubby laughing Buddha.

'Good choice.' I reach out and take his forefinger. 'This is how you rub his belly. It brings you good luck.'

Adam continues to rub Hotei's belly. 'I've been seeing Buddhas everywhere lately. Have you noticed that, Arkie?' he says.

I laugh.

'What?' he looks at me, still rubbing. 'I'm a bit slow to pick up on it, am I?'

I nod.

'What's it all about, do you think? What does it mean?'

I shrug. 'Remember to be kind? Be in the moment?'

He smiles and meets my eyes. 'Well, there's nothing wrong with that, is there?'

I shake my head. 'Nothing at all.' I pull four envelopes out of my backpack. They are addressed to Max (at the Big Pineapple), Bertie (in Greenland), Chris (at the Big Redback) and Haruko and Ebi (in Tokyo). Inside Max's envelope I slide Fukurokuju, the god of wisdom, happiness and wealth. To Bertie, I send Bishamonten, the warrior god. To Chris, I send Jurojin, the god of knowledge, who is like the gnome we found in the garden of the Big Redback. This leaves three gods.

My eyes linger on Benzaiten. She looks serene and happy in her pink kimono. I wonder if Haruko still wears her pink kimono every now and then. And if she thinks of me when she does. I imagine her multicoloured nails twinkling, her pink beret perched jauntily on her head as she strides down the streets of Harajuku. Tokyo must be full of girls with a quirky sense of style but somehow I think that Haruko would still stand out.

I place Benzaiten inside the last envelope. With her goes Ebisu, the god of fishers, who brings luck and congratulations. I think he is the right one for Ebi. *Happy New Year*, I write on four cards and place them in the envelopes.

There is now only one god left for me. It is Daikokuten, the god of farmers and fertility. I place him on the table next to Adam's Hotei – *luck and fertility.*

'What's next on the program?' says Adam.

'Bedtime.'

'Excellent.'

We collapse in a heap on the bed, our arms around each other. And he feels as he does every time, familiar and yet different. Our time apart has changed us both, but only in good ways. It is like the clock has started again. Every day he surprises me. Adam is a library I will be happy to wander through for the rest of my life.

We lie intertwined. The windows are open and I can hear the roar of the road. Above us the ceiling fan pushes sluggish air around the room. From where we are lying we can just see the Scotsman's head. 'I think Haruko would have liked it here,' I say.

Adam's eyes meet mine. He smiles. 'I'm sure she would.'

'Adam?'

'Yes?'

'Draw me a picture of my Lucky Gods before we go to sleep? If I put them under my pillow and dream, then I will have a lucky year. That's what Haruko said.'

'Does it work?'

'It worked this year.' I lean over and pull out his sketchbook from his bag, hand it to him.

Propping himself up on the pillows, he opens it, flicking through the pages. *Two Faces* isn't there anymore. In its place is a sketch of the photo I emailed him, dated the night I sent it.

'I have never understood how that photo ended up on my iPad,' I say. 'Did you send it to me?'

Adam gazes at his sketch. 'No. I took it with my phone. You looked so beautiful. But then I deleted it after you left that morning with the divorce papers. Or I thought I did. I meant to.' He looks up. 'I really have no idea how you got it.'

'A mystery, then?'

He nods. 'Maybe it got stuck onto one of my Big Scotsman raves somehow.'

'Those digital Scotsman footprints sure get around.'

'When you emailed it to me that night though, it seemed like a sign. I realised . . . I couldn't let you go that easily, Arkie.'

Tan, tan, Tanuki's testicles.

'What's that you're humming?' His brow crinkles.

'Just a little Japanese song.'

'It's kind of catchy.' He hums it too.

I remember something else Haruko said – *On New Year's Day we do something special. Something with friend.* 'What are you doing tomorrow?' I say.

Adam reaches out to squeeze my hand. 'I don't know, but whatever it is, I'm pretty sure I'm doing it with you.'

'Would you like to walk the Appalachian Trail with me when we're seventy?'

'Sure. I'll put it in my diary right now. But only if you're going to walk it in your pantywaist.'

'Oh, Scottie, you are a devil.'

He winks. 'I'll show you who's the original and still the best.'

I place Adam's picture of the Lucky Gods under my pillow before I go to sleep. And I wonder what I will dream of – maybe a daughter or a son? It hasn't happened yet, but perhaps there is still time.

'I love you,' says Adam as he turns off the light.

'I love you too.' And there is not the tiniest hesitation, not even the tiniest doubt.

In our Blossom Road bathroom, Dali's drooping clocks have pride of place. Every time I brush my teeth I contemplate them.

And it seems to me that if a tree full of cherry flowers can appear in the middle of a Brisbane summer, if a doll can take my bad luck with it, if noodles can give you long life and if my name can mean beautiful blossom then who knows?

Perhaps, under the right conditions, time might bend like melted cheese.

Acknowledgements

I have had support from many places while writing this book. Much heartfelt gratitude must go to the following people.

My tireless agent, Sophie Hamley.

Inga Simpson, who read my early draft and kept me updated on progress at the Big Pineapple.

My wonderful writing group: Helen Burns, Jane Meredith, Jessie Cole, Siboney Saavedra-Duff, Michelle Taylor and Jane Camens. Without you I would have given up before I reached the Big Redback.

The whole team at Random House. Special thanks to my publisher, Beverley Cousins, for loving Arkie as much as I do, and to my editor, Lex Hirst, and publicist, Kirsty Noffke.

The Northern Rivers Writers Centre has been a constant source of support and encouragement, thanks to all staff, past and present.

My family, Simon, Tim and John – you guys are my rock.

And to my parents, Eric and Judy. Thank you for buying me my first chocolate-coated banana at the Big Banana. Thank you for everything.

Book Group Questions

1. Do you think it's possible, as Arkie says, that people in long-term relationships sometimes know less about each other than those who have only recently got together? If so, why is this?
2. Arkie talks about the surrealist game Exquisite Corpse, where you put together random words or pictures and look for links between them to create new meanings. Have you ever played this game? One theory of creativity suggests that it arises from bringing together two or more contrasting ideas or frames of reference. Is this how you experience creativity? What experiences have you had with creating original work this way?
3. According to the latest census, Buddhism is now the largest religion in Australia after Christianity. *'Do you think that sales of Buddhas are indicative of a new desire*

for spirituality in our everyday lives?' Arkie asks. What do you think? What is it about Buddhism that appeals to us?

4. It has often been said that there are only seven basic plots in fiction and all stories are versions of these. *The Wonderful Wizard of Oz* is a recurring motif in the book. What similarities can you see between the plot and characters of *Arkie's Pilgrimage* and those of *The Wonderful Wizard of Oz*?
5. *'In Japan, we have shrines for children who die. Or babies who aren't born. They are called mizuko,'* says Haruko. Memorials to unborn and dead children are a common sight in Japan. Do you think our culture could find better ways for people to remember and mourn their lost children? What form could this take?
6. *'It's an interesting idea, the object as a storeroom for a memory. My hand drops into my bag and I finger my Seven Lucky Gods – souvenir of my re-entry back into life.'* The word souvenir is French for memory. Do you buy souvenirs or collect objects that remind you of holidays or significant times in your life? What feelings do these objects arouse in you?
7. Arkie says that her shop will *'celebrate the good old Aussie love of surrealism as it expresses itself in the pursuit of Big Things.'* Do you think that Big Things are surreal? What does the Australian love of Big Things say about our culture?

Author Q and A

1. *Where did the idea for the pilgrimage to the Big Things come from?*

I originally wanted to write a story about a woman doing the Shikoku pilgrimage in Japan. I read a lot of books about it and it sounded wonderful, but I wasn't sure when I was ever going to find sixty days to do it – I have a job and kids – and I didn't think I could write about the walk without doing it. So, rather than hold off writing the book until I could do the pilgrimage, I decided to write about someone who wants to do it, but can't.

And the Big Things . . . I was trying to think where you would go to do a 'temple' pilgrimage in Australia and the idea came to me one day as I was driving past the Big Prawn – more or less as it does for Arkie. I suppose Big Things appeal to my sense of the ridiculous. I like the way they become totems of the towns that have them and how surprisingly passionate people become about them. For me, they evoke a sense of nostalgia. I have extremely vivid memories of visiting the Big Banana and the Big Pineapple as a child and they seemed like the most exciting places in the world. Like Arkie, I still think there is something 'weird and sweet' about them.

2. *Arkie's Lucky Gods play a significant role in the book. Where did they come from?*

I have been to Japan four times, so clearly I like it. One of the things I particularly enjoy is seeing the Shinto shrines dotted all over the country. Everywhere you go there is a tori gate that welcomes you to the spirit world. The Shinto religion has many gods and even objects like trees or rocks are revered for their kami or spirit.

On my second trip to Japan I discovered the Seven Lucky Shinto Gods. Soon I started seeing them everywhere. They seemed to be calling me, so I bought a little model of the gods and took them home.

I am a bit of a collector of significant objects. When I start a new writing project I am often scanning for a touchstone that will symbolise the story. The object sits next to my computer while I write and it gives me courage. I suppose that's superstitious, but writing is a leap of faith and you take help where you can.

It wasn't until I had those gods sitting on my desk that this story really started to take shape for me. While I'm a pretty rational person usually, when it comes to writing I need my lucky object.

3. *There is an element of magic in the story. Is that something you believe in?*

Yes and no. I come from a scientific background, so I'm basically a pragmatist. But on the other hand, I tend to think that there's more going on in the world than meets the eye. I think every writer has moments when life imitates art in a way which raises hairs on the back of your neck. Coincidences multiply until you start to feel that the act of writing is almost magical.

I had a couple of funny experiences when writing *Arkie's Pilgrimage*. I wrote the scene at the Big Redback where Arkie and Haruko find a garden gnome that looks like one of the Seven Lucky Gods early on, before I'd been to any of the Big Things. Eventually I decided I'd better go to the Big Redback and check it out. And lo and behold when I got there I saw this gnome nestled among the bushes exactly as I had already described it in the story.

Another strange thing happened one day when I was struggling with the story and decided to go down to the beach for a swim. I threw down my towel and noticed an abandoned dog collar next to it. The rusty old tag on the collar read *mojo*. Just like Arkie, I had found my mojo!

The mojo dog tag immediately joined my little shrine of lucky objects next to my computer.

I don't think that there's anything magical about these events, but it is so interesting the way that once you tune in to something you start to see it everywhere. I expect that's because you're so hyper-alert to your story you start to feel like you're inside it.

I introduced a dash of magical realism into my story in order to give Arkie's quest a bit of a fairytale feel. I wanted to lift it a little above the mundane. I love Japanese magical realists like Haruki Murakami and with a bit of luck some of his playful 'anything goes' spirit has infused itself into the book.

4. *Have you visited a lot of Big Things?*

The part of the world I live in is great for all sorts of reasons; surf, lifestyle, sun and . . . Big Things. In the course of researching *Arkie's Pilgrimage* my son and I embarked on a Big Things tour. He's a keen filmmaker so he made a short film about it. Our tour included the Big Banana, Prawn, Avocado, Pie, Redback Spider, Pineapple, Macadamia, Cow, Shell, Pelican and Lawnmower. We had a lot of fun doing the sorts of things that Arkie does – eating a pie at the Big Pie, eating fruit at the Big Avocado and cruising the kinky banana souvenirs at the Big Banana. My visit to the Big Macadamia was a bit like Arkie's too – very intrepid.

At the time I did this tour, back in 2011, Ballina's Big Prawn was just a shell and the closure of the Big Pineapple was breaking news. A local newspaper had a picture of a sad family who had supposedly driven all the way from Sydney just to go to the Big Pineapple, only to find out it was closed. But since then, both the Big Prawn and the Big Pineapple have happily experienced a new lease of life so I have reflected these changes in the book.

5. *Have you ever undertaken a pilgrimage?*

I haven't, but I know people who have and some of them have changed their lives profoundly as a result. There is clearly a transformative aspect to the process and that interests me. While writing *Arkie's Pilgrimage* I read a lot of books – both memoir and scholarly works – about pilgrimages and found them all fascinating. The concept of the pilgrimage as a spiritual journey seems to go across so many cultures.

While the idea of doing a pilgrimage certainly attracts me, when I travel my priority is usually to visit wild natural areas. I have a background as a wilderness guide, so being in the bush is something I treasure. I do love seeing temples and shrines in wild places, the way you find them in countries like Japan and Nepal. They add a spiritual dimension to being in nature which I enjoy.

6. *Why surrealism?*

I've had a bit of a thing about surrealists ever since I visited Salvador Dali's house in Spain, a long, long time ago. I loved the floppy clocks, the faceless women and the strange titles.

Debris of an Automobile Giving Birth to a Blind Horse Biting a Telephone is a personal favourite.

I go through a phase when I'm writing where I become a total bowerbird. If something interesting happens to me at this point it often makes its way into the book. It was at this stage that I attended a fantastic exhibition about surrealism in Brisbane.

I was young when I visited Dali's house and less bothered by the fact that I had no idea what it was all about. However, visiting the surrealists in Brisbane I found myself rather perplexed. Why was there a table with the head of a wolf, why a woman's face with breasts for eyes and a crutch for a mouth, why was a coffin reclining on a chaise longue? Damn it, I wanted to know.

Then I had a light-bulb moment. The reason surrealism speaks to me is because it joins two or more disparate objects or ideas to create new meaning, which is exactly what I do when I write. In this book I have the unlikely assemblage of a Japanese pilgrimage, Big Things and *The Wonderful Wizard of Oz* – it's textbook surrealism.

In a way, I think surrealism is a 'make your own fun' kind of art form. It's enjoyable to find your own meaning in works of art – and that goes for novels too.

7. *Why did you choose to reference* The Wonderful Wizard of Oz *within your story?*

I didn't! Writing is a very organic process for me. I never plan and I often don't make connections about the overall themes of books until quite late in the piece. I had basically written the whole book when I went on a five-day writing retreat with a group of other writers. I took a break from wrestling with the editing one afternoon to do a bit of yoga. And there in down-face dog I had an epiphany – my story was basically a retelling of *The Wonderful Wizard of Oz*.

At that stage I tinkered around a bit, including a couple of details from *The Wonderful Wizard of Oz* within the story. The basic plot and the characters were all there. I think *The Wonderful Wizard of Oz* is just such an archetypal story about overcoming obstacles on a journey that it found its way in. The mind works in mysterious ways.